DESTINED

THE ARC SERIES BOOK FOUR

ALEXANDRA MOODY

D1737030

Edited by Pete Thompson
Cover Design by Alexandra Moody

ISBN-13: 978-1535179980
ISBN-10: 1535179988

For Phoebs, everyone deserves a beautiful best friend like you.

CHAPTER ONE

I shouldn't have come.

It's all I can think as I approach the busy market square. I can already make out the brightly coloured canopies of market stalls and throngs of people moving between them at the end of the alley. Their movements are stilted and disorderly as their indecisive eyes move from one stall to another.

It's busier here than I expected, but I shouldn't be surprised. I glance up at the dark clouds that gather overhead. Their presence feels like a bad omen and a chill runs down my spine. What if something goes wrong?

I harden my expression and attempt to dismiss my fears. Nothing will go wrong. April has been planning for today ever since Joseph announced this appearance last week. This will work. It has to.

I pull my hood up over my head and step out from the alley and into the crowd. I keep my head down as I wind my way cautiously between the men and women, and move towards the large square where people are gathering.

'Hope City is our chance at a new beginning,' a man's voice

echoes across the square. He stands atop a rickety looking platform that's been hastily erected.

There's a cautious, almost distrustful air to the people watching him in the square. Fear practically radiates from them, emphasised by their stiff postures and furtive glances at their neighbours. There's almost a question in their expressions as they face the man—what do you want now?

I find a spot to stop near the back of the crowd. It's close enough to hear, but far enough back that I shouldn't be noticed. As I scan my surroundings, I catch sight of April standing at the foot of a crumbling wall near the stage. I pull the hood of my jacket further forward, cloaking my eyes in shadow. If she recognises me, I'm dead.

I allow my gaze to drift across the people who have amassed. There's desperation in so many people's eyes, but it's tinged with caution and fear. No one seems impressed by the pretty speech they're being given. The words are another set of empty promises and these people need more than that right now.

A woman in front of me moves so I can clearly see the man speaking to the crowd; the leader of Hope City, Joseph. Surprise registers on my face as I take him in. His usual cool demeanour has somewhat changed. There are bags under his eyes and his skin is ghostly pale. It's hard to ignore the authority in his voice though and his eyes are as cold as ever.

The sight of him causes me to take an involuntary step backward. Fear slowly licks its way up the back of my spine as I remember the things this man has done to me. The things I have done to him. My hands tingle as a mixture of anger and talent ripples down into my fingertips.

I slowly exhale, trying to ignore the sound of his voice and calm myself. All I can hear though, is him. All I can think about is the weeks I was held hostage in the West Hope hospital and experimented on. All I can see is Will's cold, dead body as we lowered him into the ground just a few weeks ago. I tighten my hands into fists. I was right. I shouldn't be here.

I feel movement at my side and glance to my right to see Sebastian looking down at me. 'I thought you'd been told not to come,' he remarks, with an approving grin. His expression changes as he catches sight of the look on my face. 'You okay?'

'Fine,' I respond, through clenched teeth. His presence relaxes me enough that I no longer feel my talent awakening inside me. I take a breath in and then slowly blow it out. 'How did you know it was me?' I ask, feeling a little calmer.

I'd done my best to disguise myself, but clearly I haven't done enough. I glance at the people around me, but no one has noticed I'm here. There's certainly no one cowering away from me or shouting out in fear.

'I could feel your body calling out to me from a mile away,' he jokes, causing me to roll my eyes. 'Also, you're wearing my hoodie.'

'I'm not wearing...' I peer down at the dark grey hoodie I have zipped up to my neck. He's right; it's his. I cross my arms over my chest before looking back at him. 'Why are you here? I heard April give you the exact same speech I got.'

He gives me a conspiring smile. 'And miss this? Never.'

The smile drops from his lips as he looks out at the crowd that has gathered to listen to Joseph. His eyes are serious, and as he scans the people around us he moves slightly closer to me. He places a hand on my lower back and leans in. 'When do you think they'll start?'

The sound of a hundred chimes rings out over the crowd and I lower my voice to respond. 'Now, apparently.'

Every head in the crowd moves down to look at their Commu-Cuff, and I do the same.

'*Everything Joseph has told you is a lie...*' is written in glowing blue font across the glass cuff's display. '*Our chance at a new beginning is being wasted...*'

The people around me utter several mumbles of agreement. I glance up to gauge Joseph's reaction. He hasn't lowered his head to his cuff, but his eyes are like ice as he stares over the crowd. He continues his speech though, barely missing a beat.

'It's going to be a long winter and, as such, we will be installing measures to ensure that everyone is well fed,' he says.

'In other words, expect to go to bed hungry every night for the next few months,' Sebastian says, grimly, in my ear. 'Did he even notice the comm everyone received?'

I watch Joseph as his eyes fall on one of his recruiters. He gives the man a small nod before he looks up at the crowd again.

'Oh, he noticed,' I reply.

A small girl holding her mother's hand in front of us turns and looks directly at me. A hint of recognition lights her eyes and I quickly turn away. Even wearing this hood low over my face, I'm too easily recognised.

My face has been broadcast all over the city for weeks since we infiltrated Headquarters. I would be much safer back at our new camp. If that girl has noticed me, maybe she's not the only one.

I can easily picture the looks of fear people would give me. I can clearly imagine the panic that would fill their eyes if they realised the rebel girl who terrorised Headquarters and nearly killed Joseph, their leader, was among them.

I hazard a look back at the girl, but she has turned away from me. I let out a small sigh, but the tension in my shoulders refuses to let up. I suddenly feel aware of how many people there are in this square; of how open it is and how easy it would be for recruiters to blockade us in. Towering buildings of glass and steel line the square and their shiny faces feel like watching eyes.

Another round of chimes rings out and the square goes deadly quiet as people look down at their cuffs again. *'How can we start a new life when we are separated from the people we love?'*

The comm is closely followed by another: *'Joseph is building an army in North Hope.'*

And then another: *'He's experimenting on children in West Hope.'*

Gasps rattle through the audience and, as one, they slowly lift their heads to stare accusingly at Joseph. Joseph stares back, his face the picture of innocence.

More chimes sound off in an endless barrage. Ringing across the square, they grow louder and louder, drowning out the sound of Joseph's voice. Again and again the same message appears on everyone's cuff: *'There is no Hope for us under Joseph's rule.'*

'What is the meaning of this?' one man yells above the commotion.

'My son is in West Hope, is he being experimented on?' cries another.

Joseph slowly lowers his head to his wrist. He blinks at his cuff before raising his head to the crowd.

'I can assure you these comms are fabrications. This is a cyber attack by the callous terrorists who bombed our celebration day.' His attempts to appease the crowd fall on deaf ears. The individual shouts from the crowd are joined by others, and as one the angry mob begins to surge towards the stage, demanding answers.

Sebastian's blue eyes cloud over as he eyes the three alleys that lead from the square. With this many people it will be nearly impossible to reach them and make a quick escape.

'That's our cue to leave,' he says.

A high-pitched shout rises up from the crowd and I whip my head around to look at where it's come from. Two recruiters are wrestling a man to the ground as he attempts to climb onto the stage. As one pins him down, the other spins a ring of flames from his hands, hovering it dangerously close to the man's neck.

I stumble backwards, moving to get away, but the people behind me are pushing forward. I glance up at the stage to see more recruiters appearing beside Joseph.

He appears agitated as he looks out over the crowd. His eyes are calculating and his lips form a hard line. Recruiters move to create a circle around him, trying to get him to leave before he gets hurt, but he continues to survey us like he's waiting for something or someone.

His eyes dance across the mass of people who fight to reach him. But he seems disinterested in them, barely bothered by the shouts they hurl at him. This look of disinterest continues until his eyes fall upon me.

My body goes cold, like I've just been doused in frozen water, and a familiar crackle ignites in my veins. His eyes light with recognition and, despite the hood I wear low over my face, I know he can tell it's me standing here. I feel hooked by his stare, unable to move and unable to look away.

'Elle!' Sebastian shouts at me, but even his voice sounds like an echo from far away.

My body is thrown forward as someone hurtles into my back and I'm finally able to break Joseph's stare. My hands and knees slap against the hard concrete as I hit the ground, but I quickly scramble back to my feet.

I stagger sideways, my pulse racing, as people continue to barge past me. He knows I'm here. Joseph knows I'm here. I look to where I'd last seen Sebastian, but he's gone. I stand on my tiptoes to try and see his head over the crowd. I catch sight of him being pulled away in the current of people.

My heart beats faster as I try to move towards him, but I struggle to make my way through the surging crowd. We need to get out of here and I need to stay calm, which is becoming increasingly difficult. With each step I take, unbridled energy seems to pulse faster and stronger though my veins.

'Elle!' I hear Sebastian shout again, though I can no longer see him.

'I'm here!' I yell in response, but my voice is lost in the crowd. Panic coats me in a cold sweat as I push my way forward. I need to get out of here. I can't be caught by Joseph again. He'll have his recruiters after me by now and if I don't get out of here soon I'll be trapped. My breaths come in short and sharp as I consider being captured. I can't go back to the hospital again.

My talent surges through me as my panic rises, growing stronger with each moment that passes. The danger posed by Joseph's recruiters suddenly becomes the least of my worries as I feel the familiar tingle awakening along my skin. A dead certainty enters me; I'm going to lose control again.

I take a breath in and attempt to calm myself, but my tentative grasp on my talent is slipping. I can feel it thrumming through me, almost thirsting to be free. I shove my way past people, no longer attempting to be gentle as I try to move faster. I can't lose control here with all of these people gathered. I don't want to hurt anyone and that seems to be what my talent does best. The fear pulsing through me only seems to make my control slip further.

Power charges over my skin and when I look at my hands they are covered in tiny sparks of electricity. They spit and hiss as they slowly grow larger and wind their way up my arms until I am engulfed in the deadly raw energy. I hear gasps and shouts of fear around me. People back away, tripping over themselves as they attempt to flee the monster I'm becoming.

I have to get away. I close my eyes tightly, desperately needing to escape; frantically wishing I was anywhere but here. *I can't hurt these people.* I feel a rush of frigid air hit my body, before it just as quickly disappears. My eyes dart open, and the crowd of people shying away from me are no longer there. The bright market canopies are gone, replaced with the foul stench of rubbish and the narrow, dark walls of an empty back alley.

I can still hear the commotion of people in the marketplace, but they sound far off in the distance. I've teleported to safety and must be blocks from there now.

I sink to my knees with relief and sudden exhaustion. Sparks still dance across my skin, but they crackle contently and ever so slowly they begin to disperse until they are totally gone.

I lower my head down into my hands, rubbing my eyes tiredly. That had been too close. I could have killed all of those people in the square. I look down at my hands, which now appear so normal, and tighten them into fists. Things have been better lately. I shouldn't have lost control.

A chill works its way down my spine and I look up. The hairs on the back of my neck stand on end, and I no longer feel alone. I slowly stand, looking up and down the alley. It's just as empty as when I arrived.

'Hello?' I call out, wrapping my arms across my body. I can almost sense someone there, but there is no answer to my question. I take a step backward, glancing over my shoulder to the entrance that lies a few feet behind me. There's a wide street there, which is brighter than the alley and certainly feels safer.

I take another step backward towards it, unable to fight the sensation of being watched. A glass bottle clangs to the ground and I jump. My eyes dart to a small gap between the buildings up ahead. I can hear the bottle rolling to a stop, and I'm certain the sound is coming from in there.

I go to run to the safety of the street behind me, but then an elderly man steps from the shadows where I'd heard the sound. He has greying hair and kind blue eyes. There's an old scar running through his eyebrow and he wears an easy smile that's directed at me. I calm at the sight of him, but my heart still races from the fright he's given me. I'm just glad he wasn't a recruiter lurking in the shadows.

He walks towards me, leaning heavily on his rusted metal cane. His steps are painfully slow. 'Hello Elle,' he says, smiling widely as he approaches. He's looking at me like I'm some sort of mirage.

I take a hesitant step back. 'Do I know you?' Something about his voice sounds familiar, though I can't quite put my finger on what it is.

'Yes. Well, no, you don't know me.'

I frown and take a closer look at the man. I don't recognise him; how could he possibly know my name? Fear races through me. 'You've seen the broadcasts about me around town,' I whisper, my eyes darting to the end of the alley. I have to run before he comms for a recruiter.

He raises a hand out to me. 'Please don't leave. I've seen them, yes. But that's not why I'm here. I've come a long way to speak with you.'

'Where have you come from?' My mind races as I try to sort through the questions this man raises. Is he stalling me, waiting for recruiters to arrive? There's something about his kind eyes that makes me disregard that idea. He looks at me like he knows me, like he actually cares about me. Who is this guy?

'That's not important.' He pushes a hand through his hair and sighs. 'Elle, I'm here to warn you...'

His voice is anxious and his eyes are darker, more serious than they were before.

'Warn me about what...?

'You are destined to bring great pain to the people of Hope,' he says, with almost a tinge of sadness and regret to his words. 'But, some destinies can be changed.'

'What are you talking about?' I ask him. I'm trying to decide if the man is crazy or if he's for real—probably a mixture of both.

'You are coming to a crossroads. One road will take you to your death, the other to the death of someone you love. The only way to change the future is by taking the wrong path.'

'What do you mean change it? What am I going to do? Who's going to die?' My last question is whispered.

'I can't say.'

'Well, how do you know this? Why should I trust you?'

His eyes sadden for a moment, but then he smiles at me brightly again and winks. 'Because you've always trusted me.'

'Who are you?' I whisper, cautiously. Before I can hope to get an answer, shouting in the street behind me causes me to look over my shoulder. The crowd from the market is coming this way, and probably recruiters with them. I turn back to look at the old man, but he's nowhere to be seen. Stunned, I run to the entrance he'd appeared from, but the small lane between the buildings is empty. He's disappeared without warning.

I stand there shocked, my mouth parted in surprise. 'Who the hell was that?' I murmur, under my breath.

'Elle?' Sebastian's voice sounds from right behind me and I jump, turning to look at him.

Before I can respond he grabs me up in a hug, his strong arms wrapping around me tightly. 'Are you okay?'

I don't answer straight away. My mind is still trying to understand my encounter with the strange, elderly man. Was he telling me the future? It's not unheard of for people to have visions, but they rarely show anything other than snippets of a larger picture. He seemed to know things—to know me. Why would he say I've always trusted him when I've never met him before?

'Elle?' Sebastian asks.

I shake my head, tossing thoughts of the strange man from my mind. 'I'm fine. How did you find me?'

'I told you—I can totally sense where you are,' he jokes, reluctantly dropping his arms and taking a step away. I'm almost beginning to wonder how much of a joke that is.

'Did everyone else get out okay?'

'Yes. April's on her way back with Dalton and the others now. I'm sure she's going to chew both our ears off for being there today.'

I smile, glad for something as normal as being in trouble with April.

'We should go. It's probably not a good idea to stay too close to the market right now,' he suggests.

'No,' I agree.

He glances up at the dark clouds that fill the sky. They look ready to shower us with rain and are already stained with the deep blue colour of nightfall.

'Looks like we're in for a stormy night,' he says, tucking his hands into the pockets of his jeans, as he heads towards the road beyond the alley.

I move to follow him but, as I do, I hazard another look down the alley and push down a shudder. I pull my jacket in closer, adjusting the hood to cover my features again. That man had been warning me, but I have no idea what he could possibly mean? How could I ever choose between my own death and that of someone I love? I would never hurt anyone. I swallow tightly though as I remember how I used my talent to encase Joseph in ice. Maybe that's not completely true.

The disturbance in the marketplace and the strange man's words cause a bundle of mixed emotions to war within me and I walk along in silence. Even now, I can still feel Joseph's stare on my skin. It's like his eyes have tattooed their mark on me, and I feel as though it won't easily be washed away. In the square he had watched me with the focus of a hunter and his eyes had held a promise I can't easily forget. He's coming for me. Only this time I'll be ready.

CHAPTER TWO

I t is night by the time we reach the first lookout. The deep black clouds overhead blot out any light from the moon and the buildings that surround us rear up like menacing shadows in the dark. The lookout watches the street from behind the broken window of a dilapidated townhouse. The place has bricks crumbling from its façade and its roof has almost completely caved in. With moss and lichen coating the exterior, it's like every other place in this forsaken area of South Hope—a decaying and forgotten ruin.

In the darkness it's difficult to see who's manning the watch point. If you didn't know where to look, you would walk past the house without a second glance. Sebastian and I pause as we wait for the lookout to wave us on. Only when a hand appears through the shattered hole in the window do we continue forwards.

We're silent as we walk. Even though we have people watching the area from different points, it's difficult to feel safe. Especially not when a patrol of recruiters was seen only blocks from here last week.

It has just started to rain when I see the subway entrance up ahead. An old sign hangs by one wire over the wide opening, and though the letters have faded with time, you can just make out one word: Subway.

We approach the building slowly, giving the lookout waiting there time to identify us. She's standing in the mouth of the entrance, the shadow of the opening mostly cloaking her from sight.

'Where have you been?' Jess asks, stepping from the entrance as we approach. Even in the darkness I can see the worry in her eyes.

We both go to answer, but she proceeds to shake her head. 'Never mind, you both better get out of the rain.' She steps back, ushering us through the entrance and down the stairs that lead to our current home.

The steps widen as they reach the open concourse. Shiny white tiles cover the small hall and thick pillars reach up for the roof. There are several sets of steps that lead even further down towards the train platforms that lie underground.

I reach down to take a torch but pause. I can't stop thinking about the man in the alleyway; about the potential future he painted for me. He said I needed to take a different path than the one I'm already on. Was he saying my future is already written? Like I don't have a choice?

'Sebastian?' I ask, looking up to him. 'Have you heard of talented people who can really predict the future?'

He frowns. 'Why are you asking?'

'I'm just curious,' I say, looking down at my feet.

When I look up he's watching me closely. 'Some people at the Academy were said to have visions,' he says. 'I don't know if what they saw ever actually happened though.'

'If they saw something bad, do you think it's possible to change that?'

'Where's this coming from, Elle?' He looks at me with concerned eyes. I can understand why he might be worried, after everything that's happened to me.

'I was just wondering,' I insist.

He's silent for a moment, deep in thought, before he responds. 'I don't know. I guess it's possible. Some people think the future is set in stone, but I believe I'm in control of my own destiny.'

He leans over and grabs a torch from by the stairs. 'Got any more questions tonight?' he jokes, winking at me as he flicks the light on. I shake my head.

'You go on without me,' he says, nodding towards the stairs the lead down to the platform. 'I want to check in with April. She's going to be busy dealing with the fallout from the square today.'

'Oh, okay. Come get me if she needs any help,' I say.

I watch him as he walks over to a door marked, 'staff only.' There's a security office down the end of the hallway that lies beyond. I have no doubt that's where April will be. Only when Sebastian disappears behind the door do I start to make my way across the concourse towards a staircase leading downwards with, 'Platform 2,' displayed on a sign overhead.

I carefully take the stairs down to the platform, shining my torch in front of me to avoid the wooden steps that are cracked and damaged. I try to push any thoughts about the old man in the alley out of my head. I don't have time to worry about my future. There's too much going on in the present.

When I reach the bottom of the steps I shine the torch around the platform to see if anyone's here. The light skims across the faded red letters imprinted into the green tiles on the wall that read, 'Alta Park.' There's no sign of anyone here. I walk to the edge of the platform and swing myself down onto the train tracks. The gravel crunches beneath my feet as I land.

I follow the tracks until the dark mass of the deadened train I've been sleeping in looms up ahead of me. I pass three carriages until I reach the one I share with Kelsey. There's a soft light glowing in the windows, and when I climb into the carriage I find her already asleep on the makeshift bed we share.

I flick my torch off and leave it by the door, before I make my way past the worn red seats that line the walls and head straight for the bed. I intend to crash for the remainder of the night. But, like every other night, sleep doesn't come easily and I am consumed by the grief I fight so hard to ignore during the day.

For hours I stare at the faded route map on the wall, listening to the high-pitched whistle of the wind. It howls as it whips its way over the rubble and through the narrow tunnels of the subway. The sorrowful wails of the wind seem to be mourning with me and I long to cry out with it. Instead, I keep my grief silent, holding it tightly within my heart.

The candle by my bedside sputters as a draft comes in under the door. It is all that lights the dilapidated cavity of a train carriage and is dangerously close to dying. I cup my hands around the flame until it ceases flickering and returns to a straight, unwavering flame. Dark shadows already haunt the edges of the room and creep up the walls. I need this small spark of brightness. I can't stand to be in the dark. Not when it's already a struggle to keep control of myself during the daylight.

Kelsey sleeps soundly tonight, her face is relaxed while her fingers pull the threadbare blanket I scavenged for her close to her chest. We've only been hiding here for a couple of weeks, but it feels like an eternity has passed since the night our camp was torched.

I try my best not to think of that night, but it still haunts me and I know I'm not the only one affected. We all seem to be handling that night differently. Most are shaken at best; angry and out for vengeance at worst.

There seems to be an overarching question that hovers unspoken over the group. How can we hope for a better future when M, the man with the vision of how to make it happen, has been kidnapped? April is trying her best to continue his mission, but I think we all worry that it may be doomed without him. Even the comms she arranged to be sent to everyone in the square today were just a small bump in the road for Joseph. We'll need to do a lot more than that to remove him from power.

I curl my legs to my chest as I look up at the tall dark windows that line the carriage. The wind continues to wail through the tunnel, but in here it is deadly silent. My chest tightens as I think of Will. He never should have died, and I've felt his absence keenly in the weeks since.

The hairs on my arms stand on end and my skin buzzes as I picture his cold, dead body in my arms again. I quickly push the thought of him from my mind, feeling my talents awaken in response to the raw emotion that stirs inside me whenever I think of him. I chew on my lower lip and close my eyes as I take a calming breath.

No one knows that I left my inhibitor band behind. Even today, Sebastian was completely oblivious to the fact that I managed to escape the market square by teleporting. I know I'm still struggling to control my talents, but I made the right decision the day I stopped wearing the inhibitor.

Joseph needs to be stopped, and I can't do that if I spend my life fearing the talents within me. I worry that my need for revenge is putting the people I care about at risk. But, if I can help stop Joseph from hurting anyone else the way he hurt Will, a little danger is a small price to pay.

The door to the carriage creaks as it is pushed slightly ajar.

'Elle?'

I look over to see Sebastian peering at me through the crack. By the soft glow of the candlelight I can see he's drenched from head to toe and dark wet strands of hair hang over his blue eyes.

'You're soaking!' I say, jumping up and walking to over to him, pushing the door wide. 'Are you okay?'

I pull him in through the doorway and he towers over me. A shiver runs through me as I take him in and I glance over at Kelsey who is still in a deep sleep on the floor.

'I'm fine,' he replies, pushing one hand through his wet hair. 'I've been on lookout since I left you. It's a nightmare out there. I've never seen a storm like this before.'

'You should change into something dry. You'll get sick if you keep those wet clothes on.'

'I'll be fine,' he replies. 'Why are you still up?'

I give a mere shrug in response. My lack of sleep is nothing new. I've barely slept in weeks. I sit down on one of the seats that line the wall and hug my knees to my chest.

'Have you been having nightmares again?' he asks, softly.

I slowly nod and he kneels down next to the chair, taking care not to let his wet clothes touch it. 'You've got to stop blaming yourself. It's not your fault what happened.'

'Isn't it? If I hadn't destroyed Joseph's office and nearly killed him, he never would have retaliated. M wouldn't have been captured, the camp wouldn't have been torched and Will…' My voice breaks and I fail to finish the sentence.

He lightly touches my cheek. 'Joseph did those things, not you. He started all of this and he will pay for it.'

I look down at my hands as I pick at my nails. I take a deep breath in and slowly blow it out, trying to calm the tingles that have begun vibrating down my arms. I'm getting too emotional and my talent is quickly responding.

I've become much better at keeping myself calm over the past few weeks, but after losing control today I feel less certain of myself. It's only a matter of time before people figure out I ditched my inhibitor. I'm a ticking time bomb and conversations about Joseph don't help.

'Anything strange happen while you were on watch tonight?' I ask, trying to avoid thinking of the man who had me tested on like a lab rat for months and turned me into the monster I am today.

'No,' he says, yawning. 'There have been more recruiters in the area after what happened in the square today, but even they were sane enough to give up the search once it started raining. April certainly wished she was inside rather than keeping watch.'

I frown as I picture April keeping lookout on a night like tonight. She must have hated it, but since M disappeared she's become the person everyone turns to and she wouldn't have felt comfortable making anyone else do it—anyone besides her brother Sebastian that is.

'You should have got me to come help,' I say.

'Then you would be as wet as I am,' he replies, waving his hand at his damp clothes.

I pat the chair next to me, signalling for Sebastian to come and take a seat. He must be exhausted after being up all night, and it doesn't matter if he gets the seat a little wet. It would just be nice to be close to him right now.

He shakes his head and moves away from me. 'I should go...'

I glance down at my CommuCuff to see it's 4:00 A.M. A sense of dread pulses through me as I picture him leaving. I don't want to be alone, but I can't ask him to stay.

I nod slowly. 'Yeah, go dry off. You must be miserable in those drenched clothes.'

'It's not so bad.' He moves to the door, but as he grasps the handle he hesitates. 'I'm just in the next carriage if you need anything...' he says.

'Thanks.' I smile. 'But, I'll be fine. I wouldn't want to disturb April.'

'Screw April,' he mutters, shooting me a grin. 'Seriously though, come get me if you're worried about anything.'

As he leaves, the door clicks quietly shut behind him. It almost seems colder in here without his presence. I glance over at Kelsey who has one eye open, peeking up at me from under her covers.

'I think he likes you,' she says.

'And I think you should be asleep,' I respond.

She giggles and rolls over to face away from me. I return to bed and close my eyes, but nervous energy runs through my body and sleep feels unattainable. I can't seem to switch my mind off. Every time I shut my eyes I feel a sense of dread in my gut and I see Will's face. I failed him. I couldn't control the wild talents inside of me and because of my actions Joseph saw our group, The Movement, as a danger and retaliated.

A noise in the tunnel outside the train reaches my ears and I jerk up in bed to stare at the window looming over me. I slowly ease my way off of the mattress and creep over to the door at the end of the carriage. I open it and look into the tunnel.

The small glow from my carriage is all that lights the dark tunnel, and looking up and down it I see nothing out of place. Everyone must be asleep. I go to return to the safety of the carriage but hear the noise again. It's the sound of voices talking, but it's coming from down the tunnel, somewhere only my talented hearing can reach. As I try to listen closer, the howling wind and rain from the raging storm outside makes it difficult to tell how many voices there are. It could be two, maybe three, maybe more. Who could be out there at this time of night?

I glance back at Kelsey, who hasn't moved. Her chest rises and falls in a slow rhythm and she appears to have fallen back to sleep. I don't want to leave her in here alone, but Sebastian is next door and she should be fine for a minute while I investigate the source of the voices.

I take my torch from just inside the door and flick it on as I slip into the tunnel. There's a chill in the empty tunnel and the ground is cold and damp beneath my bare feet.

The network of tunnels is a bit of a labyrinth, but I've come to know the ones near the train we've been sleeping in quite well. I look back down the tunnel towards the platform and focus on my hearing. There are two entrances down that way. One of them is through the main subway entrance accessed by the endless flights of stairs that lead up from the platform. Beyond the platform, further down the tunnel, is another exit. A manhole cover that can be reached by narrow ladders cut into the walls of the tunnel. All I can hear that way is silence.

The third and final exit is in the other direction, past all the carriages and down into the tunnel, where the train tracks gradually veer up to the surface and continue on through South Hope above ground. I can easily hear the rain pouring down outside the opening through the darkness. The voices must have come from up there.

I walk alongside the row of carriages, deeper into the darkness.

This place gives me the creeps, especially when I'm traipsing around the empty tunnels while everyone else is asleep. The light from my torch does little against the all-consuming darkness down here and treacherous black shadows line the concrete walls of the tunnel. My keen sight helps me navigate without too much difficulty though. Where once I would have seen nothing in the darkness, deepest night has become more like twilight with my talented sight.

When we first moved here, I'd been surprised by April's choice of hideout. Returning underground? I would have preferred to stay in a crumbling house in South Hope or perhaps one of the abandoned warehouses that line the far side of West Hope. Hell, anything would have been better than the dark depths of the subway system under Hope. But April had been adamant and, as much as I hate this place, it does feel safer than all the other options.

There had been a layer of dust covering everything, from the train carriages to the ground, when we arrived in the subway station. The place had smelt stale, like the air inside had been bottled up and soured over time. It was the smell of a place long forgotten and even now my nose tickles at the dust in the air.

There is no power in this area of the city, which is great for keeping our location a secret, but not so good for the computers they are trying to set up in the security office of the station—or for midnight walks through the tunnel. Most of our supplies went in the fire that destroyed our camp, and we've been slowly scavenging more to get our operation up and running again.

As I move down the tunnel, past the carriages, the only sound that reaches my ears are my soft breaths and near silent footsteps. I listen carefully for any sound of movement or conversation to indicate where the voices have come from, keeping my senses alert in case the sound echoes down the tunnel again.

All the carriages are silent and I think of the people sleeping soundly inside. I feel so sorry that they have been forced back underground again but we had no choice other than to leave our old hideout after it was attacked. Not with the constant risk that recruiters would return to finish the job they started. I was more than happy to leave the charred remains of our camp. There were too many bad memories from the fire to stay.

Eventually, far beyond the final carriage, the tunnel widens and opens up to reveal an area covered in train tracks. Tall stone pillars divide the tracks and there are six different lines all running alongside each other. I can see the end of the tunnel from here and the rain pelting in through the gaping mouth that opens onto the surface.

I pause as I look across at the other tracks, a frown crinkling my forehead. There should be a lookout at this point, but I can't see anyone here. Shivers crawl up the back of my spine as I look around for them. I extend my senses out to see if I can hear the voices that brought me from my bed or at least catch the sound of a lookout nearby.

The silence becomes deafening as I listen and, after minutes of not hearing anything out of the ordinary, I heave out a sigh. I should head back and tell April about the missing lookout and the voices I'd heard. I'm sure there's a valid explanation for their deserted post, but I'd rather tell her just in case.

I turn to leave, but then I hear the voices again. I freeze and my head whips back to look at the opening at the far end of the tunnel. The voices came from outside.

I follow the train tracks to the opening of the tunnel, carefully avoiding the pile of rocks and rubble that have collapsed from the roof and block part of the mouth. The howl of the wind is louder outside and the constant patter of rain on the concrete is more defined.

A breeze brushes against my face as I hesitate by the entrance. The train tracks beyond are covered in rugged and untamed weeds. Overgrown bushes line the rusted wire fences that border both sides of the tracks. There's a large and empty field beyond the fence on the right side of the track. The other fence separates the track from an empty street. The rain falls so heavily, that even with my enhanced eyesight it's difficult to see as far as the other side of the road where I know a row of houses stands.

My heart beats faster and my skin hums with my talent awakening as I look out into the night. I take a deep breath in. I need to stay calm. I can't allow myself to lose control.

I place one hand up against the damp concrete wall of the tunnel and I look out into the darkness, narrowing my eyes in an attempt to see more clearly. The thick deluge of rain slaps harshly against the ground, creating a torrent of water that washes down along the tracks. There is no movement in the dark shadows but, as I listen, I catch a whisper of sound. A voice. No, two voices talking.

I stop breathing as I extend my senses out to listen. Though I can't hear their words clearly, I can tell the voices are coming from behind the fence, amongst the houses on the other side of the road.

I should go back to the train and warn the others that someone is out there. A feeling in my gut stops me though and, instead of heading back to the safety of the tunnel, I step out into the rain.

CHAPTER THREE

Within moments of leaving the tunnel I am drenched from head to toe. Water rushes over my bare feet, and my clothes and hair are completely soaked. The wind buffets at my wet clothes. Coming in waves, it whips against me like an icy lash biting into my skin. I'm aware of how cold it is, but the temperature doesn't seem to bother me the way it should and I'm not even shivering.

I clamber down the side of the tracks and over to the rusted wire fence. I pull back a loose section and crawl under it. Bushes scratch at my arms as I push my way through them to get to the road. I hope I'm not making too much noise, but the rain is making more than enough racket to cover the rustling sound from anyone without talented hearing. All the same, you can never be too careful.

I look up and down the dark street before stepping onto it. The storm is still raging out here, and feels even more violent without the small protection the bushes by the fence provided. I'm exposed out here in the open, so I keep as close as I can to the bushes in case I need to hide.

Looking back at the tunnel entrance, I feel a stab of longing for my bed. For a moment I truly miss the comfort and small safety the space seems to provide. I know I won't be able to sleep if I go back now though, not when there could be people out here lurking in the shadows.

I turn back to survey the street. Water pelts against my face, rushing down it so fast I feel more like I'm swimming than walking. It makes it difficult to see anything out of the ordinary. I cup my eyes with my hands and blink them open to take in the area. As I concentrate on my surrounds, my senses heighten. My sight becomes keen and unnaturally perceptive.

With an uncanny efficiency, my eyes focus in and out on the smallest details as I look for where the voices have come from. They scan the street and I notice everything, from the way the rain ricochets off the ground to the leaves on the bushes nearby that shudder in the breeze. I search for movement, for any sign of people out here, but I can't see anything out of the ordinary. Even as I focus in on the darkened shadows that crawl up the buildings nearby, I'm unable to see any people out here.

I'm beginning to wonder if I imagined the voices when I hear them once again, louder and more clearly this time, despite the deafening downpour of rain. I know immediately who it is.

'Look, I don't have long; the next lookout is scheduled to start in fifteen minutes. Why are you back here?' I hear April ask, her voice unmistakable.

I frown and turn to where her voice is coming from. She sounds close by, somewhere down the street in one of the houses that face the tracks. I move in that direction, pulling my arms tightly around my body as I go. I can't understand why she's out here in the rain of all places. Who could she be talking to? Why has she left the tunnels to seek them out? Is she in trouble?

I follow the sound to a house several doors down and pause when I catch sight of her. She's standing on the patio in a doorway that provides some protection from the wind. There's a man standing beside her, but he has his back to me and I can't see his face.

'You know why,' comes the man's response. His voice is surprisingly familiar and a strange pit forms in my stomach. I move closer to get a better look at him and recognise Ryan standing in the doorway with April. What is he doing here?

'You shouldn't have come...'

'I know,' comes his strangled response. 'But I have to keep trying. Even if it does seem impossible.' He pauses. 'I thought I could save her from all this, but each time I try to help, it only seems to put her more on course for what's to come.'

My heart races as I listen to his words. He sounds so serious and April sounds scared. Who are they talking about?

I move closer to the house, hiding under the shadow of a tree by the small fence that borders it. It's unlikely that they'd notice me out in the rain, but I don't want to risk being caught eavesdropping.

'Have you tried telling her the truth about you?' April asks.

Ryan sighs sadly. 'I don't think that will help. If she knows the truth it will only scare her. I think a part of her knows already, but still, I have no idea how she'll react.'

'Don't you?' April responds, cautiously.

'Look, if we can pull this off without her knowing, all the better. I've come to terms with my fate, but if I can fix hers...well... it'll all be worth it then.'

I find I've stopped breathing as I listen. I'm desperate to hear more. Ryan has always been mysterious but, right now, I feel like I'm finally getting close to answering the many questions I have about him.

'Have you told Sebastian?' he asks.

April pauses. 'No, I don't think that's a good idea. He might do something stupid.'

Ryan laughs under his breath. 'True.'

April sighs and then I hear a sniff. I glance around the side of the tree and see her face is in her hands. 'I don't want to lose you,' she says. 'But, I don't want to lose her either.'

He slowly puts his arm around her shoulders. 'It will work out,' he says. 'You'll see.'

He steps back, still grasping both her shoulders. 'Now, you better get going. Tomorrow is going to be a big day for you and you need to get some sleep.'

I hear her laugh under her breath. 'No clues about what to expect then?'

'No. You'll know soon enough...'

She takes a step away from him, turning towards the street. I have so many questions for April about what I've heard, but I know I can't ask her them. Not without admitting creeping out into the darkness to listen in. Yeah, I can imagine that would go down *really* well.

Through the rain I can see April making her way towards me. I don't have time to linger over their conversation now. My hands drop from shielding my eyes, allowing the rain to run down my face and, before April can catch me, I hurry back to the tunnel. As I descend into the darkness I find myself wondering about the girl Ryan is trying to protect. It sounded like she was in trouble and I worry that perhaps he was talking about me.

THE CARRIAGE IS quiet when I wake in the morning. It's impossible to tell the sun has risen on the surface, but the lamps in the tunnel are always lit during the day and the light filters in through the carriage window. I ease myself from the bed and immediately notice that Kelsey is no longer with me.

The floor is cold beneath my feet and I pull my cardigan in close to my chest as I move for the carriage door. I'm surprised Kelsey didn't wake me when she got up. It's not like her to creep out without telling me where she's gone.

Yawning and rubbing the sleep from my eyes, I make my way down the carriage steps and begin to slowly move through the tunnel towards Alta Park Station. I hear the rumble of voices well before I reach the platform. They drift down the tunnel to me like a lost echo.

28

When I reach the platform, I can see a group of people standing around in the corner of the station, where the food rations are stored. Someone is handing out cans of food to the people lined up before her.

As I climb up onto the platform and make my way over to the crowd I realise it's Mia. She smiles warmly as she shares out the rations. With her stunning short black hair and cloudy grey eyes, most of the men down here ogle her, but she's so sweet I doubt she even realises she has their attention.

She's ten years older than me and has a daughter, Amber, who is hugging her leg tightly today. She often helps me out with Kelsey, so we've formed a firm friendship over the last few weeks.

'What are we having today?' I ask, when I reach her.

'Oh hey, Elle,' she says, smiling kindly. She glances at the can in her hand. 'Corn today.'

'Thanks,' I reply, reaching out and taking the can. The canned food is always well beyond its best before date, but we've been eating it for weeks and no one's been sick from it yet. The camp's crops all went in the fire and it's risky to go to the market for food too often.

'Sebastian and Kelsey are over there,' she says, nodding over my shoulder.

I follow her gaze to see the two of them sitting on a set of bucket seats. Kelsey has a small frown and a look of complete concentration on her face as Sebastian shows her how to open her can by herself. She claps with delight when she manages it. I try to cover a smile as I watch them. For just a moment they both look so carefree. The smile falls from my lips as I am struck by how different life would be if we weren't in hiding.

A man clears his throat in the queue behind me and I turn back to Mia, giving her a smile. 'Thanks again. I'll see you later.' She nods and smiles back before turning to the next man in the line to hand him some corn.

'Are those from yesterday,' she asks him, pointing at the two empty cans he holds in his hand. He nods. 'Just put them on the floor down there,' she says, pointing to the ground by her side.

Once he does as she asks, Mia reaches out and holds her hand above the empty cans. A small black hole gradually appears in the air between her hand and the ground. The metal cans begin to rattle and shake before slowly lifting up off the floor. In a flash they shoot up towards the tiny dark abyss and disappear into the darkness, gone forever. Without glancing away from the line in front of her, Mia closes her hand and goes to grab a can of corn for the next person. I don't understand where the cans go, but her talent still amazes me every time I see it.

I turn and walk away, ignoring the looks some of the people in line shoot me as I pass them. Some blame me for what happened at our old camp. Not everyone, but enough that I never feel truly welcome here. I don't hold it against them, not when I blame myself too. I think they would be happier if I were to disappear from here. Seeing me every day is a reminder of what we've lost, so I can't hold that against them either.

I approach Kelsey and give her a cuddle. 'What's for breakfast?' I ask her.

'Corn,' she says, a large grin on her face. 'Do you want some?'

'I got my own Kels,' I say, holding up the can in front of her.

'Can I open it?'

I laugh and pass it over to her, going to sit in the spare seat next to Sebastian as I wait.

'Did you sleep okay?' he asks. 'You were out cold when I poked my head in this morning, so I brought Kelsey here for breakfast. I didn't want to wake you.'

'I slept okay,' I respond. I reach over and steal a piece of corn from his can and pop it into my mouth. 'It took a while though, I heard voices in the tunnel after you left last night.'

Sebastian's eyes shoot up to mine and I immediately realise my mistake mentioning them. 'But I couldn't find anyone there,' I quickly rush on. I can't imagine he'd be happy hearing about April's middle of the night meeting with Ryan on the street. He's as protective of her as he is of me.

'What do you mean you couldn't find anyone?'

I glance away from him. 'I went and took a look, but there was no one there.'

'You shouldn't be walking the tunnels by yourself at night. You *know* that. What were you thinking?'

I frown. 'I was thinking that I wanted to know if there were people out there. It wasn't a problem, there wasn't anyone there.'

'And what if it was a recruiter and you'd been found? You know they're looking for us.'

'I'm not completely helpless,' I mutter in response.

Sebastian sighs. 'You've been getting better with your talents, but you're not ready to face a recruiter with them. They're too unpredictable. What if they'd got to you and you didn't have a chance to remove you inhibitor band?'

I unconsciously pull at the long sleeve of my top that covers my wrist where my inhibitor band should reside.

'Well, it was fine.'

He nods, trying to keep the anger from flashing in his eyes. I know he's only looking out for me, but I really was fine last night.

'Are they still holding the meeting today?' I ask, hoping to change the topic.

'That's the plan,' he replies. 'April's hoping she can get everyone to finally agree on a more effective plan of action. We can't keep talking about our options forever and that stunt with the cuffs yesterday isn't going to change things. Something needs to be done about Joseph.'

He sighs, and reaches over to take the can from Kelsey who is struggling to open it. He lifts the ring tab on it to start her off and passes it back to her. 'If M was still here, there would be no problem. People follow him without question. But, April? She's just turned eighteen and, while I know she's led important assignments for M in the past, the others don't see her as their leader.'

I purse my lips. 'The crazy thing is, she could easily have everyone follow her without question if she used her talent on them.'

Sebastian glances up at me. 'Yeah, but can you really imagine her doing that?'

'No. She would never do that,' I agree. 'So, do you think they're just going to keep arguing forever?'

He shrugs. 'I have no idea, but they need to let her take charge or have someone else step up to the plate otherwise nothing will ever get done.'

'I did it!' Kelsey squeals, passing the can over to me.

'Thanks Kels, what would I do without you?'

'You'd be hungry of course,' she replies, shaking her head at the silliness of my question.

I smile into my food. I'd definitely be missing something without her in my life.

'I'm just going to check with Mia about looking after Kels tonight. I'll be back in a sec,' Sebastian says, standing and moving over to her. The line has gone now and she's busy packing away the boxes of cans.

A cold shiver passes down the back of my neck and I look over to see Luke emerging from the darkness of the tunnel. Bright purple flames dance along his fingertips, and he only extinguishes them once he reaches the light of the platform. I immediately look back at the can in my hand and try to stay calm.

I've only known him a few weeks, meeting him for the first time when we moved into these tunnels. But, even from our first meeting I've felt uncomfortable around him. He's a little older than me and is covered with toned muscles, which he wears like a threat. There's an aggressive scar running down one of his cheeks and with short, white blonde hair he's difficult to miss in a crowd. He looks at me like I'm vermin and the things he has to say to me usually make me feel like I am. I'm not sure what I've done to him, to put him so off side, but he treats me like I'm not good enough to be the dirt beneath his shoes.

'Morning Luke,' I say, as he approaches. I attempt to sound as pleasant as possible, but my effort is lost on him. He merely grunts in response and I actually feel grateful that's all he has to say to me.

I listen for the sound of him moving on, but it doesn't come. Out of the corner of my eye, I can see him standing there watching me.

'You're still here then,' he says. 'You know, we'd all be a lot better off if you weren't.'

I fumble with my can, causing it to fall out of my hands and crash onto the ground, spilling corn and liquid everywhere.

'Excuse me?' I reply, my voice small with shock. I slowly pick the can back up, clutching it tightly in my hand.

'You're a liability. We would all be much better off if you'd stayed in the hospital. Everyone knows it, but they're all too scared you'll freeze them like you did to Joseph if they so much as mutter a word.'

I swallow slowly, glancing around the platform. There are still a few people here and those closest to us are staring determinedly into their cans of food, refusing to meet my eyes. They can clearly hear what Luke's saying.

'Well, I'm here now and I'm not going anywhere,' I respond, trying not to let my hurt seep into my voice. Does everyone really feel the same way? Do they all think I'm a monster? I knew a few people must, but everyone?

'We'll see,' he responds, turning and walking away.

A shiver works its way down my spine and I try to take a calming breath in. The can in my hand turns icy cold and I throw it away from me as it begins to freeze. I stand and try to move away from Kelsey, but my seat has already become covered in frost.

My heart beats faster and my breath comes quicker. I'm losing control again. I have to get out of here. Without another thought, I run for the steps at the end of the platform. I pass Mia and Sebastian on the way, but I don't acknowledge them as I rush past.

I can't lose control of my talent in here. The more I think of trying to stay calm though, the more out of control I feel. My legs pump beneath me as I fly up the staircase. I can't move fast enough, can't get away quick enough. When I reach the top, I launch my way over the turnstiles, leaving an icy handprint in my wake.

There's no one in the station concourse and I race across the empty hall before launching myself up the stairs to get to the street. Reaching the entrance, I still don't feel far enough away.

'Where are you going?' Dalton grunts as he appears beside me. He must be on lookout up here. He stands there frowning down at me, with his hulk-like frame taking up a large portion of the entrance. I ignore his question and bolt past him, out onto the road. It's still pelting down with rain out here, but I know I need to get as far away from the station as possible. I keep running, ignoring the downpour, which quickly soaks my clothes.

'Elle!' Dalton shouts after me, his voice almost inaudible over the rain that smacks loudly against the pavement.

The droplets that hit my skin begin to turn hard as they roll off me, falling onto the ground as small icy pellets. I drive on, through the torrent, aiming for an alley a few blocks away.

When I reach it, I run into the alcove of one of the doors and sit on the ground, curling up into a little ball as I try to calm myself down. I hug my knees tightly to my chest and ever so slowly count to ten.

I need to learn to control my outbursts. I've been better in the weeks since I removed my cuff. But, in moments where I'm slightly scared or hurt, they rush out of me and I lose all ability to contain myself.

The ice always seems to come the easiest when I'm upset. Though when I'm more affected it can be the wind that whips up or flames that erupt from my hands. Teleporting rarely happens and in moments like these I truly wish I could easily disappear, and get away from the people who are at risk because they're close to me.

'Elle?' I look up at the sound of my name to see Sebastian standing at the end of the alley, which has been frosted over with thousands of tiny balls of ice. He's completely soaked from the rain and when his eyes lock onto mine, my heart begins to race faster.

He takes a step into the alley. 'Are you okay?'

I shake my head. 'Please don't come near me. I just need to calm down right now. I don't want to hurt you.'

He doesn't listen and walks swiftly to me. He sits beside me and wraps his arm around my shoulders causing me to gasp. 'But...'

He silences me by turning my head to look at him, his bright blue eyes looking into mine. 'When are you going to learn? You will never hurt me and I will always be here for you when you lose control.'

I nod and try to stop a tear from running down my cheek. He pulls me close and I tuck my head into his shoulder. I fit perfectly in the nook between his arm and his chest and having him so close eases me in a way I haven't been able to manage alone. As we sit there the frozen hailstones slowly start to melt and I can feel myself calming in response to Sebastian's presence.

'Why did you take your band off?' he asks, when he can tell I've recovered from my outburst.

I keep my eyes focused on the ground, hesitating. I know exactly how he'll react if I tell him it's been gone this whole time. He'll be upset I didn't tell him and I don't want to deal with his disappointment in me. Not today.

'It's been irritating me so I started taking it off when I try to sleep at night. I must've forgotten to put it back on this morning,' I lie.

He raises one eyebrow at me, and I wonder if he can tell I'm lying to him. He doesn't push me for the truth though. 'What made you lose control? You were fine at breakfast.'

'Luke,' I reply. Luke isn't particularly nice to anyone here, but he's been giving me an especially bad time.

'What did he want this time?' Sebastian's voice is gentle, but when I sneak a glance at him his eyes are hard and unforgiving as he glares holes in the building across the alley.

'He said that I shouldn't be here, and that he and everyone else want me gone—nothing unusual really. I'm just tired this morning and it upset me more than his taunts normally do.' I huff out a breath and rest my chin on my knees.

Sebastian drops his arm and rubs my back. 'I'll talk to him.' His eyes are still brimming with anger and I can tell he's imagining exactly the kind of talk he'd like to have with Luke.

I pull his chin so he looks at me. 'Don't you dare Sebastian Scott! Things are bad enough as it is. I can only imagine how bad he would become if you went in there, all guns blazing. It will be fine. I just need to grow thicker skin.'

'And remember to wear your band,' he adds, his eyes softening. I don't miss that he hasn't agreed to leave Luke alone.

'Yeah,' I respond. 'That too.'

'Come on,' he says, standing and holding out his hand to me. 'We need to get back in time for the meeting.'

'Thanks.' I grab his hand and let him help me up. His palm is large and warm around mine. I pause before letting it go, enjoying the feeling more than I should. 'Do you think it's a good idea for me to go still?'

'Why wouldn't it be?'

'Well, I'm worried that people don't want me here. Luke isn't alone in that wish.'

'Don't be silly; of course people want you here. You're our greatest asset.'

'Or our greatest liability,' I mutter in response.

Sebastian shakes his head at me. 'One day you're going to surprise everyone, but mostly yourself, and I'll be there to say, "I told you so," because I believed in you all along.'

I lift my eyes to the sky. 'You really missed your calling in life,' I say. 'You'd do wonders writing self-help books you know.'

Sebastian laughs deeply and takes my hand in his again, which causes my heart to flutter. 'Well, that was always my fallback career. I do quite like the ring of Sebastian Scott, "rebel," though.'

I smile and shake my head at him before looking out at the falling rain, steeling myself for our return. 'We better run back to the station if we don't want to get soaked again,' I say.

He gives the sky a disparaging look, as though he is truly pained at the thought of getting wet again. But then his eyes light up and he grins. 'I have a better idea,' he says. He pulls me close to him, wrapping his arms around my body.

'Hold on tight,' he whispers, leaning his head close to my ear. I feel the tingle of his talent vibrating through the air around us, before we both disappear from the side alley.

CHAPTER FOUR

The meeting is set to take place on the platform. Most of The Movement are already packed into the area by the time Sebastian and I arrive. It's the easiest place for us to all meet, and the largest. But with people standing all along the platform, it seems a whole lot smaller.

I spot Kelsey with Mia as soon as I walk down the steps and she runs over to me, taking my hand in hers as we search for a space to sit. We end up settling against one of the walls; the few seats down here must have been taken a while ago. Kelsey happily curls up on my lap and Sebastian sits next to me, his knee brushing against mine.

I catch sight of Lara and her parents standing over by one of the graffiti covered pillars. She gives me a warm smile, which I return to her. It's good to see her here. She's been struggling since we rescued her from Headquarters, and has avoided interacting with other people—even me. Not that I hold it against her. She deserves as much time as she needs to recover.

She looks comfortable despite the crowd and my eyes naturally seek out her wrist. She's wearing her inhibitor band, which explains her ease. I can't imagine how hard it must be for her in a room filled with the emotions of so many people.

I peer around for sight of Aiden, but it's no surprise he's not here. He's barely left the old veterinary clinic we're using as a medical centre since we got here. His girlfriend, Jane, still hasn't woken up after what the hospital did to her and he refuses to stop working on a way to fix her. Leaving the clinic for a meeting isn't nearly a good enough reason.

'What's *he* doing here?' Sebastian grumbles.

I follow his gaze to see Ryan standing over by the steps. He keeps looking up them, as though he's concerned.

'He's a part of The Movement,' I say. 'Why shouldn't he be here?'

He shrugs. 'I just don't like the guy.'

'Why not?'

He folds his arms across his chest and scowls, refusing to explain. I roll my eyes at his stubbornness and glance down at the time on my cuff. The meeting was supposed to start ten minutes ago and there's no sign of April anywhere. I look to Sebastian. 'Where's April?'

The scowl on his face drops and he stands, trying to see her in the crowd. When he can't find her, he looks back down at me. 'She should be here by now.'

'She's not coming,' Kelsey says, quietly.

We both look at her. 'Do you know why?' I ask, lowering my voice to match hers.

'I have a feeling something bad has happened.'

I immediately lift her off my lap and stand. Sebastian follows me as we shuffle through the crowd and walk up the steps that lead from the platform to the surface. Kelsey's had these gut feelings before and they're usually pretty spot on. Aiden thinks she has some sort of heightened intuition, maybe even foresight. We have no way to test it though as it always comes and goes. I've had enough experience with her feelings now, that when she has one, I know it's usually right.

'Do you know what's happened?' Sebastian asks her, once we reach the turnstiles at the top.

'I just had a feeling,' is all she says in response. She seems confused and worried about letting us down.

I smile down at her, encouragingly. 'That's okay. You've been a great help.' I look up at Sebastian. 'Have you seen April this morning?' My heart slowly beats faster. The last I'd seen April, it was the middle of the night and she was out on the street. What if something happened to her after I left?

Sebastian frowns. 'Yeah, I saw her briefly this morning. I think she was going to go check on the computers they're setting up in the security office. They acquired a generator a few days ago and it sounded like they were close to being up and running again.'

I nod and let out a slow breath, trying not to appear too relieved. I don't know what I'd do if something had happened to her. Hopefully the reason for her delay is just a minor problem with the computers.

'Let's see if she's there,' I suggest.

Sebastian pulls Kelsey into his arms to carry her and we hurry through the turnstiles and over to the door marked, 'staff only.' We push through the door and walk down a long corridor before reaching the room that we're after. I've only been here once before and it wasn't a very pleasant experience. The whole room had flooded after a rainstorm. Hopefully they've managed to find a way to stop it from happening again or I can very well guess what's going on in there now.

I'm relieved to find the security office is dry. Everyone in the room is silent though, and there's a tension to the air I can almost feel rubbing against my skin. April, Soren and Dalton, along with two guys working at the computers, all have their eyes riveted to a screen that's up on the wall.

I move towards them, but when I see the contents of the screen I stop. The pictures show Joseph standing on what looks like a rooftop with his cold eyes staring down the lens of the camera. Even though he's not in this room I can feel his gaze cutting into me like a frozen dagger to my heart. Sebastian grabs my hand, squeezing it tightly as Joseph begins to make an announcement.

'Hope City is under the threat of terrorists,' he says. 'They call themselves "The Movement," and they have committed inexcusable acts of violence against our people over the last few weeks. They have spread lies and deceit, and created fear throughout the city.

'We have spent years building our new home here on the surface and I will not stand idly by while this happens. We cannot allow these rebels to tear our community down. We will not bow to radicalism. Not even for family...'

'What does he mean by that?' I whisper to Sebastian.

He looks at me, his eyes as lost as mine. I turn back to the screen, my heart racing. Is he talking about Hunter? What could he have done? Would he really hold his son accountable? I chew my lower lip. This isn't good.

Joseph turns to look at a door behind him, which two recruiters open to reveal M standing there in shackles. He is shoved out into the open, tripping over his feet as he staggers towards Joseph. His clothes are in tatters and his skin is drawn and ashen.

'What have they done to him?' I wonder aloud, knowing the others in the room feel as worried as I do. I squeeze Sebastian's hand tighter.

'This,' Joseph waves his hand towards M, 'is my brother, Michael.' Several in the room with me gasp, clasping their hands over their mouths. I glance at April who doesn't appear shocked at all. Has she known all along?

'He has been arrested for masterminding the attack on Headquarters. This act of terrorism was planned and executed under his orders and resulted in the deaths of innocent people. He has betrayed his family and his people.

'It gives me no pleasure to say, that all attempts at negotiations with this terrorist and his supporters have failed. As of tonight, any individuals found associated with The Movement will be arrested. If they are found guilty of acts of terrorism, they will be subject to the same fate as their leader.'

He pauses, allowing the words to settle on his audience before he continues, turning to M. 'This man's actions, and those of his follow-ers, are so heinous that we are left with only one option to ensure the safety of everyone in Hope City. For the first time since we have returned to the surface, we will be employing the death penalty. He will be executed in two days, on Friday at 12 P.M.'

The camera flashes to M, whose eyes refuse to show the slightest hint of emotion. He doesn't look surprised or worried by Joseph's announcement.

I lean in to Sebastian, my mind whirling as I process the informa-tion. 'He's had M for weeks. Why is he doing this now?'

'He knows how quickly the people will turn on him when given the right motivation,' he growls in response. 'He doesn't want us gaining a foothold. Yesterday in the market square he saw how Hope would react to the truth. He's afraid.'

Our eyes both focus back on the television screen as the recruiters drag M back to the door he came through.

'Anyone with any information on this group's activities should report to a recruiter immediately,' Joseph continues. 'We will not stop until this threat to our future is eradicated. There is no sanctuary for them in Hope City. There is no place for them to rest and no place for them to hide. We will find them.' The way his last words are hammered down through the screen, it feels like they've been targeted directly at me—like he's talking to me and me alone.

One of the guys sitting at a computer switches the screen off and turns to April. 'He's made us into terrorists. What do we do?' he asks her.

April glances our way, acknowledging us for the first time since we arrived in the room, before turning back to the others. 'We need to send in a rescue team for M.'

'But you saw the way Joseph was taunting us. It's clearly a trap,' the other man says.

Her eyes flick to him, cold and calculating as she stares him down. The man swallows tightly, sheepishly looking away from her.

'That's probably true, but he would do the same for any of us,' she responds. 'We need to rescue him. I won't let him die a terrorist. We have some time to come up with a good plan and get him out of there before it's too late.'

'How do we convince the others? We can't send a rescue team without their approval and they're all downstairs waiting for the meeting to begin,' Sebastian says.

'Let me talk with them,' April replies. 'We need M back and they will understand that. Joseph is more cunning that we thought. With that pretty little speech he's turned us into the bad guys. Without M's help we'll never gain the support of Hope's citizens now.'

She moves past us to head down to the platform for the meeting. As I go to follow her I can't fight the dread I feel in my gut. What if M isn't as important to these people as she thinks? What if they see what Joseph has planned for M and decide that maybe rebelling against him isn't such a good idea? We all know the risk of being a part of The Movement now, and it's not just a slap across the wrists.

Sebastian catches up with April in the corridor. 'You knew he was Joseph's brother, didn't you?'

'Yes,' she replies. 'I think that's part of the reason he's so opposed to what Joseph has been doing. M knows the truth behind Joseph's motives. He knows what he will sacrifice to get what he wants.'

Her words cause me to involuntarily shudder. I already know exactly what Joseph wants—more power. I experienced his thirst for it first hand in the hospital, with his experiments to develop a way to force talents upon people, like he did with me. Like he tried to do with Will and Jane.

I've seen the way he commands this city with the brutal force of his recruiters. And Sebastian was practically a recruit in the talented army he's building in the north. He has divided Hope and manipulated the people with lies to keep them powerless to oppose him.

He wants the ability to choose who has the power in this city and who doesn't. If he's able to select which people receive talents, he'll have a following of highly powerful talented individuals.

But his actions today show he's scared things aren't going to plan. He's getting desperate, which only makes him more dangerous.

'Why didn't you tell me the truth?' Sebastian asks.

'Would it have made a difference?' April replies. 'Besides, it's not like it matters now. The whole of Hope knows the truth about M. Joseph may have shown that he's willing to punish anyone who steps out of line, including his own family, but he also exposed the fact that even his own brother is against him. It might make people question his authority. This could be the turning point we need to gain traction with the people of Hope.'

'Maybe,' Sebastian says. 'But his speech about our supposed terrorist acts was pretty convincing. I mean, he told people we're murders! How do we get them to see the truth after that?'

'I'm working on it,' she mutters in response.

As we pass the turnstiles and walk down the steps towards the platform, I can clearly hear disgruntled rumblings from the crowd waiting below. They've been waiting 20 minutes for April and there's an air of restlessness on the platform as we arrive.

The crowd falls silent when April comes into view. The room becomes so quiet that you wouldn't need talented hearing to catch the sound of a penny dropping against the concrete floor. The atmosphere has completely changed since we left and I can almost feel people's anger and suspicion buzzing through the air. Some have their eyes focused down on their cuffs. Others are watching April with distrusting eyes, like she's let them down.

'You've heard,' she says simply, as the crowd erupts in a series of angry outbursts.

CHAPTER FIVE

'Did you know?' one man shouts.

'How can we trust him?' comes another woman.

'He betrayed us!'

Shouts of hurt and anger fill the station and I glance between the fired up rebels and April, who appears completely calm even though most of the people's rage is aimed at her.

She walks to the front of the crowd and waits for their shouts of dismay to slowly quieten. It takes over five minutes, but only when no one speaks at all, does she respond to the group.

'I realise you are surprised to learn that M is, in fact, Joseph's brother. But you should not allow this to cloud your judgement of him. M is both brave and smart for realising how dangerous Joseph is and for wanting to do something about it.

'I have known about their relationship for a while and never once has it caused me to doubt M. Everything he has ever told me turned out to be the truth, and we would be stupid if we threw away everything we have worked so hard to achieve simply because he shared the same parents as Joseph.'

I look around the room at the people gathered. Some are slowly beginning to nod their heads in agreement as they listen to April's words.

'You all have friends who have been affected by Joseph's division of the city,' she continues. 'You know about the experiments he undertakes on innocent people in his hospital. Some of you have seen first hand that he is creating a talented army in North Hope to do his bidding. And I know you all want to see your loved ones who still remain in the ARC brought safely to the surface.

'All these things are worth fighting for, and M was the man who banded us together. We can't leave him to die.'

The place stays silent and I glance around to see if anyone will object. April's impassioned words have most people speechless. Being reminded of what they're here for seems to have done the trick. I catch sight of Luke and see one of his friends nudge him hard in the ribs as he goes to open his mouth. He quickly closes it and glares at his friend who subtly shakes his head. I'm not surprised he wants to object. He was probably the one who got everyone here all worked up to begin with. That guy is bad news.

When no one responds, April continues. 'We need to send a team to retrieve M.'

'But it's too risky, isn't it? We already agreed on this,' a woman in the crowd says, gaining several mutters of agreement.

'It would be volunteers only. I won't ask people to risk their lives if they're not willing to,' April responds.

Sebastian immediately steps forward and so does Soren. 'I volunteer,' Sebastian says. 'Me too,' adds Soren.

I place my hand in the air. 'Count me in,' I say.

'Well, if she's in then you may as well just kill the other volunteers now,' Luke interrupts. I can practically hear the smirk on his lips. I refuse to turn around and acknowledge what he's said, but I hear some voices agreeing with him. They think I'm a danger.

'She's the reason M was captured in the first place,' Luke continues. 'What will they do to us if she loses control again? I for one am

48

not prepared to pay the price of recruiter retribution a second time around.' The mutters of agreement become louder.

April's eyes look to me, pleadingly. 'I'll stay behind,' I say to her, my voice low and dejected. 'I don't want to put anyone in danger.'

She nods with authority. 'I appreciate the offer Elle, but it would be best if we had more experienced talents go in.'

The room seems to breathe a communal sigh of relief that I won't be going. I don't want to put people in danger and I don't want people to be scared, but it hurts that the people here have so little trust in me.

Several others put their names forward to volunteer. No surprises that Luke doesn't put himself forward. I don't know why he's even here. It's pretty clear he's not interested in anyone but himself.

I am a little shocked to see Lara raise her hand for the mission. April happily accepts her offer of help, which I don't anticipate. She's still wearing an inhibitor band and has been struggling with her talent after what happened in the hospital. The look of determination on Lara's face says it all though. She's clearly ready to fight back after what Joseph put her through.

April continues the meeting, gaining support from people for her rescue mission. It's incredible how much she's matured and stepped up since M was taken. I know she's young, but I truly believe she'd be a great leader for this group if they would only let her.

When the meeting ends, most people move to the edge of the platform and make their way into the tunnel. I follow them but hesitate before I swing myself down onto the tracks. Instead, I sit and dangle my legs over the edge of the platform, watching as people are swallowed by the darkness of the tunnel.

I hear the tread of footsteps approaching and look up as April crouches down to sit next to me.

'Please don't look at me that way,' I say, when I see how her eyes fall on me. There's pity in her stare and she's watching me like I've just been dumped and am broken hearted.

'I'm sorry you can't go Elle,' she says. 'Look, it's not because of what Luke said. You're too easily recognised, and you could be playing right into Joseph's hands. Your talents are too important to him and we can't risk you being captured again. I don't know what I'd do if you ended up in that hospital again.'

Her face is filled with total dismay at the thought. She's right. If Joseph has the chance he'll return me straight to the hospital to continue his experiments. If he wants to be able to dictate who has talents and who doesn't, he needs to figure out why it's worked on me. I reach out and touch her hand. 'I understand why I can't come. It's fine.'

She shakes her head. 'No, it's not fine. Everything's a mess, and the way those people misjudged you? It makes me so angry. I want to lead this group and I want their trust, but I don't want to lose my own principles to make them happy.'

She sighs and places her head down in her hands. 'I just want them to see me as the leader I know I can be to them. They need someone to guide them and I've tried to do that, but ever since M was taken our whole group has been flailing. I've been with these people since the beginning and it hurts that they won't listen to me.'

I gently rub her back. 'You've been doing an amazing job. I just think everyone here is still in shock after what happened to the camp. Just keep doing what you're doing and give them the time to come to terms with what has happened.'

'We don't have time,' she responds, her fingers gently rubbing the ridge of her nose. 'Joseph already has his recruiters combing the city for us, and now every person in Hope is going to be looking for us too. We need to do something and we need to do it fast. Our peaceful attempts at gaining support in Hope aren't working, and every day we waste is another day that he's getting away with the terrible things he's doing.'

'If we get M back, it will make all the difference,' I say.

April nods, but I can see she's not convinced. There are doubts clearly lurking behind her eyes, but she won't share what they are. Leadership weighs heavily on April and the sleepy bags under her eyes have only gotten darker since the fire. I guess we both have that in common.

I look away from her and glance back down the tunnel. It's quiet on the platform, but I can still hear the shuffles of people moving along the train tracks.

'Sebastian was talking about you last night,' April says, drawing my attention back to her.

'Oh?' I respond. I glance over my shoulder to see him standing over by the steps with Kelsey, chatting to Mia.

'Have you been leading my brother on?'

My cheeks warm in response and I tear my gaze from him. 'I have no idea what you're talking about.' I try not to look her in the eyes.

'Uh huh.' She smiles.

'I just remembered, I'm meant to be helping out in the clinic today,' I respond, trying to sound as casual as possible, though she can probably tell I'm desperate to flee her questions.

Her smile broadens as I stand, and I try to keep my face passive as I make a beeline for the steps leading up to the surface. I wonder what Sebastian has said to her. She didn't sound upset or angry about it, so whatever he said can't have been too bad. Still...

I have tried to create distance between us, but it doesn't seem to be working. The truth is, I want him in a way a friend shouldn't, but I'm scared of allowing myself to become too close to him. I've lost him once and I'm not sure I'll survive if that happens again.

The rain has stopped when I reach the surface, and the air is crisp and fresh. I'm only wearing a light cardigan, but I'm surprisingly not cold. Whilst I can feel the temperature is cool against my skin, I don't find it uncomfortable. In fact, I don't think I've felt the cold properly in a long while.

'I'm going to the clinic,' I tell the lookout, who stands just inside the subway entrance. He pulls a radio from his belt and checks with the other lookouts that the street is clear.

He gives me a small nod when he gets the fuzzy reply. 'It's clear, but keep an eye out for recruiters just in case,' he says, his gaze looking past me to the street beyond. 'There were some a few streets over last week.'

I follow his gaze to the street beyond. The black clouds that gather overhead shadow the road in darkness. In the day's gloom, the colour is almost leeched from our surrounds and everything feels like it's a varied shade of grey. Even the leaves on the bushes that grow untamed and wild along the sidewalk seem to lack any colour.

I smile and thank the lookout for giving me the heads up before leaving. I move away from the safety of the subway entrance and along the road, keeping close to the walls of the buildings that line it. It's unnervingly quiet up here, and my feet move quickly beneath me as I walk. I feel so exposed on the street by myself and I can't wait to get to the clinic.

A few weeks ago I wouldn't have been so eager to get there. It had been hectic when we first arrived. With so many injuries from the fire, it was both physically and emotionally draining helping with patients every day. I found it difficult to stay strong, especially when the place brought up painful memories of Will.

Most people have recovered now though. So my days at the clinic are spent assisting Aiden and Henry, Lara's father, with the cure—not that I'm a great help other than running errands and cleaning up after them.

Any help I can give though is important. If they find a cure, it will mean they can stop the mutations that happen when people are brought up from the ARC too soon and exposed to Lysartium. If this happens, everyone will be able to return to a life above ground. No more secrets; no more broken families. And, I will finally be able to see Quinn again.

Henry's wife, Jess, has a unique talent that means she doesn't age and he's convinced it will help them find the cure, but they still haven't figured it out. They've still been taking samples of my blood for their attempts too, but I don't think my talent for absorbing other talents is helping as much as they'd like.

The clinic is oddly quiet when I arrive. The entrance foyer is dark and there's not so much as a murmur from the rooms down the hallway. A gust of wind comes in through the open door, flapping at some of the old veterinary flyers that sit on one of the tables. I ease the door shut behind me and take a step into the clinic.

'Hello?' I call out, expecting to hear movement down the hallway or a shout of greeting in reply, but no response comes. I continue past the foyer and further into the clinic, only pausing when I reach the door that leads to the room Aiden and Henry have been conducting their research in. The door is slightly ajar and as I move to push it open I catch the sound of voices inside causing me to pause.

'It didn't work, did it?' comes Aiden's voice. I can practically hear the sorrow in his words. I wonder which experiment he's talking about. When Aiden isn't working on the cure, he's looking for a way to fix what the hospital did to his girlfriend, Jane. Either way, if what they've been working on hasn't been a success, it won't be good.

'I'm sorry Aiden. I really thought I had it this time,' Henry says, softly.

A hand slams down on one of the tables. 'We're running out of time,' Aiden responds hotly. 'She can't last much longer like this and she's only getting worse.'

'I know, Aiden, I know. What's been done to her; having all those talents forced on her. Her body has rejected them. I'm just concerned there's no way back from it.'

'Of course there is,' Aiden growls.

My heart tugs in my chest as I listen to his despair, and there's something about Henry's words that worry me. The way he's talking, it sounds like he's preparing Aiden for the worst.

I step away from the door, not certain I feel comfortable listening to any more. Instead, I move on down the corridor to the room Jane's in.

She's alone in there, but next to her bed is a bright bunch of wildflowers. Considering winter is nearly upon us, I have no idea how Aiden could have found them.

I pull a chair up next to Jane's bed and take her hand in mine.

Her skin is so fair and her bright red hair is soft next to her full lips. It looks like she's merely resting, but I know that's not the reality.

I've never had an actual conversation with the girl, but I feel such a connection to her. It so easily could have been me in Jane's position, if not for my ability to absorb the talents given to me. I know how deeply Aiden cares for her and I desperately just want for her to wake up and for both of their pain to end.

I've spent weeks in the clinic with her and though I'm never certain if she can hear me, I always have chats to her. I think a part of me hopes my words will help draw her from her slumber.

Kelsey was convinced that all she needed was a kiss to awaken her from her sleep, just like Sleeping Beauty. It really upset her when Aiden slowly bent down and gently kissed her lips and she didn't wake up. I've been hesitant to bring Kelsey back since.

I bring my other hand up and clasp it around hers. 'Jane, I know you've been sick, but you really need to wake up now,' I say to her, softly. 'Aiden needs you here and I for one would really like to meet you properly. We can't keep having these one sided conversations.' I try to joke, but inside my words only make me sadder.

'Please just wake up,' I urge her. I rest my head down on her hands and as I do I feel a surge of energy pulse through me. It rushes from my heart, down my arms and through my hands, and then leaches out where my skin touches Jane's.

A wave of dizziness comes over me. I drop her hand and push back from the bed, staggering to my feet. I feel nauseated, weak and tired, and I rest my hand on the back of the chair to steady myself as I watch Jane.

Did her eyelids just flicker? She lies there, just as still as always, but there seems to be a little more colour in her cheeks. Fear coats me like a slick sheen of sweat. What did I do to her?

I stumble as I rush to leave her room. Reaching out, I steady myself on the doorframe. Maybe I need some fresh air to try and clear my mind.

Once I'm steady I proceed into the hallway. Henry is walking towards me and as I focus on him my nausea seems to subside.

'How are you today Elle?' he asks.

'Fine,' I respond, nodding my head as the dizziness I'd felt moments ago starts to fade.

'Are you helping us today?' he asks.

I hesitate with my response. I need to clear my head and try to figure out what just happened with Jane. I'm saved from answering as Aiden appears behind Henry.

'Elle, you're here,' he says.

His eyes look red and exhausted. It pains me to see him that way, especially when it looks like he's been crying.

'Henry was just telling me about M,' Aiden continues. 'I'm glad they're planning to send someone for him.'

I nod, in a very non-committal way.

'Will you be going with them?' he asks.

Henry shoots a nervous glance my way as I shake my head. 'I'm too much of a liability.'

Aiden folds his arms over his chest. 'Well, I definitely don't see you that way. You've been such an amazing help here. This place wouldn't run without you.'

I smile up at him. He's totally exaggerating, but it makes me feel good to know that I'm appreciated here in the clinic. After those weeks captured in the hospital I thought I'd never want to see the inside of one again, but I've surprised myself. Being in the clinic gives me a sense of purpose I wouldn't otherwise have.

'I'm sure it would run fine.'

'Don't sell yourself short,' Henry says, patting me on the shoulder. He glances over his shoulder towards his lab at the back of the clinic. 'I'd better get back to work.'

'Before you go, Henry,' I say, causing him to pause. 'How's Lara doing? I saw her at the meeting today.'

'Much better,' he responds. 'She's seeming more like her old self now. I think she's really turned a corner.'

I smile at him. 'I'm glad she's feeling more herself.' In the last few weeks she's spent so much time alone I've barely seen her at all. Henry gives me a warm smile, in complete agreement with me, before he continues on his way to the back of the clinic.

'Aiden?' I ask, slowly turning to him. He raises one eyebrow looking at me questioningly. I want to get his opinion on what just happened with Jane, but I don't want to upset him. He's got a lot on his mind right now and what if I've somehow made her worse?

'Could you check on Jane?' I ask. 'I think she has more colour in her cheeks today.'

He gives me a sad smile. 'I was just going to check on her now. Do you want to come with me?'

I nod and follow him back down the corridor to Jane's room. I hover by the door, chewing on my lower lip, as I watch him check her over. I've watched him do the same tests checking for her response so many times now. As he opens her eyelid to check her pupils, I know he's nearing the end of them.

'How is she?' I ask.

He slowly straightens his back and looks at me, giving me a small shake of his head. 'The same.'

My shoulders slouch and I can't bring myself to look him in the eye. Not when there's so much pain visible there. Did I really see her eyelids flickering? I felt certain I had, but maybe I imagined it.

'I should go,' I say.

He nods. 'I'll see you later.'

I walk to the door and pick up the radio there to call the lookouts to check if it's all clear. As I glance back, I see Aiden huffing out a deep sigh and his shoulders hunching over. He needs for Jane to be okay, but I don't know what I can do to help.

It's lightly raining when I get outside. The droplets are so soft they almost tingle as they touch my face. I pull my hood up to cover my head and glance up at the sky, before I begin to walk back to the subway.

Even though the lookouts gave me the go ahead and I know there are no recruiters in the area, I don't feel completely safe. I've made this walk countless times, but each time makes me just as uneasy as the first. The clinic is three blocks away from the subway, but the short distance always feels impossibly far. Large townhouses line the street, their tall, crumbling facades making me feel like I'm constantly being watched from the dark shadows that pool in their empty windows.

I pause when I reach the end of the first block of houses, pushing my senses out to see if I can catch the sound of anyone else on the street. My eyes scan across the wide square of grass on the other side of the road. There's a small playground there with wild grasses that grow around the swing set and a slide that is covered in rust.

I can't hear anything other than my deep breaths in and out, and the ever soft rustle of the breeze through the grass. The coast is clear. I move to walk across the road, when my cuff suddenly vibrates. I glance down to see the message I've received. The comm is from one of the lookouts.

'Hide,' is all it says.

I swear under my breath and race for the park across the road. Throwing myself into the long grasses, I lay my body flat on the ground. It's muddy and my clothes are immediately caked in the wet dirt. But that's the least of my worries. A recruiter must be in the area and until I get the all clear, I need to stay as hidden as possible.

We've practiced what to do when a recruiter is in the area before, but this is the first time I've been out in the open when a message has come through for real. They must be close. I try to recall April's exact words. She told us to hide, stay quiet and keep out of sight; not to move until a message is sent saying it's safe to return.

My heart races as I wonder at how close they could be. Is there only one recruiter or are there more?

I don't want to get caught and it makes me so nervous being out in the open like this, but I don't want to risk making a run for the subway. I close my eyes and try to concentrate on what I can hear.

It doesn't sound like anyone is close. All I can hear is the sound of the wind as it softly rustles in the grasses I hide in. I shuffle in an attempt to get comfortable. I could be here for a while.

Twenty minutes pass and still there's no sign of any recruiters. I glance at my cuff, yet again, waiting for the comm that everything is fine. Maybe they're not sending one? Maybe they can't.

I lift my head slightly to look around. The park I'm in is a small square that's surrounded by townhouses. I was stupid to choose the park to hide in. It's way too open and exposed. Breaking into one of the abandoned townhouses would have been a much better idea. I hadn't put much thought into it when I'd received the comm though. All I could think was that I needed to hide, and the long grass in the park was the first place my eyes had fallen upon.

I continue to scan the edge of the park and the houses that surround it. I freeze as I catch movement at the end of one of the roads that lead to the park. A figure comes into view that causes me to gasp.

The man looks up and across the park, his eyes immediately latching onto mine. It's Hunter. He's dressed in a recruiter's uniform and from the moment his eyes meet mine, I know I've been caught.

CHAPTER SIX

I flatten my body to the ground, my heart pounding wildly against the wall of my chest. I can hear it thudding in my ears as though it were the only sound in the world. I take two deep breaths in before glancing up again. Hunter continues to watch me, his eyes bright with recognition.

I curse at my stupidity and take a quick look over my shoulder in the direction of the station. Do I make a run for it? I quickly dismiss the thought. I'd be leading him straight to the others.

My pulse quickens and I feel the tingle of my talent awaken over my skin. I close my eyes tightly and concentrate on trying to teleport out of here. If I can manage it, there's no way for him to follow me. Seconds pass though, and I'm still lying in the mud in the park. My body tenses as I urge for it to disappear. I try to focus completely on the task, but a small part of my brain seizes with terror as I imagine letting my talent loose.

The more I will for it to happen, the more grounded I feel.

I exhale the breath I've been holding as I give up. Teleportation clearly isn't going to happen. I sneak another look at Hunter. He's still watching the grasses, his eyes zeroed in on where I hide. He hasn't made a step towards me though. There's a slight frown on his forehead and he looks like he's thinking hard.

Another voice calls out to him and he slowly turns his head to the side. 'There's nothing down this way,' he yells in reply. 'Let's try back towards the edge of East Hope.'

He moves back down the street, glancing over his shoulder just once as he moves away.

My heart still hammers as I sink back into the ground. I'm certain he saw me, but why didn't he give me away? Why did he let me go?

When the comm finally comes in that it's safe, it's well into the afternoon and the sky has begun to darken. I'm dirty, wet and completely miserable as I trudge back to the subway, but at least I still have my freedom.

Sebastian is pacing inside the station entrance when I return, and I find myself in his arms before I have a chance to warn him about the mud all over me.

'You're okay,' he says, breathing a sigh of relief. 'And you've been rolling in the mud.' He chuckles as he pulls back to take a look at me.

I look down at my clothes and cringe. They're even worse than I thought. 'I got a warning comm while I was walking back from the clinic, so I hid in the park. It wasn't pleasant. Where's Kelsey?'

'She's with Mia, playing with Amber. I've been going crazy waiting for you. I knew you'd gone to the clinic, but I had no idea if you were safe.'

I smile at him. 'I came back as soon as I got the all clear. How many were there? Did they get close?'

I follow Sebastian down into the station. 'There was a team of them, about six guys. They were checking houses the street over from the station. It was close.'

I chew on my lower lip. They've never been that close before. It's only a matter of time before they're back, and we may not be so lucky next time.

We walk down the steps and onto the platform. There are a handful of people there, preparing to go on a scouting mission for food. One of the girls eyes me strangely and I follow her gaze down to my wet and dirty clothes.

'I should go change.'

'I quite like the look you've got going,' Sebastian replies, his eyes bright with amusement, as he looks me up and down. 'And I'm slightly jealous. You look like a kid who just couldn't resist the big pile of mud in front of them. I wish I could have been there to roll around in it with you.'

I give him a playful shove. 'You're impossible.'

This only seems to make his smile wider. 'Come find me when you're changed?'

I raise an eyebrow, questioning him.

'I have a surprise...'

'If it's an extra training session, you know that's not much of a surprise.' He's been helping me practice to use my talent over the last few weeks. I'm guessing he's got some time to help me today.

He shakes his head and looks away, as though suddenly unable to meet my eyes. 'Nah, it's not that. You'll like it, I promise.'

'Okay. I'll meet you back at the platform in ten minutes.' I smile and try to ignore the way my heart races as he beams back at me.

It takes me twenty minutes to get ready. I hadn't realised that my hair was coated in a layer of mud and I have to hunt down some water to try and wash it out.

I walk back along the tunnel, emerging by the platform. Sebastian is sitting on the edge of it and his eyes light up when he sees me. He looks excited as I approach him and I wonder what he wants to do.

'Hmm, maybe I don't prefer the mud,' he says, reaching a hand down to help me up onto the platform.

I can feel a blush forming on my cheeks. 'So, what do you have planned?' I ask him.

'If I told you now that would just ruin it, wouldn't it?'

I fold my arms over my chest and try to come up with a reason why telling me now wouldn't ruin the surprise, but give up. If he wants to surprise me, I don't want to spoil it by finding out.

'What are you guys doing?' April emerges from the tunnel behind me. There's a serious look on her face and she looks distracted, like she has too much on her mind to even listen to our response. She smiles as she approaches, but the smile doesn't meet her eyes.

'Nothing,' we both say at the time.

'Don't forget we're meeting in the morning before going in to rescue M,' she says to Sebastian, as she climbs up onto the platform.

Sebastian nods, a flicker of worry entering his expression as she strides past us, making for the stairs at the end of the platform. She hesitates when she reaches them and looks back at us. Her eyes are clouded with concern, and she looks like she wants to say something else, but she shakes her head and starts up the stairs.

'She's worried,' he says, quietly.

'We all are,' I reply.

He frowns and then dismisses the expression, replacing it with a grin. 'Let's just pretend for one night that we're not hiding out in an abandoned subway station; that our world is not all messed up. Tonight, let's just be two regular teenagers.'

He offers out his arm to take mine and I smile. I don't even remember what it feels like to be a regular teenager, but it sounds amazing.

'Where to?' I ask, linking my arm with his. He begins walking, but instead of heading back to the tunnel we follow April up the steps towards the surface. He leads me over to the staff area of the station.

'The security office?' I ask, frowning.

'Just trust me,' he says.

I nod and nervously follow his lead through the door and along the corridor. I can't imagine what is waiting for us in there. He seems excited about it though; I don't think I've ever seen him walk this fast before.

When he pushes the door to the security office open I stop, my jaw dropping open. The room has completely transformed from its usual bare attire. The roof is covered with twinkling fairy lights and there are piles of cushions set up facing the large screen on the wall. My pulse races with surprise as I take it all in.

'You did this for me?' I whisper.

'I know it's not much, but I wanted tonight to be special.'

I reach out and grab his hand, squeezing it tightly. 'It's more than special.' No one has ever done anything like this for me before.

He beams at me, his eyes sparkling with happiness.

I take a step into the room. 'Where is everyone?'

'They're setting up a backup office in a house in South Hope. They don't want a reoccurrence of what happened last time.'

'And the fairy lights?'

'Found them on one of my scavenger hunts. Do you like them?'

'Like them? I love them,' I gush.

He grins and leads me over to the piles of cushions. I sit down and when I look at my feet I find a bowl of popcorn there. I love popcorn, but it was always difficult to get in the ARC. I can't imagine how he's managed to get a hold of some up here.

'So, what are we watching?' I ask, guessing at what he has planned.

He lowers himself onto the cushions next to mine. 'Movie marathon,' he says.

I clasp my hands together in delight. 'Which movies?'

'I have a whole selection,' he says, picking about five DVDs off the floor.

'Are we going to watch all of them?' I ask, my voice going up an octave in excitement.

He laughs. 'If you like.'

'Yeah, I'd like.' I smile.

I snuggle into the cushions, ready for the first film. I love watching movies so much, no matter what the genre. But, as it starts, all I can think of is Sebastian's hand that rests so close to mine.

He glances over at me and catches me watching him, so I quickly look away. It feels so nice to be doing this together. My life has felt so crazy for the last few months and I can't remember when I felt a semblance of anything that looks even remotely close to normal. I don't know how he knew I needed this, but I appreciate it so much.

I notice his hand move slightly closer. Our hands are nearly touching now and I can feel charged electricity racing between the small gap between them. Does he feel the same thing that I do?

He slowly reaches out and pulls my hand into his. My heart races as he grips it firmly and slowly traces his thumb along the edge of my fingers. I feel like I'm about to self-combust and all he's done is lightly touch my hand.

I sneak a glance at him again and find he's watching me intensely. His blue eyes are charged and I struggle to look away from him.

I try to remember all the reasons why I've been keeping my distance from him. How messed up I am right now; how I don't want to risk losing him again if we allow ourselves to get too close. But, in this moment my reasons don't seem strong enough. I should drop his hand and look away, but the line I'd drawn in the sand between him and me has been blurring and it's a struggle to continue fighting the pull I feel towards him.

His eyes suddenly look down from mine at our hands that are clasped together and I gasp. I've somehow made them glow a soft warm yellow colour. I quickly let go of his hand and pull mine back to me. It immediately stops glowing, thankfully.

'I'm so sorry,' I stutter.

Sebastian shakes his head. He pauses the movie and turns back to me. 'Don't be sorry, it didn't hurt. I wouldn't mind you telling me when you decided to stop wearing your cuff though. This isn't the first time I've seen you using your talents recently.'

I sigh and try to stop the tears from falling from my eyes. I've been so pent up trying to keep it secret and trying to keep my talents under control.

'I'm sorry I didn't tell you,' I say.

'I understand that you want to keep it to yourself. I figured it out about a week after we got here when I was passing your carriage and found the handle had been frozen solid. I think you're the only person here who can do that.'

I drop my head into my hands. 'I've tried so hard to keep it down. I wanted to be the person you believed I could be. I wanted to embrace who I've become, but it's useless. I still have no control.

'What about your senses,' he asks. 'Your hearing and sight?'

'They are easier to control,' I respond. 'But they can still be unpredictable. I'm not worried about them. They can't hurt anyone...'

Sebastian gently places his hand on my back. 'You don't have to be so secretive,' he says. 'I want to help you in any way I can; you don't have to suffer this alone. But look at how far you've come. When you first came out of the hospital you never would have believed you could go an hour without the inhibitor band let alone live without it. You're already doing it.'

'For now I am, barely, but it's only a matter of time before I truly hurt someone.'

Sebastian pulls me into him and holds me close. His slow, deep breaths calm me and I concentrate on listening to the beat of his heart, which I can hear so clearly in his chest.

'These talents can be overwhelming, but only if you let them be,' he says. 'I'm still only coming into my own with my talent and there was a time when I was ruled by it. Any time I got angry or upset or frustrated I would teleport without warning. It was usually only a few meters away, but it scared me. I feared my talents when I couldn't control them, but the fear only makes the lack of control worse.

'While I know it's nowhere near to what you're going through, the only way I could control myself was to become mentally strong. You have to move past the fear if you want to overcome this and learn control.'

I sigh. 'I know what I have to do. It's just, it's one thing to know and something else completely to actually do.'

'I know we've practiced together a few times, but maybe we need to step it up a little?'

I pull back to look at him. 'You think that would help?'

'You fear them because you don't know them or understand them. Maybe if you understood your talents better and spent more time using them you'd have better control? You keep bottling things up and it only makes everything worse for you.'

I frown as I consider his words. Could he be right? Could repressing my talents make it harder to control them? 'Are you sure you don't mind. What if something goes wrong?'

'It won't,' he says. 'We'll make this work. I promise.'

I give him a small smile. I don't want to cause him any trouble, but this is something I struggle with alone.

His eyes suddenly light up. 'I nearly forgot...' He stands and moves towards the door.

'Forgot what?'

'The best bit of your surprise. Wait here, I'll be back in a sec.'

I wrap my arms around my knees and wait in the security office for his return. My thoughts quickly drift back to my talent. Sebastian is right. I am terrified of using my talents and my fear only seems to make them worse. I just don't want to hurt anyone and I don't know how to overcome that fear.

I hear footsteps in the corridor and turn to them.

'Close your eyes,' Sebastian calls out. I oblige and close them, but my curiosity is killing me. What does he have planned?

I hear him move around the cushions and then settle down on the ground beside me.

'And open,' he says.

I open my eyes and Sebastian holds a cupcake out in front of me with one candle burning at its centre. 'Happy birthday,' he says.

'But my birthday's not for...' my voice trails off. I haven't kept track of the date since before I was in the hospital. 'Is it really my birthday?' I ask, completely dumbfounded.

'Yes,' Sebastian laughs.

'I could have sworn...'

'Elle?' I glance up at him. 'It's not every day you turn eighteen. Make a wish.' He nods at the burning candle.

I smile and blow the lone candle out, closing my eyes as I make my wish.

'What did you wish for?' he asks, his eyes burning with curiosity.

'I wished that we had another cupcake so I didn't have to share this one,' I reply, poking my tongue out.

He laughs and pulls out another one from behind him. 'Your wish is my command.'

I grin and take one of the cakes from him and take a bite. It's incredibly delicious and I can't remember the last time I had cake.

'Where did you get this?' I groan, enjoying every bite.

'The market the other day,' he says. 'I saw a stand selling them and couldn't resist.'

I smile and take another bite. I chew slowly, wanting to savour every mouthful.

'What did you really wish for?' he asks, quietly.

I sigh. 'I can't tell you, because this is one wish I really want to come true.'

He looks at me gravely, but then his eyes spark with a hint of mischief. 'Maybe it's about to,' he says, with a smile.

He leans in towards me and I'm about to lean into him, when a scream shatters the silence from down the corridor. We both freeze, our faces so close I can feel his breath on my lips.

The scream comes again and we jump up, both racing for the door. That voice sounded like it was April.

CHAPTER SEVEN

We rush along the corridor and burst out into the entrance foyer of the station. April stands against one of the walls, cowering away from a large, mangy looking animal that heaves and pants at her.

'What the hell is that!' she yells, almost trying to push her body into the wall.

'It's a dog,' I respond with certainty, though I've never seen one in real life. I move towards the animal cautiously. It has a dark russet coloured fur with two large white patches on its back and a small white mark on its ear. It wags its tail and looks at each of us, excitedly. It doesn't appear particularly dangerous, but it has got really sharp looking teeth.

Sebastian stays next to me as we move closer to the dog. The animal is no higher than my knee but we still approach it cautiously.

'Where did it come from?' Sebastian asks.

'I-I don't know,' April says. 'When I came in I was attacked by the thing.' She slowly edges her way along the wall, attempting to get further and further away from the dog.

'I don't think it's dangerous...' I hedge. I crouch down and hold one hand out towards it. The dog slowly approaches me.

'What are you doing Elle?' April hisses.

'It's fine,' I respond. 'I saw this in a movie once. I think this is how you approach them.'

'Are you sure?' Sebastian asks, coming to crouch beside me. Instead of reaching his hand out to the dog, he lightly holds one hand on my back as if waiting to teleport me away from the animal if it decides to use its razor sharp teeth on me.

The dog sniffs my hand, inspecting it before panting and giving it a slobbery lick. I giggle. 'I think it's friendly.'

I move closer and lightly place my hand on the dog's head. Its fur is thick and a little matted. The animal nuzzles its head into my hand as though it enjoys being touched.

'It likes you,' Sebastian says, grinning beside me and slowly reaching his own hand out towards it. The dog eyeballs him, but allows Sebastian to pat him with me.

'Are you guys crazy?' April asks. 'It looks like it's about to attack.'

I laugh. 'April, don't worry. He's just a little dirty.' I was just as dirty a couple of hours ago.

The dog pauses and almost raises one of his eyebrows as if to say, 'it's really not my fault.'

I smile and raise my other hand to pat its head. 'I know you couldn't help it. It's not very nice outside.' I feel myself getting lost in the dog's deep brown eyes. 'How did you survive out there?' I ask aloud.

April whimpers. 'Elle, the dog's feral. You need to put it outside.'

The dog lets out a soft growl in response. I look behind me at April who has picked a rotting plank of wood from the ground and holds it out between her and the dog.

'Don't be silly. He's fine.'

'Yeah April, he seems really friendly,' Sebastian agrees. 'What should we call him?' He turns to me to ask.

'Don't even think of naming it,' April says. 'Naming it means you intend to keep it and I won't have that thing staying here!'

Sebastian and I both ignore April's comment as we both back and forth with different names for the dog.

'Max,' Sebastian suggests.

'Lucky?' I counter

'Jack?'

We continue to try different names, but none of them seem right. I shake my head and look deep into the dog's eyes. Then it comes to me.

'How about Copper,' I say, lifting my eyes to Sebastian's.

He smiles in response. 'Copper,' he tries the name aloud. 'I like it. Are you a Copper?' Sebastian asks the dog, ruffling up his fur with his hands.

The dog jumps up and licks Sebastian's face causing us to laugh. 'Well, that's settled,' we both agree.

'You guys aren't keeping him...' April says, but I barely hear her words. Something about Copper being here feels right and he keeps a smile plastered across my face as we continue to pat him.

'We should go show him to Kels, she's going to flip!' Sebastian suggests. 'She's just down in Mia's carriage.'

I grin in response. 'She's going to love him!'

We both jump up and call Copper to follow us downstairs. I hear April groaning behind us, but it's a groan of begrudging acceptance. She may not like the dog, but it's clear Copper is here to stay.

Kelsey does flip out when she sees Copper. The dog is gentle with her, even when she's a little rough with patting him.

'Where did you find him?' Mia asks us, as we watch Kelsey playing with the dog.

'Actually, he found us,' Sebastian responds.

She frowns. 'But where did he come from?'

'We don't know,' I say.

'Well, wherever he came from, he looks like he's had a bit of a rough run. It'll be nice to have a dog around again.' She smiles down at the dog. I'd never really thought about how families used to keep pets. The concept had always seemed strange to me, but after meeting Copper I totally get it.

We spend a while chatting with Mia about things we need to do to look after the dog. She used to have one and her eyes become sad as she talks about it. They wouldn't let anyone in the ARCs keep their animals when they came in, so a lot of people lost beloved pets on the day of impact.

I take Kelsey with me when we leave Mia's carriage and we head along the train tracks to our own. Sebastian walks us to the door and Copper follows, keeping close to my heels.

I let Kelsey and Copper into the carriage but pause before I enter myself. I turn to face Sebastian who stands right behind me. 'I didn't thank you for tonight,' I say to him. 'I absolutely loved it.'

'No problem. I'm sorry we didn't get to finish the movie.'

I shrug. 'I wasn't really watching it anyway,' I say, with a smile.

He grins back at me, causing my heart to flutter.

'Well,' he says, lifting one hand up to my face to slowly tuck a stray hair behind my ear. 'Happy birthday.'

He leans forward and gives me a kiss on my forehead. I close my eyes and breath in deeply, wishing he could stay close to me for a moment longer.

He pulls back and I open my eyes to him, smiling. 'Thanks.' The word gets stuck in my throat, as I catch his gaze. His eyes are smouldering as he watches me, and my heart races as tingles work their way down my arms. For once, they are nothing to do with my talent.

I hear movement in the tunnel and look over to see April creeping towards the carriage next to ours. She clamps one hand over her eyes. 'Just pretend I'm not here. I know I am,' she says, rushing to get into the train.

Once the door is closed behind her we both let out a laugh. 'I guess that's my cue to go to bed,' I say.

Sebastian takes a step back and I feel colder now that he's moved away from me. 'See you in the morning?' he asks.

I nod, sad to see our night end. I don't want to say goodbye right now. 'See you then,' I reply. I turn to my door and let myself into the carriage, softly closing it behind me.

I lean my back against the door, waiting for my heart to stop racing. The dog is already settled on the end of our makeshift bed and giving me a puzzled look.

'You better not snore,' I tell him, pushing myself off the door and getting into bed. Copper snoring is the last thing on my mind though, as I find my way under the covers. All I can think about is what would have happened with Sebastian if April hadn't interrupted us.

THE STATION IS a flurry of activity in the morning as April prepares everyone for M's retrieval mission. I want to help, but April thinks it will look bad if I'm involved in the planning.

The people here don't trust me and she's already struggling to keep them all in line. She doesn't want to push against them and cause any discord, so I'm left completely out of the loop. Instead of getting in the way, I head to the clinic to help Aiden and Henry.

Copper seems to follow me everywhere I go, but when we get to the clinic he gravitates immediately towards Jane's room. I follow him in and find him sitting at the end of Jane's bed with his head resting on top of her feet. I pull a chair over and pat him. 'I still think she'll get past this,' I say, hopefully.

Copper almost seems to nod in agreement with me and I know he feels the same way I do. I rest my head on top of his. 'She's going to be okay,' I whisper, mostly to myself.

'I heard we had a new addition to the group' Aiden says, from the doorway.

I lift my head to look at him. 'Yeah, sorry. I hope it's okay I brought him here. He seems to like it.'

'It's no problem' he responds, smiling and coming to sit in the chair on the opposite side of Jane's bed. 'I once read a study on how companionship could help patients become stronger. Maybe he'll help her.'

'Maybe,' I respond. I hesitate before continuing and asking the question I've been dreading. 'How is she Aiden?'

He sighs and rubs the ridge between his eyes tiredly. 'She's not doing so well today. Henry thinks it's a waste of resources to continue searching for a way to help her, but I can't just give up.'

I look at Jane, wishing I had the knowledge to help her. 'What's been the problem? Why isn't she waking up?'

'She's been dosed with talents, like you were in the hospital, but she doesn't have your ability to adapt so her body rejects it. The talents they injected are like a strong infection. Her body's trying to fight it, but she's not strong enough and she's losing. If we can't neutralise them or treat them, she will die.'

I chew on my lower lip as I watch her. 'And my blood samples haven't helped?'

He shakes his head. 'What you have is so unique, I'm not sure it can be replicated. Henry thinks we can find a way to stop the cells from mutating any further, but we can't reverse what's happened to them. In Jane's case, the damage is already done. He doesn't think it's possible to reverse it.'

He pulls Jane's hand into his own, clasping it tightly. His eyes are wet with unshed tears.

I look away and focus on Copper. His eyes seem sad as he looks up at me. 'We should go,' I say, as much to the dog as to Aiden. 'April's going in for M tonight. I want to be there when she leaves.'

Aiden nods, but doesn't look my way. His eyes are totally focused on Jane.

I don't need to tell Copper to get down. He hops off the bed and follows me from the room as though he can sense it's time to go.

The station is quiet when we return and as I walk in through the entrance Copper growls. I look behind me to see Luke following me down the stairs. He must be returning from a stint on lookout.

He smirks as he looks at Copper, like he doesn't believe the dog could hurt him. With Luke's talent for creating fire, he'd probably be right, but I'm sure Copper could get in a few choice bites if he ever needed to.

I turn away and continue down to the staff entrance, ignoring the creepy feeling I have on the back of my neck. I can tell Luke's still watching me.

The team going in for M are all in the security office. April glances at me as I enter and gives me a brief nod. I give her a slight nod in return, hoping the others are okay with me being here.

She has a team of five people gathered. There's her, Soren, Sebastian, Lara and Dalton. I *should* be going too, but being left behind has only made me more determined to be in control of my talents for next time. I won't be left behind again—not when I know I could be of help.

April finishes briefing the group and they slowly break apart. 'How are you feeling?' I ask Lara, as I approach.

'Good,' she says, smiling. 'I'm bringing my inhibitor band with me just in case I run into any trouble with my talent, but I think I'll be okay. I refuse to be the victim any longer. I need to do this.'

I smile at her. 'I'm sure you'll be great.'

She shakes her head as she watches me. 'You don't need to worry so much. We've planned this; it's going to go without a hitch. You'll see.'

I wrap my arms over my chest, feeling unexpectedly cold. 'I know, it will be fine. I can still worry though, right?'

She lets out a small laugh. 'I'd feel much better if you didn't.'

I take a step back from her and try to control my feelings. 'Sorry, I sometimes forget how it affects you.'

'It doesn't matter,' she replies. 'I'm used to it.' She nods her head to the other side of the room, where Sebastian stands. 'I think someone wants to see you before he goes. I could practically feel his heart leap the moment you walked in the door.'

'Really?' I look at him and try not to smile too widely when he looks back at me. Does he really feel so strongly for me? I suddenly feel self-conscious as I realise Lara will be reading my emotions.

'Yes, really,' she responds. 'I wish I had someone who felt that way about me.'

I open my mouth to remind her about Josh in West Hope. I didn't need her empathy talent to know how much he cared about her when I met him, but Lara begins talking again. 'Well, I'll catch you on the other side,' she says.

I nod. I want to give her a hug, but don't want to overwhelm her with my emotions. 'Good luck,' I say.

'Thanks. I'll see you once I'm back,' she responds, moving towards the door.

Sebastian breaks away from talking to Soren and moves over to me. He immediately pulls me into him and folds me within his arms.

'Be safe,' I say, suddenly lacking words.

'I will,' he murmurs back.

We stand like that for several moments before April calls Sebastian. 'It's time to go guys. Seb?' she says, pointedly.

'Coming,' he replies, pulling away from me. 'I'll come see you when I get back,' he says to me.

I nod. 'Look after the girls. Lara's still so fragile and April's tough, but she's been different lately. Her mind is so involved in looking after everyone else, I'm worried she'll forget to look after herself.'

'I'll get them back safe,' he responds. He gives me a reassuring smile before his eyes harden and he turns to focus on the task at hand. He walks past me, following April through the open doorway.

As they leave I feel like I have cement forming in my gut and I get a bad feeling that not everyone will be returning from this mission.

CHAPTER EIGHT

I sit and wait in the security office for ages. The men who work here don't seem to mind my presence. They're all busy on their computers and barely seem to know I'm there. I feel tense as I wait. The men are barely talking to each other and I have no idea what's happening with the group. They must be nearly at Headquarters by now.

Unable to keep quiet any longer, I push myself off the ground and walk over to Thatch who is sitting at one of the computers. He's around Mia's age and can be a bit quiet, but he always has a smile for me, so I'm sure he won't mind giving me an update.

As I approach I realise he has his eyes closed and his hands rest lightly on the keyboard of the computer in front of him. He must be using his talent to connect with the computer. Since Gadge disappeared before the fire at our last camp, Thatch is the only one in the group with a similar talent.

'Hey, Thatch,' I say, carefully placing my hand on his shoulder. His eyes flick open and he spins his chair around to look at me.

'Hi, Elle,' he replies before glancing down at my feet. 'I'd heard about the dog,' he says, smiling as he looks at Copper, who's waiting patiently beside me. Copper immediately goes up to him, knowing he's in store for a good pat. Thatch smiles warmly as he rubs his head.

'His name is Copper,' I say, giving the dog the same smile I've seen on doting mothers. I only met him yesterday and I'm already infatuated with him.

'Copper? That's a great name. Seems to suit him perfectly.'

'Thanks, he seems to think so too.'

My eyes flicker to his computer. 'Are you getting updates on what's happening with the team who have just gone after M?'

'I'm able to track their cuffs but, unless we get a comm, that's it for the moment.'

'Where are they now?' I ask, peering over his shoulder at the computer screen he sits in front of.

'They've just arrived and are making their way to a back alley behind Headquarters.'

'Do you know where they're keeping M?' I ask.

'From what we can tell, they're keeping M in the sub-level 1 confinement. It's been a little hard for us to get information like we used to since Gadge died. He was our best technical talent and I'm nowhere near as effective.'

My face drops and I instinctively raise my hand to cover my mouth at Thatch's words. 'I thought he was still missing?'

Thatch's eyes sadden. 'I'm so sorry Elle, I thought you knew.'

I shake my head. 'What happened?' I ask.

He sighs. 'We found him in the forest near our old camp after the fire. He was a wreck, rambling about how Joseph's men tortured him and attacked his mind to get information. He wasn't the same person after everything they'd done to him. We tried to bring him here, but before we could get him back...' Thatch bows his head slightly, looking blankly at the ground. 'Well, he didn't want to live knowing he'd betrayed us...'

My eyes widen. I can't believe Gadge is gone. He didn't deserve this. If he was tortured for information it's not his fault he gave our location away. Not only that, but he gave us the information about Henry. Without Henry we'd be nowhere close to a cure.

It hurts that April never said anything to me. She's been so focused on leading though, I can't blame her for not telling me.

'Thatch?' One of the men at the desk opposite calls out to him. 'You need to see this...' He stands and turns on the large screen on the main wall of the room.

I follow Thatch and stand just behind him and the others. I don't want to be too obvious in case I'm noticed and they decide to send me away.

The screen comes to life and I gasp. Joseph is standing there surrounded by recruiters. The tops of tall buildings can be seen behind him. It's the same rooftop view as his last speech. It's not Joseph or the view that I focus on though, but Hunter who is standing in line with the other recruiters, his face blank of any emotion.

'Citizens of Hope,' Joseph begins. 'It is with a grave heart that I must announce the planned execution of the terrorist leader has had to be moved forward.' The men around me still and one of them races to the corner of the room to put in a comm to April.

'The terrorist group, The Movement, has made an attempt on innocent lives today. They planted a bomb in one of the school lockers at East Hope High. Thankfully, our recruiters were able to stop the attack before it was carried out, arresting the guilty culprits.'

'He's lying,' Thatch growls. He glances at the man trying to contact April. 'No answer?'

'I can't get through.'

Thatch rushes to his computer screen. 'They're in the building,' he says, looking up from his computer to the others. 'But it's difficult to pinpoint their location. Is something blocking the comm?'

'I can't tell...' the other man responds. 'I'll try to comm again...'

I look back to the screen as Joseph's gaze flickers off camera. He licks his lips as a feral grin curves at the side of his mouth. Turning back to the camera, I feel as though his eyes are cutting through the screen and staring straight into mine as he eyeballs the lens. 'The terrorists who were caught planting the bomb will face the same fate as their leader.'

Joseph waves his hand to someone off camera and three hooded people are brought over by recruiters. They are violently thrown down onto their knees, each person struggling not to collapse completely onto the ground. The first hood is removed to reveal M.

He may have been calm when they'd first announced the execution, but there is fear in his eyes this time. He looks exhausted and extremely unwell. He's always had a slight frame, but he's clearly lost weight. His clothes hang loosely from his body and his face is hallowed and gaunt.

The recruiters hovering over the other two hooded people rip the material from over their heads. Lara and Sebastian's faces are revealed and my heart stops beating in my chest.

'No,' I whimper, both my hands moving to cover my mouth in distress.

The two of them look completely dazed and sway on their knees. I can clearly see inhibitor bands on their wrists and tears freely flow down Lara's cheeks.

'They have them,' I say, causing the others in the room to look at the screen again. My body shakes and small trembles cover my skin. They have Sebastian. My heart begins to race. They've taken Lara. She can't be there again. They can't have her again.

'Elle?' I hear Thatch ask, but his voice barely registers.

My breathing becomes short and shallow as I continue to look at the screen. They look like they've been drugged. They can't fight back and they seem to be trapped within bodies that won't respond.

'Do something,' I whimper, looking to Sebastian. He promised he'd get them out of there. He *needs* to get them out of there.

Ice-cold chills cover my skin as I continue to watch the screen. Joseph walks towards Sebastian, who is too disorientated to even recognise who he's looking at. Joseph nods at the recruiter who pulls Sebastian up by the scruff of his collar.

A sick certainty enters my stomach. Joseph is going to make a spectacle of them. He's going to kill them all.

A ball of sparking electricity erupts in the recruiter's free hand. I scream and cover my eyes with my hands. The sound of my scream is lingering and I feel a rush of adrenaline pulsing through my body. A strange pulling feeling tugs at my belly and a rush of cold covers my skin.

I feel a strange breath of air ruffle my top and I pull my hands away from my face. I'm on the rooftop, with Joseph and the others. The recruiter stands over Sebastian with electricity frying between his fingertips while Joseph looks on with triumph in his eyes.

I gasp and Joseph's head snaps to look over at me. His manic grin becomes positively frenzied as he eyes me standing there. I don't have time to try and consider how I made it here, as Joseph slowly approaches me. I feel unsteady on my feet and a little dizzy as I turn to face him.

'If it isn't my favourite runaway,' Joseph says, his voice taking on a cooing tone.

'Stay back,' I warn, holding my hands out in front of me as if to defend myself. I know my talents are powerful enough to take him down, but I've never been able to use them as I want. There's no way Joseph could know that though. For once, I have the upper hand.

Joseph eyes my hands warily and stops where he stands. 'You gave me a lot of trouble when you decided to give my office a makeover. I'm lucky I had a talented healer on hand to help my son and me.'

'Let them go,' I say, nodding at Sebastian and the others.

Joseph laughs and glances over his shoulder to where they kneel. 'When I have you right where I want you? I don't think so.' I follow his gaze and catch sight of Hunter standing there by the others.

I can feel my anger keenly in my stare as I glare at him, and he looks away as soon as I catch his eye. He almost seems disappointed in himself too.

I try to concentrate on the power that pulses beneath my skin, but the threads of it feel loose and intangible. I can't manage to grasp them and I can't urge it to rise to the surface and spill out no matter how hard I try.

'You can't do it can you?' Joseph taunts. 'After everything I did for you, all the time and energy I spent giving you those incredible gifts, you're still just a scared little girl.'

He laughs to himself and his shoulders relax, the hint of worry I saw in his eyes completely disappearing.

'Lots of people had to die so you could become the way you are Elle,' he continues. 'You don't deserve those talents you're too afraid to use. If you thought that the tests I did on you were bad, that's nothing compared to what I will make you do now that I know my experiments have worked on you.'

I growl as I launch myself at Joseph, determined to take him down with my bare hands alone if I can't get my talents to work. I'm only a few steps from him when a pair of arms latch around my waist and I'm thrown to the ground.

'Let me go!' I yell, struggling against the recruiter who holds me. The man is strong though and barely lets me squirm beneath his grasp. I throw my head back against his chin, but the man's face must be carved from solid rock for all the good it does me. He clamps an inhibitor band over my wrist and I feel the cool numbness of my talents being repressed in reaction.

Tears pool in my eyes and I kick and scream as I try to free myself from the man's arms. I've ruined my one chance at saving M, Sebastian and Lara. The man has my arms locked behind my back as he pulls me from the ground. I stomp on his foot and try to throw my head back into his chin again, but it's no use. The man's too strong for me and there's no way I can escape his iron grip.

'Stop!' roars Hunter, his voice strong and powerful. Everyone on the roof freezes, no one even moving a finger in reaction. I try to free myself from the recruiter's arms, but I can feel Hunter's compulsion coursing through me too.

'You will let them go,' he commands. The recruiters who hover over Sebastian, M and Lara step back, and the man grasping my arms releases me.

Hunter looks at me, his eyes haunted as they stare into mine. 'Get them out of here,' he says, and I feel his compulsion to stay motionless release from me so I can move again.

Sebastian, Lara and M all look like they've awoken from a dream. I start to run over to them but then stop. Joseph and his recruiters stand frozen to the spot. He has no means for defence, now's the perfect chance to finally stop him.

'Quick Elle! I'm loosing them,' Hunter yells, as one of the recruiters standing next to him starts to flinch aggressively, as if trying to rip free from invisible ropes that tie him down.

His shout launches me into action. The recruiters are slowly regaining control over their bodies, and I can't risk them returning to full strength while the rest of us are still talentless.

I grab a swipe card from one of the recruiter's pockets and tap it against the black, glass inhibitor band on my wrist. The band opens and tumbles to the ground. I then rush over and do the same to the others.

'What happened?' Sebastian asks.

M stands weakly. 'You were caught coming for me. The recruiters had your minds numbed to control you,' he says, calmly.

'We have to get out of here,' I say.

Sebastian looks between us. 'I can't teleport all of you out of here,' he says.

I shake my head. 'Just get M out. He's the important one.'

Sebastian looks like he wants to object, but I touch his shoulder gently. 'Go,' I urge.

He nods and walks over to M. He takes hold of his arms tightly and looks over his shoulder to me as he disappears, his eyes full of anguish.

'Come on,' I say to Lara, moving towards Hunter and the door that leads from the roof. I have so many questions to ask him, but there's no time for them now.

Hunter's face is full of determined concentration and there's a drop of blood slowly beginning to drip from his nose. 'I couldn't save you before, but I can now,' he says, through gritted teeth. 'You guys have to get out of here.'

'But...'

'I can't hold them much longer, get out of here!'

I nod and move past him, pulling open the door to lead us downstairs. I glance over my shoulder one last time, focusing my gaze in on Joseph who still stands there frozen. This was my chance to take my revenge against him, but I couldn't do it. Not when I could be sacrificing my friends just to make him hurt. Joseph got lucky today. Next time things will be different.

I turn back to the stairwell, which is dark inside with only the dim emergency lights flashing on. I feel a wave of unease rush through me as I close the door behind me.

I know Hunter was the one who tormented me, but the other day when he saw me hiding me in the park, he didn't alert the other recruiters. Now tonight, he was the one who saved us. It doesn't make any sense.

Lara and I run together, down the stairs heading for the ground floor.

'Where are the others?' I ask her as we run.

Lara breathes heavily. 'We split up when we went inside. Sebastian and I were heading for the elevators. The next thing I know I'm opening my eyes and I'm on the roof. We never even saw them coming.'

'Where were you meeting the others?'

'We planned to meet in an alley a few blocks away...' she pauses, as realisation dawns on her. 'This whole place is locked down and crawling with recruiters. How are we going to get out?'

'We'll find a way,' I reply, hoping Lara doesn't feel the fear that pounds through me, just beneath my skin.

We come out on the ground floor of the building by the elevators. The area before us is open and as soon as we leave the stairwell we are totally exposed. The front entrance is just behind a row of turnstiles that recruiters scan their badges at to gain access to the building.

Small lights glow by the turnstiles but, aside from that, the large foyer is dark. We don't have time to try and find another way out though. We'll have to risk it.

We silently rush across the room, jumping over the turnstiles as we each head for one of the glass doors. We both try the handles, but they're locked.

'Elle,' Lara says, her voice quivering. 'Can you get us out of here?'

'I ... I don't know,' I reply. Not knowing isn't good enough though. I need to get Lara out of here. I can't let her be captured by these people again.

I push one hand against the door and focus my will on my hands, so I can try to make a window and get us out of here. With my talent I should be able to sense the microscopic matter of the door that stands before me, but all I can manage to feel is cool glass beneath my fingers.

The warm tingling place in my chest where my talent resides buzzes, so I know my talent's still there. But, as I try to tug and pull at the power, forcing it to my hands, it doesn't respond.

'It's not working,' I say, keeping my voice low. Although I'm whispering there's panic evident in my voice. The recruiters could find us any second. I have the power to save us, but I just can't control it. Joseph was right. I'm just a scared little girl.

'Elle, you can do this,' Lara says. 'Don't be afraid of your talent, just let it loose. It won't hurt us.'

I nod and focus back on the window. I'm still terrified of the recruiters finding us, but I push aside the fear I feel of letting my talent surge to the surface. My talent tingles within me, but instead of trying to restrict it I coax it to the surface and allow it to run freely through my body.

Warmth floods through me and there's an almost prickling sensation all over my skin as my talent begins to surge through me. I welcome the power into my fingertips, and it slowly seems to build. Inch by slow inch it gathers and pulses towards my hands. When my hand glows I nearly drop it away from the door in surprise. I hadn't believed I could really do it.

I swallow tightly and tense my body for fear of losing the progress I've made. I raise my other hand and begin to trace a circle in the glass, large enough for us to step through. A soft glowing light trails my finger until a full circle is made. I take a deep breath and close my eyes to imagine the matter I feel with my hand dispersing. In my mind I command every molecule to slowly separate.

When I open my eyes there's an empty space within the circle I've drawn. I did it! I take another deep breath, attempting to hold it steady. I hear the sound of an elevator dinging behind me.

'Elle...' Lara whimpers, but I refuse to look behind me and see what's there. I'm already guessing there are recruiters, and if I see them I may lose control of the window I've created. Then we'd be really screwed.

'Quickly,' I whisper to Lara, nodding my head at the window.

I don't have to tell her twice as Lara darts through the window and I quickly follow her through. I remove my hand from the window and the glow that surrounds the hole I've made disappears and the glass door becomes whole again.

I catch sight of recruiters on the other side of the door. There must be ten of them running towards us from the lifts.

Lara grabs my hand and tugs me as I swear. 'Let's get out of here!'

I nod and follow Lara at a run as we rush through the streets to the meeting point. We've got a good start on the recruiters, and as I push my senses out I can't hear them chasing us. They must be struggling to get out of the locked building.

A sense of accomplishment fills me as we run. I have finally been able to do something with my talent, something I wanted. I try to think of what I had done differently. I had been scared, but for once I wasn't scared of the power within me when I used it. My terror for Lara had allowed me to do the one thing I never thought possible— embrace my talent. Maybe I can get control of it after all?

I glance back at the street we've just come down and watch Headquarters disappear behind a building as we run. I feel a twist in my gut as I watch it go. We shouldn't have left Hunter behind. He's not safe there anymore.

CHAPTER NINE

When we get to the meeting point we find the rest of the team there, including Sebastian and M. Sebastian rushes towards me and catches me up in his arms. I sag into them, finally feeling safe again.

April approaches and hugs me too. She looks angry and emotional, like she might be about to cry. 'You are crazy,' she reproves. 'Sebastian just told me what happened and I'm totally locking you in your carriage when we get back.'

I smile and hug her back warmly. 'Yes Mum,' I murmur, with a laugh.

She pulls back and laughs herself. 'Sorry,' she wipes one hand under her eye. 'I don't know why I'm so emotional about this.'

Lara clears her throat, guiltily. I glance over and see tears in her eyes. 'Sorry, it's my fault. I'm projecting my emotions. I've got it back under control,' she says. 'I'm just so happy we got everyone out safely.'

April smiles at Lara. 'Well, that explains it,' she says, winking at me as she turns back to the others.

Sebastian resumes his place next to me, placing his arm over my shoulder. I feel like he doesn't want me anywhere he can't get a hold of me right now.

He leans in close to my ear. 'Did you teleport all the way from camp?' he asks quietly.

'Yeah, why?'

'That's a *long* way,' he answers. 'It's definitely further than I've ever been.'

'Really?' I ask.

He nods. 'I think we're only just starting to see your potential.'

I fall silent at his words. Can I really teleport further than him? I hadn't even planned it. I was just so terrified for them all. Perhaps it was only possible because I had some serious motivation.

'Let's get back,' April says, looking to M for approval. 'Joseph will send people after us. We need to get out of here as quickly as possible.'

M nods tiredly and stands, using Soren for support.

The streets we walk through are dark and uninviting as we head back to South Hope. M is weaker than I'd initially thought and needs longer and longer breaks so our progress is slow.

Sebastian keeps my hand held tightly in his. I think what I did tonight has shocked him more than he's willing to admit and he wants to keep me firmly by his side. I'm not about to object though. It feels good to have him there for comfort.

When we arrive back at the subway the entire team gathers on the station platform for a debriefing. Though it's well after midnight and we're all exhausted, April doesn't want to wait until morning in case we miss something that happened that could put us all in danger.

Lara's parents are waiting on the platform and break down crying as they pull her into their arms. Copper is also waiting for me. He leaps up at me, placing his paws on my chest, and licks my face. When he gets back down he gives me an accusing look, and I get the impression he's not very happy about my unexpected departure.

He then decidedly ignores me and walks over to Thatch, who is standing by Lara's family. I follow the dog over to him.

'He was worried about you,' Thatch says, scratching behind Copper's ears. 'I thought he was going to tear the station apart looking for you. You have a very smart dog here.'

'I'm sorry if he caused you any problems,' I reply. 'My leaving, it wasn't exactly intended.'

'Oh, I know,' he replies. 'You gave us a scare though. Watching you disappear, then reappear on the screen with Joseph...' His voice trails off before he continues quietly. 'I thought you were all going to die. He's even worse than I thought.'

I nod. I've known for some time now how evil Joseph is. The one thing I have learnt from tonight is how badly he wants me back in the hospital. I wouldn't be surprised if that whole show on the rooftop was all aimed at trapping me and returning me to the lab.

'I just hope that anyone else who was watching was able to get a true glimpse at their leader. Did you see what happened with Hunter?' I ask Thatch.

'Once you were gone, it appeared like he was trying to escape too. Whether he did or not is a mystery. They cut the feed right after you left.' He laughs. 'You certainly made Joseph angry tonight. I'll give you that.'

He has that right. Joseph was crazed tonight and our escape will only make him step up his attempts to quash us. We probably only gave him more ammunition against us. I can't imagine the people of Hope being on our side when he continues to tell them we are dangerous terrorists.

He may paint us as the enemy but surely people are beginning to see the truth about him. Surely people aren't going to continue to stand for his rules and restrictions. We saw how fragile his power was in the market square that day. If we could only show people there's a better way...

I feel exhausted from using my talent so much tonight and don't waste time getting back to my carriage. Sebastian walks silently along the tracks with me and Copper, despite his obvious mood with me, stays close by as well. I think he's scared I'll disappear again, and wants to keep an eye on me.

I push open the door to my carriage when we get there and stand on the steps looking in. Kelsey is staying with Mia tonight, which is a weight off my mind.

I glance at the cold, empty space and shiver. Part of me wishes she was fast asleep in here. The place is so uninviting and I could really use the company tonight. I turn to Sebastian.

'I don't want to be alone tonight,' I say, so quiet I worry he may miss my words.

I see him slowly swallow. We slept in the same room for years when I used to live with his family, but asking now feels so different. He doesn't answer but simply takes my hand and climbs into the carriage with me, shutting the door behind him.

We both take our shoes off and collapse onto my bed. Sebastian wraps his arm around my shoulders and I snuggle into the crook of his arm, feeling safer than I've felt in a long time, and immediately fall to sleep.

When I wake I forget that I'm not alone and nearly let out a scream when I find an arm draped across my waist. It takes me several moments to remember Sebastian is there and, when I do, I immediately relax.

I glance at the time on my cuff. It's well after 10:00 A.M. and I'm slightly surprised Mia and Kelsey haven't come in to wake me yet. I consider getting up in search of them but look down at Sebastian's arm over me and decide I can probably wait a few more minutes.

I can hear him breathing deeply behind me. We didn't get to bed until the early hours of the morning, so he'll probably continue sleeping for a while longer.

I huff out a breath and decide to get up, my body protesting as I slip out from under Sebastian's arm and stand. I feel weak and shaky this morning. My body is completely exhausted and I suspect it has more to do with the talents I used last night rather than the lack of sleep.

I pause before leaving the carriage to look at Sebastian, who sleeps soundly. His hair is ruffled and there's a smile touching his lips. My insides tingle as I look at him and I have the sudden urge to return to bed.

Instead, I leave quietly and head down the tunnel to the station platform. My feelings for him are growing stronger, but I don't know what to do. Every day we are in danger and every day I risk losing him again. I need to stop caring about him so much because I won't be able handle it if he's taken from me again.

There's no one at the platform when I arrive. I slowly move to the boxes of food at the end of it and take out a tin of corn. My movements are tired this morning and simply walking to a seat and opening a can seems like an effort.

Footsteps sound down the tunnel and I look up as April emerges from the darkness. Her eyes are heavy and her shoulders sag. She looks as tired as I feel. She slowly pulls herself onto the platform and makes her way to the food, pulling a can from one of the boxes.

'Food,' she groans happily, as she comes to take a seat beside me.

'Did you sleep okay?' I ask.

'I should be asking you that,' she says. 'Sebastian never made it to our room last night...'

I glance away and look decidedly down at my corn. 'Nothing happened,' I say quietly.

She gives a soft laugh. 'I'm only messing with you. Whatever's going on with you two is fine. I just don't want to hear any details.' She gives an overacted shudder, which makes me smile. It's good to know I have her blessing and she better believe I would never give her any details if anything did happen. Something would of course have to happen, which I don't currently feel certain it will.

'Have you checked in on M?' I ask, deciding it's definitely a good point to change the topic of conversation.

'No. I've asked Henry to take a look at him this morning and make sure he's okay. He may need to be moved to the clinic for a little while. They treated him very badly while he was in Headquarters. He won't talk about it, of course, but I think they tortured him. There's a look in his eyes that wasn't there before...'

I place my hand on hers. 'We've got him now. He's going to be okay.'

She nods and I can see tears springing to her eyes. 'I tried so hard to be a leader while he was gone, but I'm worried he's going to be disappointed in me. Our people wouldn't listen to me and it's my fault we didn't get him out of there sooner.'

I give her hand a squeeze. 'I've never seen anyone try as hard as you did to make the right choices for everyone in this group. You made the right decision choosing to wait until now to rescue him and he'll understand. We nearly lost Lara and Sebastian trying to get him out. It was always going to be dangerous.'

She nods, but it doesn't look like she believes my words. I've never seen her so emotional before, she always puts up such a strong front. All the pressure of being in charge must really have gotten to her.

'Look, if you hadn't taken charge we would have been caught a long time ago. You had to make hard decisions and you chose what was best for everyone. That's what true leaders do. There are always going to be people who disagree with what is decided, but that's the nature of people, it doesn't make you wrong. You're only eighteen, you need to remember that.'

April laughs sadly. 'Most days I feel much older than that,' she responds. She sighs and slowly stands. 'Well, for now, I still have to look after our group while M recovers. So, I better get back to it.'

She leaves via the stairs at the end of the platform, her shoulders slouching as though they buckle under the weight of all her worries.

After I've finished breakfast I check in on Kelsey, who is playing happily with Mia and Amber in their carriage. She pouts when I tell her I'm on lookout this morning. Her pout changes to a grin when I tell her she can look after Copper while I'm gone.

Copper doesn't seem quite as happy at the idea of being left behind with Kelsey though. He keeps shooting worried looks in her direction. She's accidently pulled his tail a few times while playing and he's grown a little more cautious of her. He gives me such a disapproving look I laugh out loud. It almost seems to say, 'you're leaving me, with *her?* Are you serious?'

'You'll be fine,' I say, patting him on the head. I look up at Mia who is doing her daughter's hair. She has an intense look of concentration on her face as she attempts to braid it. Amber is wriggling like mad, and she throws an empty food tin she's be playing with onto the floor.

Mia huffs out a breath and glances at the tin. She flicks out one hand and a gaping black hole opens under the tin. The tin drops through it, disappearing completely, and a moment later the hole closes with a strange suction noise.

Mia smiles as she catches me staring at the spot where the can had once stood. 'It's the handiest talent for cleaning up,' she replies. 'All mums should have it.'

'But, where does it go?'

She shrugs. 'I have no idea. But wherever it is, it's filled with a lot of rubbish thanks to me. I wish I'd had this talent for a few of my ex-boyfriends.'

I laugh. 'Remind me never to get on your bad side.'

'Never get on my bad side,' she parrots back, making me smile.

'I'm headed on lookout, but I'll be back later this afternoon. Are you sure it's fine for Kelsey to stay?' She's already been looking after Kelsey since yesterday and I don't want her to overstay her welcome.

She nods, focusing back on the intricate braid she plaits in Amber's hair. 'It's no problem. The two girls love playing, so it makes my life easier.' She briefly looks back at me, and gives me a warm smile. 'I'm glad you're okay. What happened last night with Joseph, well, I hope he never comes near you again.' She shakes her head, as though trying to push the thought from her mind.

'Me too,' I reply.

IT'S FREEZING on the surface today and I bury my hands into my jacket pockets as I walk. I had hoped we still had a while before winter hit the city, but the weather appears to have other intentions. At least it's just bitterly cold today and there's no rain pouring or wind biting into my face, though the dark billowing clouds in the distance don't seem promising.

The lookout point I'm heading for is in a building only another block away from where I am, but instead of continuing on towards it I pause at the intersection. The park I'd hidden in the other day is just across the street and for some reason I feel drawn to it.

I've barely stepped off the sidewalk to cross the road and head for the long grasses when a voice sounds from behind me and causes me to spin around.

'What are you doing?'

I gasp with surprise as I see Ryan sitting on the stone steps that lead up to one of the abandoned townhouses lining the street. He leans lightly on his knees and while he seems a bit agitated, he looks quite well. My eyes naturally draw to the scar that runs through his eyebrow and his warm brown eyes assess me as I turn to him. I've known him since I was in the ARC, but he's always been a bit of a mystery to me. After overhearing his conversation with April the other night, I don't feel like I know him at all.

'Ryan ... you scared me,' I accuse, making my way over to him.

'Sorry about that,' he responds. 'Where are you going?'

I shoot a nervous glance in the direction of the park. With the added restrictions April imposed last night, I'm lucky to be allowed out of the station at all.

'Just walking to the lookout point down the street,' I respond. I quickly rush on before he can question why I'm heading for the park instead. 'I haven't talked with you since before the fire took the camp. Where have you been?'

He eyes me gravely and completely ignores my question. 'You

should be staying within sight,' he says. 'No one can see you when you're in the park.'

I sigh. 'Yeah, I know'

He stands and walks down the steps to stand beside me. 'You need to take better care of yourself.'

I grimace. 'I'm guessing you heard about what happened last night.'

He nods. 'Yes, I heard. What you did was foolish and very dangerous.'

'It was an accident,' I reply.

'You can't afford to have accidents. Your talents are not a toy and running around the city with them out of control is a hazard to you and everyone around you. Especially given the things you can do.'

I look down at my feet and nod, trying to keep tears from my eyes. Everyone else had said how brave I was. He's the first person who's honed in on the truth of the matter. My lack of control is dangerous and I know that, but hearing it hurts all the same.

'I'm trying to get control of them,' I reply.

'Not hard enough,' he responds. Each word is like a slap across my face and I feel like a child who's being told off by a parent.

I take a deep breath and push down the wave of disappointment I feel in myself in response to his words. All I know is, I will prove him wrong. I will get control of my talents.

When I look up, my face is a mask hiding the emotions I feel swirling within me. I won't give him the satisfaction of knowing how much he's affected me with his words.

'Why *haven't* you been around?' I ask, still not looking him in the eyes. I've seen him around the place a couple of times but not once has he talked to me. Whenever he does appear he disappears just as quickly. It's like he's a ghost, only materialising when he wants. I would have thought he'd have been here more since M was missing and our world was thrown into turmoil.

When he doesn't answer me, I continue. 'And you somehow

managed to find me in the hospital to get me out of there. Why didn't you teleport into Headquarters for M?'

'I haven't been here because I didn't need to be and I didn't attempt to retrieve M because getting him out of Headquarters is not important right now.'

'I'm pretty sure we could have used you here. And getting M not important? Are you crazy? He's the most important one of us all and they were going to kill him,' I respond.

Ryan sighs. 'Actually, he's not, but it would be too difficult to try and explain to you why. Besides, M didn't need my help, he was always going to escape.'

I shake my head. 'What are you talking about?'

'M was never going to die there.'

'How do you know that?' I ask.

He looks away uncomfortably. 'I've told you before, I have some insight into these events.'

'What does that mean? You can teleport and tell the future?'

'No, I can't tell the future, but that doesn't mean I don't have some idea what will happen.'

I shake my head at him. He's just as cryptic as ever. 'When will you ever answer me for real?'

'One day you will know the truth about me, but until then...'

'Until then, I'd much rather be left alone,' I respond. I turn from him and continue on my route to the lookout point. I don't know what to believe about Ryan and it's clear he's hiding so much from me. Deep down I feel I can trust him, but right now my brain keeps telling me otherwise. This man is hiding one too many secrets and I worry about why.

CHAPTER TEN

The moment I'm relieved from keeping watch, later that afternoon, I feel a strong urge to return to the park. It's a strange sensation and, as I return to the subway, the closer I get to the park the stronger the feeling gets. I feel drawn to it in a way that's hard to explain. It's almost like the thought of avoiding the place is painful and my feet can't help but walk towards it.

When I reach the park I glance at the steps of the building Ryan had been sitting at earlier. I feel a wave of relief to see they are empty. I'm not sure if I'm up for another dressing down like I received before. He's always been cryptic, but never mean. The things he said to me before hurt. I feel like he doesn't trust me, but expects me to blindly trust him. It makes me angry that he thinks he can act that way.

As I approach the park my pace seems to naturally slow. The place is quiet today and not a breath of air moves through the long grasses by the swings. Shivers run down my spine as I consider the place. I know I need to keep going to the station, but I can't seem to get the park out of my mind.

I cautiously make my way out into the open grass area that

leads to the swing set. The small hairs on the back of my neck stand on end and I almost feel a feather-like brush against my mind.

'Who's there?' I say aloud. Despite the fact I'm alone, it doesn't feel like a stupid question, even though my words hang unanswered in the empty air. The silence makes the back of my arms crawl and when I look down I notice a thin layer of icicles forming on my arm hairs.

'Who's out there?' I repeat, louder this time.

I hear a scuffle of movement behind me and I whip around to look at the bushes nearby. The leaves rustle as someone emerges from behind the shrubs.

'Hunter?' I ask.

He turns and grins at me. 'Winters. I knew you'd come,' he replies, taking a step towards me.

'Don't come any closer,' I warn, holding my hands out in front of me. 'What are you doing here?'

'Well, I can't exactly go home right now...'

I shake my head. 'No. Why have you come here?'

'Because you're the only person I can trust.'

I laugh darkly under my breath. 'After the things you've put me through? Unlikely.'

The grin on his face drops and he runs a hand through his hair. 'I can explain...' his voice trails off.

I wait, as the silence grows longer. 'Well?'

'It's a long story,' he replies. 'I don't know where to begin...'

'How about with the part where you tortured me in the hospital? Or when you had Lara taken away and you tortured her too? There was that time you handed us over to Joseph. There's also the time you took me to North Hope, raised an alert for my capture and left me to be abducted by recruiters. Take your pick.'

The colour drains from his face as he listens. 'When you put it like that, it sounds pretty bad.'

'Pretty bad? I thought you were my friend and you left me to become a lab rat for your father. You *helped* him do it. In what world would you think you could trust me after that?'

'We *are* friends,' he replies.

I glare at him. 'I tried to kill you with my talent. In case you didn't realise, that was me terminating our friendship.'

He takes a step towards me and lifts his arm out as though to comfort me, but I quickly step away. As I do, a small surge of talent pulses through me and the ground frosts over and icicles begin to grow on the small shoots of grass by my feet. 'Don't come near me.'

He nods and steps back again. 'I know you may never forgive me, but will you at least listen to what I have to say? It might make you understand.'

I nod for him to go ahead, but he hesitates. 'It's freezing out here and I've been waiting in that damn bush since sunrise. There's a house I've been staying in since last night on the other side of the park. Can we go there to talk?'

I eye him closely. He seems sincere, but I don't know if I can trust him. I thought he was completely sincere when I met him at East Hope High and look how wrong I was. It could easily be a trap. His lips are blue from the cold though, so he's definitely freezing out here.

'I'll come but only if you answer one question. Why have you been helping me?' First he spotted me here in this park and led the recruiters away, and then at Headquarters he helped us all escape. Those weren't the actions of the same Hunter who tortured me when I was in hospital.

He looks down at his feet. 'I'll explain that when I tell you everything...'

I fold my arms across my chest, refusing to budge unless I get even a small explanation.

He sighs and glances up at me. 'Because I care about you and I couldn't let my father hurt you again. Look, it will all make a lot more sense if you let me tell the whole story.'

'Fine,' I agree. 'I'll come. But, if this is a trap, I *will* finish the job I started in your father's office...'

Hunter shudders and a look of terror flickers over his features. He appears to remember being frozen when I found out he'd betrayed us quite clearly.

'It's no trap,' he replies, when he finds his voice again.

I follow him at a distance across the grass to the other side of the park. The houses here are large and incredibly nice. April had considered setting us up in one of them initially, but quickly decided against it. Staying in the nicest abandoned houses is the first place the recruiters would probably look.

Hunter has, of course, chosen the largest and most obnoxious looking place on the block. It is several stories high and is set back from the street behind a tall wrought iron fence. Bushes and shrubbery grow wildly in the front yard much like the rest of South Hope.

I slow as I follow Hunter through the gate. The hinges squeak loudly as he pushes it open. This place feels deserted, but what if I'm walking into a trap? I close my eyes briefly and extend my senses out to see if I can hear anything from within the house walls.

There's nothing to be heard other than Hunter's soft breaths and the crunch of leaves under his shoes as he continues towards the house. It appears to be abandoned, but this wouldn't be the first time my senses have deceived me.

As he pushes open the front door, the nervous tension I feel increases and my heart beats faster. He stands just inside the doorway and looks back at me.

'You coming?' he asks.

I hesitate but then nod my head and cautiously approach, walking past him and into the house. I eye the place as I enter, making certain there's no one else here. I refuse to let my guard down.

The foyer has an old world charm to it, with dark wooden floorboards and a cobwebbed chandelier that hangs just inside the doorway. A large archway to the right leads through to a huge open room, which holds a majestic grand piano and chairs that are covered in an ornate red fabric.

I can almost imagine the kind of exclusive parties that would have been held in such a space once upon a time. The type of people who lived here would have been well above my station in life. Much like those who lived in the West Wing of the ARC.

Hunter moves past me and into the room, taking a seat on one of the couches. I follow him quietly and sit across from him, making certain to keep my distance.

'So, your explanation?' I say.

He smiles. 'Straight to the point, Winters?' he asks, in an attempt to lighten the mood.

I refuse to respond in kind and merely nod my head.

He moves forward on the couch, leaning his head into his hands as he gathers his thoughts. When he looks up at me again there's a kind of tormented pain in his eyes. He looks haunted in a way I never would have expected and I worry about what is to come.

'You know about my talent,' he starts. 'How I can manipulate the minds of others. I wasn't always so confident in my skills and when I first surfaced my *father* was very hard on me.' He almost spits the word 'father.'

A series of images begin to flicker through my mind. I can see Hunter, younger, with his face overjoyed as he's reunited with his father. Joseph doesn't hug the boy back though. The next image shows Hunter in a white room with his eyes closed, his brow furrowed as he uses his talent, while Joseph watches on. Another shows the two of them in Joseph's office. Hunter's father is shouting down at him as the young boy cowers, tears welling in his eyes.

'He was consumed with jealousy when he saw what I could do,' Hunter continues. 'He wanted control of my talent and he pushed me in ways I would never wish upon anyone. He scared me more than I care to admit. He wouldn't let me go to school and kept me hostage in our apartment in North Hope, pushing me further and further each and every day. One day, I snapped. I couldn't take his treatments anymore, so I escaped.

'I ventured deep into East Hope and started a new life for myself.

With my talent, I managed to easily avoid recruiters and even the school had no idea who I truly was. I thought I'd finally managed to get out.' He laughs sadly to himself. 'And for a while I had.

'When I first met you I read your mind, just like I did with almost everyone, and I found myself surprised. Your thoughts were kind and I saw you'd escaped from your ARC to find one of your friends. It was refreshing to be around someone like that, who didn't care about talents or being talented, and I found myself wanting to help you. It had been so long since I'd had a purpose, and I wanted you to trust me. I wanted you to want to be around me the way I wanted to be around you.'

The images enter my mind again but this time they're visions of me—the way Hunter sees me. He shows me the moment he first saw me in the park in East Hope and the time he used his talent to draw on my tablet in class. I see myself fall to the ground in the darkness of the loft party and watch him come to my aid. There are flashes of me smiling at him, laughing at one of his jokes. Through his eyes I am beautiful and I look down at my hands, uncomfortable with seeing myself this way. The images stop and when I look up at him he's frowning, but he continues with his explanation.

'When I suggested we go to the Reintegration Centre it was partly because I wanted to help you find your friend, but also, I'd heard rumours of a man who was opposed to my father. I'd caught thoughts from people about a group who wanted to fight against him.'

'M,' I whisper.

He nods. 'Little did I know, M was actually my uncle.' He shakes his head and runs his hand through his hair. 'So, that's when I took you and Lara to the Reintegration Centre. She was after her father, you were after Sebastian and I wanted to find any clue I could on how to contact M.'

'But you said you took us there so Lara would get caught...'

'That was a lie,' he says softly. 'I wasn't myself when I said those things.'

'Why would you lie?'

'I'm getting to that,' he says. 'When we went to North Hope for Sebastian I was severely weakened. The recruiters caught me and I couldn't fight back. They took me to my father and I will never forget the evil look on his face when they brought me in. I felt like I'd been returned to the devil and he was welcoming me back to Hell.'

I clench my teeth as I wait for him to show me in my mind, but thankfully the images don't come. His return must have been too terrible for him to share.

'He locked me up again, returning me to life as a prisoner. But this time he was angry with me. He wanted to punish me for my ways. He wanted to teach me to become just like him.

'He kept me weak, feeding me little and having his men beat me so I couldn't escape. I always thought I was a strong talent, but I was so fragile after his torture that I was easily controlled by another mind manipulator he has working for him. He had complete control over my mind and I couldn't escape.

'It was a week before I saw you again. You were in the hospital and looking so ill, I wanted to get you out of that place, but it was like that small part of my brain was trapped in a cage and the person who spoke and talked was no longer me.

'I was an empty shell doing my father's bidding and I couldn't stop it. I couldn't stop a single thing I did. He had me torture you; he had me torture Lara and countless others with my talent. It wasn't until you froze me in Headquarters, and I was healed, that I managed to get free.

'It was like a bar to my cage had been wrenched open and I could finally speak my own words and move my own hands. My father didn't realise what had happened, so I had to keep following his orders, biding my time as I rebuilt my strength—waiting for a chance to escape.

'Then, when I saw you on the roof, I knew I couldn't pretend any longer. You and Michael were going to die if I didn't do something. So I did...' He stops, as though he's run out of words, and watches me closely.

I take a deep breath and consider what he's said and the images he's shown me. The whole time I've known Hunter he has seemed so sure of himself, so free. I never imagined that anything so terrible could have happened to him. The thought of him being locked away and tortured by his own father is awful. It sounds like he was as much Joseph's prisoner as I was. It's such a terrible story I can't believe he would lie about it. But can I really trust that he is telling the truth?

'How can I believe any of this?' I ask. He could so easily be lying and I've been foolish enough to believe him once before, to my detriment. Am I stupid enough to trust him again?

He sighs. 'I don't expect you to believe me right away, but I will prove myself to you. To the others...'

'You think I'll take you to them?' I guess.

He nods. 'I can be of help. They need me as much as I need them. We want the same things. My father can't be allowed to get away with this anymore.'

'I can't take you to them; not when you could so easily be lying. You could be here to get information and turn us in to your father. It wouldn't be the first time.'

'I'm not,' he replies. 'But, I understand if you need time to see that.'

I look him closely in the eyes. He seems so sincere that he wants to help, but there's no way to be sure. Not when he could be planting the thoughts in my mind.

'I'll talk with the others and see what they say,' I decide. 'If they are willing to meet with you I will be in contact.'

He nods gravely. 'That is all I ask.'

CHAPTER ELEVEN

I 'm almost back at the subway when Sebastian emerges from the entrance. He rushes towards me, his face flushing with relief.

'Where have you been?' he asks.

I open my mouth to reply, but he cuts me off before I answer. 'You never returned from keeping watch. The other lookouts were going to issue an alert.'

I stare at his chest, as I can't bring myself to look him in the eyes. He's going to be so angry with me when he finds out. 'I'll tell you, but I think we need to find April and M first. They need to hear too.'

I look up and find him watching me with a puzzled expression, but he quickly nods. 'I think they're in the security office.'

I follow him back to the subway, and we head straight for the security office. We find M and April both inside watching one of the screens intently. There are dark circles around M's eyes and his face is still drawn. He looks like he should be resting, but I can't imagine him agreeing to take it easy and recover.

'I need to talk to you,' I say, as we enter the room, shutting the door behind us. 'Something's happened and I'm not sure you're going to like it.'

M gives me the nod to go ahead and April stands back, crossing her arms over her chest.

'You weren't the only one to escape last night,' I say, addressing M. 'Hunter also managed to get away from Joseph...' I continue, repeating everything Hunter had just told me. The only thing I leave out is his current location.

'You think we can trust him?' April's voice is thick with disapproval. 'After all he did to you? Are you crazy.'

M watches me closely and I look to him as I respond. 'I'm not sure if he can be trusted, which is why I came to you. He's your nephew and you know him best. If you're not sure, we could send someone talented who may be able to get the truth from him. All I know is what he's told me. It's up to you what we do.'

M nods and draws a long breath in as he considers me. 'You did the right thing bringing this to me. I already know of the torture my brother has put him through, so that much at least is true. But I think we should send someone to interrogate him, so we can be sure of his intentions.'

I gulp as I hear the word interrogate. It sounds unpleasant and makes me worry about what they have planned for him.

'April?' M says. 'I would like for you to go with Elle now and use your persuasion talent to get Hunter to tell you the truth. If he's been lying, he needs to be dealt with. If it's the truth, well, there will be a lot to consider before we allow him to join us here.'

April nods grimly and I shudder in response. How exactly does M 'deal' with people? I'm not certain I want to find out. Even after everything Hunter has done to me, a part of me doesn't want to see him hurt.

'I want to go with them,' Sebastian says, from beside me. He hasn't said a word since I started explaining what happened with Hunter today and has been oddly silent since. 'I won't be able to tell if Hunter is lying, but I can at least help protect the girls.'

M nods. 'That's fine with me. Now if you'll excuse us, I'd like to have a word with April before you leave.'

Sebastian and I both nod and withdraw back to the door in silence. I shoot one last glance at M as we leave. He looks so tired and malnourished, but the passion for The Movement still burns in his eyes.

Now that I look at him, I can see a certain resemblance between him and Joseph. It's not much, but they have the same thin lips and hooked nose. Looks aside though, they have very different values. I've never been M's biggest fan, but I could never fault where his heart lies.

'How did you know where to find Hunter?' Sebastian asks, once we've left the room.

I shrug. 'I didn't. I just had a gut feeling I needed to go to the park.'

'You weren't worried it was a trap? You should have taken someone with you.'

'I didn't expect to find him. I wasn't even certain I was going to look for him. All I knew was that I was drawn to the spot where he was.'

Sebastian looks unsure but then the look of confusion drops from his face and he rubs his hand through his hair. 'Well, he's the reason we're still standing here today so I'm not about to question it. I just hope that this isn't some plan of Joseph's and that Hunter is for real. It doesn't matter how many times he may rescue us though; I will never call him a friend after what he did to you in that hospital.'

I take his hand in mine. 'It may not have been him at all from the sounds of it. Let's just give him a chance. We owe him that at least.'

He nods. 'I still don't have to like him,' he replies.

April joins us several minutes later and we set off for the park. Sebastian stays quiet as we walk and April keeps shooting me uncertain glances. They're worried about me, but they have no need to be. I met with Hunter by myself and nothing untoward happened. I doubt anything bad will happen now. I'm the one Joseph wants and if Hunter had wanted to take me, he had the ideal opportunity earlier.

April gives us instructions as she walks.

'Sebastian, stay close to Elle when we get there. If anything happens with Hunter, I want you to teleport her out of there as quickly as possible.'

'What about you?' he asks.

'I can take care of myself. Just make sure she's safe.'

Sebastian nods, but he looks concerned. He clearly doesn't like the idea of leaving April behind. He's not the only one.

I take them directly to the house Hunter is staying in and April lets out a derisive snort as I push the front gate open.

'What?' I ask, pausing with my hand on the metal handle.

'Nothing,' she responds, her eyes the picture of innocence. 'I just think it's typical he chose the biggest house on the street,' she mutters.

The door opens as we walk up the steps to the porch and Hunter peers out, opening the door wide when he sees it's us.

'You're back,' he says, a hint of surprise in his voice.

I shrug. I'm back but that doesn't mean I trust him. His eyes flick past me to April.

'Beth,' he says, eyeing her closely. 'Or can I call you April now?'

She clenches her teeth tightly together, barely withholding her anger at him. 'It's April.'

'The Masons are pretty upset that you've disappeared,' he says.

I turn to face her. 'They think you disappeared?' Even though Paul Mason works with Joseph, his whole family had been so kind to me when I stayed with them. I understand why April had to convince them she was their daughter, Beth, but thinking about how worried the family must be makes me feel slightly guilty.

She shrugs. 'Things changed. I've clearly had other priorities over the last few weeks.' Her eyes flicker to mine, and for a moment I see the weight and stress running The Movement has taken on her.

Hunter looks past April to Sebastian who stands behind. 'This is the guy you're in love with?' he asks me.

I splutter in response, my heart leaping to my mouth. Did Hunter really just say that out loud? I can't bring myself to turn and see Sebastian's reaction.

April saves me the indignity of responding myself. 'This is my brother, Sebastian,' she says coolly.

Hunter nods, then steps back from the doorway and waves us in. 'Well, please step into my office,' he remarks.

I move to follow him and April grabs my arm before I walk through the doorway. 'Stay on guard,' she says, under her breath.

Once we're seated in the front entrance room, April asks Hunter to repeat what he told me earlier.

'You will tell me what you told Elle earlier, *but you will only tell me the truth about why you helped Joseph*,' she says. '*You will not lie.*' Her voice is soft and has taken on a dreamy quality as she laces her words with her persuasion talent.

Hunter's eyes cloud over and he gives her a dreamy nod in return, before launching into his speech. His words have no inflection in them and are monotone without any emotion in them. He almost sounds like a machine as he recounts the same things he told me earlier.

I glance at Sebastian, who refused a seat and stands behind my chair. There's a dark look of concentration on his face as he watches Hunter. He looks ready to move at a moment's notice if Hunter tries anything on us.

April purses her lips as she listens to Hunter's explanation. Give or take, his account is the same as earlier and he was clearly telling me the truth.

When he finishes April gives him a short nod and turns to me. 'Let's go,' she says, standing to leave.

I glance between her and Hunter. What's been decided? Is he coming with us? Does April believe the things he just repeated are true?

When we reach the door she pauses and looks back at Hunter. 'We'll let you know,' she says.

'Don't take too long. I can help The Movement,' he replies.

April raises one eyebrow but then continues as though Hunter hasn't said a word. 'Until then, I suggest you stay here,' she says. Her voice has taken on the same eerie sound as earlier. It's almost hypnotising as her lips curl around each word. '*Do not come to find us and do not seek Elle out.*'

Hunter nods and the milky tone to his eyes returns for a moment. It's not until we're at the gate and leaving that it seems to pass. He lifts his hand in one small wave to me, and then winks. There's a knowing look in his eyes, and I worry that perhaps he wasn't as affected by April's talent as he's led us to believe.

I don't wave back at him, I merely turn and follow April as Sebastian places his hand on my lower back and guides me onto the road.

No matter what April and M decide, there's something I don't trust about Hunter.

'So?' Sebastian asks, as we walk back through the park, past the swing set. Even he has to move quickly to keep up with the rapid pace April sets. She walks purposefully, like she's late and rushing to be somewhere, but maybe she's also hurrying to get away?

April glances at me before she responds to Sebastian. 'He appears to be telling the truth,' she says, almost reluctantly. She chews on her lower lip as she thinks about it. 'Everything he said fits with what Elle told us earlier.'

'You really think his father put him through all that?' I try not to sound too startled, but my voice betrays me as the words rush out of my mouth.

She nods. 'You've seen first hand what Joseph is like. I'm surprised you're surprised.'

'But to his own son?' I continue.

She sighs. 'I guess not everyone gets a father like we had...'

We all fall silent as we consider the reality of Hunter's story. It's not until we reach the other side of the park that anyone speaks again.

'I just don't understand how anyone could have thought Joseph was fit to be in charge,' Sebastian says. 'The guy is obviously not the right man for the job.'

April looks undecided before she responds, like she's considering whether she should say anything. 'He seemed like the man for the job at the time,' she says thoughtfully.

'How do you know that,' Sebastian asks?

'M told me how this all started,' she begins. 'Joseph and M were from a military family. They knew the ins and outs of military strategy before they knew their times tables. It's how they came to be in their ARC. Their father was one of the head military commanders in charge of its protection, and they were both up and coming soldiers.

'Each ARC had a chief purpose, and theirs was surface exploration after the day of impact. The problem was that people kept coming back sick—so sick they ended up dying.'

'They were mutating too fast,' I say, quickly guessing the reason why.

She nods. 'But Joseph never got sick. From what I've heard, he was on nearly every surface mission and he was never affected. Not in the slightest.'

'Because he was talented?' I ask.

She shakes her head. 'No, that's the thing. Joseph isn't talented, he's immune to the effects of mutation.'

'But he's obsessed with talents.'

'Because he doesn't have one,' she finishes for me. I can feel the shock register on my face as her words settle within me. It certainly explains his obsession with the hospital and with the experiments on Will, Jane, me and all the other patients. He wants to make himself talented.

'And that's why he was so jealous of his son's talent,' Sebastian concludes.

'I guess so,' April says, taking a deep breath before she continues. 'Because of his immunity, Joseph was in charge of settling Hope. The council knew they couldn't go above ground safely, unless they were tainted, so they gave him interim powers to take control of the surface. Initially, he was brilliant at what he did. He had the city up and running quicker than anyone else could have dreamed.

'But, he was arrogant. Once The Sphere was in place he thought it would reduce Lysartium exposure for the people within Hope, so he brought his wife, son and brother to the surface. It was too soon for his wife. His arrogance caused her death, but Hunter and M were already tainted at the time, so they survived.

'Once his wife died he wasn't the same. The traits that made him brilliant became his worst assets. It was when she died that he began building the wall and started his experiments in the hospital. He became obsessed with creating the perfect race. He's had an explanation for every restriction he's put in place so people continue to follow blindly. At first he was the right man for the job...'

'But he's clearly not anymore,' I finish for her.

We fall silent as we continue to walk, each of us deep in thought as we consider what April has said. My heart goes out to Hunter. How he's put up with such a cruel and selfish father, I have no idea. The things he's done to his own son are just as bad as the things he's done to me—a girl he doesn't even know.

We round the corner and I realise we are nearly back at the subway. I feel a chill go through me as the wind whips up. I wrap my arms around myself and look up at Sebastian. He's got such a serious look on his face and his eyes are deep in thought. He catches me watching and gives me a small smile, which makes me feel better.

He reaches out and takes my hand in his, giving it a small squeeze. I give his a small squeeze back before letting go. Everything will be okay. We will fix this somehow.

I stop at the intersection and look over my shoulder in the direction of the clinic. 'I should go see if they need a hand at the clinic...'

'Go ahead,' April says. 'I need to talk with M about Hunter.'

Sebastian looks like he wants to come with me, but I give him a small smile and tell them I'll be back later. I turn to walk to the clinic before he decides to join me. It's not that I don't want his company, but going to the clinic is something I like to do myself. It's like my own little haven away from the dark station that I can escape to and I like to help them out without any distractions. Sebastian is definitely a distraction.

The clinic is quiet when I arrive. There are no volunteers walking the corridors and no talking from the patient rooms. I walk to Aiden's office, but he's not there, so I head to the back of the clinic where Henry has his lab.

I knock once and enter to find the two of them talking excitedly. When Aiden looks up he grins at me. 'Henry's done it,' he says, finding it difficult to keep the enthusiasm from his voice. 'He's created a cure.'

'What?' I exclaim, looking to Henry who smiles encouragingly.

'We will still need to test it on humans, but I think we've found a way to halt the mutations. It could be the cure people need to leave the ARC and return to the surface.'

'Oh my gosh Henry!' I exclaim. I squeal and rush over to hug them both.

Henry clears his throat when I pull back, trying to look more formal after my enthusiastic hug. 'Well, we can't get too excited now. We haven't tested it yet.'

Aiden and I don't really hear him though, as we're too busy laughing and dancing around with happiness. I halt suddenly, looking at Aiden seriously. 'What does this mean for Jane?' I ask.

His shoulders slouch and sadness touches his eyes. 'This won't help her,' he answers softly. He quickly pushes the emotion down and allows a smile to come back to his face. 'But that doesn't mean we shouldn't celebrate this achievement.'

I smile and nod with him. 'When did it happen?' I ask, turning to Henry.

'Last night,' he says. 'I'd been working on a serum using a combination of your blood and Jess' blood. When mixed together, her cells will act as a shield against mutations, and your cells ability to absorb new talents will help the body absorb the cure. It's finally worked. I haven't slept all night,' he adds, stifling a yawn.

'So what happens next?' I ask.

They both look at me hesitantly. 'We need to start human trials,' Henry says.

I take an instant step back. After what happened to me in the hospital, I find the idea of them doing trials on people to test their cure completely wrong. 'But you can't do that,' I say, finding my voice.

'Elle, it would only be on people who volunteer,' Aiden says softly, sensing my distress.

'It's still not right,' I say.

'Maybe not, but it's the only way to go ahead with it. We cannot administer it to a whole group of people without testing it on a smaller sample first. If it doesn't work, it would affect everyone, rather than just a few.'

'Who would volunteer for that?' I ask.

Aiden shoots a glance at Henry. 'That's our next problem,' he says. 'It won't work on people who are on the surface because their bodies have already been exposed to Lysartium. We need volunteers who aren't already tainted.'

'How will you get them?' I ask, but I think I already know what he's going to say.

'We need to go back to the ARC.'

CHAPTER TWELVE

Aiden and Henry swear me to secrecy before I return to the station. They need to tell M about their cure before anyone else knows so he can form a plan of action. I don't like keeping it a secret from Sebastian and April, so I find myself avoiding them when I get back.

Copper and I sit on one of the red fabric seats in my train carriage, essentially hiding. I listlessly run my hand though the fur on his back as I stare at the thick graffiti on the ceiling. Henry's cure could mean so many things, but I still find it difficult to come to terms with the fact they want to test it on someone first. What if they got something wrong with it? What if someone dies because they made a mistake?

They both seem so certain this is it though. Henry had seemed close to creating a cure for weeks now. Maybe he really has done it.

I sigh and look down at where my hand runs through the dog's fur. 'Do you think it will work, Copper?' I ask. He swivels around to look at me and tilts his head, almost as if he wishes he could understand what I'm saying. I rub the top of his head affectionately. 'It's okay boy. I'm not sure if it will work either.'

There's a loud knock at the door. 'Elle, I know you're hiding out in there,' April yells. Before I can answer she opens the door and walks in. She stands over me with her hand firmly on her hips. 'You should really find a better hiding place to sulk in.'

'I'm not sulking,' I reply.

She eyes me closely and takes a seat opposite me. 'Are you upset after we saw Hunter today?' she asks.

'No, it's not him,' I answer.

'So, why are you avoiding everyone?'

'It's nothing important,' I respond. 'Did you and M come to a decision about what you're going to do with Hunter?'

She nods. 'We're going to bring him in tomorrow morning.'

My mouth drops in surprise. 'So, you trust him...'

'I'm not sure,' she replies. 'But I do believe what he's told us. In all the time I knew him at school, he may have been cocky, but he was never the type to torture people. I honestly don't believe that's in him.'

I nod. 'I feel the same way. Thinking back to when I saw him in Joseph's office at Headquarters, I feel like the guy looking at me then wasn't Hunter. It can't have been. He wasn't the same person.'

April looks over my shoulder and out the window at the darkened walls of the tunnel. Her eyes are troubled and her thoughts seem to have moved beyond the confines of the train.

'If M thinks we can trust him, I'm sure we can,' she says softly. She sighs and rubs her eyes before looking back at me. 'I just don't want to give him the chance to hurt you again.'

I reach out and give her hand a squeeze. 'We won't let him.'

'No. Not if I have anything to do with it.' She folds her arms across her chest and her body stiffens. Looking into her eyes, I can almost see her planning what she would do if he did hurt me again.

'How's M feeling?' I ask, trying to distract her from Hunter.

'Better, but he's not resting as much as he should be. He's been through so much, but he refuses to stop and allow himself to recover. His heart is so invested in The Movement he can't allow himself to rest for even one moment. I'm just glad we have him back,' she says, with a smile.

'People do seem more positive now that he's back,' I agree. 'But I still think you were doing brilliantly as a leader.'

'Thanks,' she says, with a smile. 'Let's just say I'm not going to miss it.'

A knock sounds at the door and Sebastian peeks his head in.

'Seb. I should have known that would be you,' April says, winking at me. 'I've just remembered I need to be anywhere but here right now.' She quickly jumps up and dashes out the door before we can say anything.

Sebastian smiles and comes to sit on the seat next to me. 'You've been hiding,' he says.

I nod.

He frowns and looks down at his hands. 'Is it because of Hunter today?'

I pause as I consider my response. 'Your sister came to the same conclusion, but no, it's not because of him. I just have some things on my mind right now.'

He gives me the same look of understanding he always does as he nods. He won't question me about it, as he knows I'd share what is bothering me if I was ready to. Instead his eyes brighten and a look of resolve settles in them. 'I thought we should train tonight,' he says.

'Are you sure that's a good idea?' I nervously chew on my lower lip as I consider it. We've practiced using my talent together a couple of times since we left the camp but, so much has happened recently, I'm worried about what could go wrong.

'Of course it is. We talked about this; we need to practice more. Now that we have M back I imagine Joseph will be stepping up his attempts to find us. I want you to be prepared if he does.'

Joseph's name being spoken out loud causes my stomach to drop. Sebastian is right. Joseph will be coming for us sooner rather than later, especially after he lost M, Hunter and me at the same time. It sounds like I'm crucial to his plans and I won't be safe until I can protect myself and those around me.

'Where do you think we should practice?' I ask.

Sebastian's eyes twinkle at me. 'I know the perfect place.'

SEBASTIAN TAKES us to an old stone building. It's a short walk from the subway and well within sight of the lookouts, who watch for recruiters from the station entrance and different points along the road.

I walk past this place every time I go to the clinic and have always marvelled at the structure but never thought to go inside. Set back from the street, the building has a peaked roof with a large bell hanging in a tower overhead and stone statues carved into the façade.

I try not to let my nerves get the better of me as we approach the building. My skin crawls as Sebastian pushes open the huge front door. The rotting wood is battered and weatherworn, and groans loudly as it slowly creaks open. A small, dark chamber is revealed within. A thick layer of dust has settled over the cold, stone tiles that run across the floor, and silence permeates the air, assaulting the senses.

The chamber is mostly empty, but for a single door on the opposite wall that leads further into the building. Sebastian pushes through the second, inner door and I jump as the outer door slams shut behind me. I rush to get closer to Sebastian, feeling a wave of anxiety run through me.

The second room we walk into is a huge open hall that takes up most of the building. It's lighter in here, with large, multi-coloured windows that allow the moon's light to shine into the room. Some of the windows are broken, but the ones that are still intact group together to form vivid and beautiful images.

Rows and rows of benches line the walls and a long tattered carpet extends down the centre of the room. Against the far wall there's a huge wooden cross. The sight of it causes me to shiver. I never thought I'd enter one of these places and I'm not sure if I feel comfortable here.

'A church?' I ask Sebastian, my voice echoing through the hall.

He silently nods and moves forward, his footsteps loud against the stone floor. Before impact religion had been such an important part of life for many people, but that changed after everything happened. While people in the ARC were entitled to their beliefs, there were no places of worship erected and few people seemed to observe religious doctrines. I've never been certain whether or not to believe in God, but it does feel wrong to use a place like this for practicing my talent.

'You really think this is the best place?' I ask him.

'Well, we can't exactly practice in the subway after you nearly caused that cave in last time, and we need somewhere large enough that you can't cause too much damage. I think this building is about as sturdy as it gets. I'd like to see you try and knock it down.' He grins at his comment.

'Don't laugh too soon,' I mutter. Knowing my luck, I'll walk away with this place a crumbling ruin behind me.

Sebastian finds a spot on the floor and sits down. I seat myself opposite him. The ground is hard and cold beneath me and the shadows that creep up the walls are long and dark.

'Let's just get this over with,' I say, wanting to get out of the church as quickly as possible.

Sebastian smiles knowingly. 'So, when we're practicing tonight, I want you to relax. I don't want you to be afraid of your talents. There's no reason to be. You are in a safe space and I can disappear at a moment's notice if needed, so you won't hurt anyone. Tonight, don't think about trying to control your talents. Just let them flow through your body. It's as natural as breathing if you allow them to run free.'

'It's easier said than done,' I murmur.

'I know it's difficult,' he says. 'But you're safe here and it's worth a try.'

I let out a breath and nod. I understand what he wants me to do, but I'm not sure I can do it. If I let my talents roam free I'm worried they will burst out and do something I'm not prepared for.

Perhaps he is right though. I've been able to use my talented sight and hearing for weeks instinctively without trouble, like they are no different from my normal senses. I think it's because I'm not afraid of hurting someone with them. If I finally embrace my other talents, maybe I will be able to keep them within my control.

'What talent do you want to work on?' he asks.

I hesitate, thinking back to the time I had been sitting with Jane and thought I saw her eyelids flicker. Aiden said there had been no change in her condition, but I felt like I'd done something to her. Maybe I had used a talent I didn't even know I had. What talents lurk deep within me waiting to come out?

'Is there a way to know what talents I might have?' I ask.

Sebastian frowns. 'There's not exactly a test. We know about your enhanced eyesight and hearing. You can make windows after Aiden gave you that talent. We've seen you teleport and freeze things. I've also seen you create balls of fire and pure electricity. I've seen you build swirling storms out of thin air. Pretty much the only thing I haven't seen you do is manipulate someone's mind.'

'Could there be other talents I haven't discovered yet?'

'I suppose there could,' he replies.

'I guess there's not really a list of potential talents?'

His frown deepens. 'Not really. Supposedly each talent manifests differently with each individual, so the possibilities are kind of endless. Everyone's brain works differently, so they can use their talents in unique ways. April and Hunter are both mind manipulators, but the way the talent has developed in each of them is slightly different. There could be endless variations on the talents we have, so nobody knows how many there are.'

'But there are others that have been identified, along with mind manipulation?'

Sebastian nods. 'Yeah, when I was at the Academy in North Hope they tried to divide talents into categories. There were the

Gifted who had increased brain capacity and the Enhanced who were physically stronger or had heightened senses. They even had a category for Healers, although I never met one. Why are you bringing this up?'

'I was just wondering.' I shrug, avoiding looking him in the eyes.

He frowns again. 'Should we get started?'

'Sure.' I lift my gaze and push my shoulders back. 'What should I do?'

'Well, we could do with a bit more light in here,' he says with a smile. Before I can respond, he jumps up and retraces our steps to the front of the church. When he reaches the final row of benches he turns and follows it to a dark corner of the room. He stops by a metal table, which stands under a huge cross on the wall there. In the dim moonlight it's difficult to see what he's doing, but his hands appear to be gathering small items that have been left on the table.

When he's done he makes his way back towards me and sits back down on the floor. He opens his hands to reveal a bunch of tiny wax candles and lets them slide out of his grasp and onto the floor in front of me. Carefully, he organises them in a neat line.

'Do you think you can create some fire to light these candles?' he asks.

I nod slowly, but I don't feel confident. I can't think of a time when I've summoned my fire talent with any kind of control. The damage it could potentially cause frightens me and I feel anxiety building up inside me.

'Don't forget, there's no reason to be afraid,' Sebastian says, as if reading my thoughts.

'Easier said than done,' I murmur. 'Should I try it?'

Sebastian nods. 'Yes, but first I want you to calm yourself with deep breaths in and out,' he says.

I try to clear my mind and listen to the sound of his voice, but I find myself getting distracted by it. Instead of clearing, my mind keenly focuses on how Sebastian's knee is so close to touching mine. They are merely an inch apart...

'Focus Elle,' he says, effectively pulling me from my wandering thoughts.

I look up at him, guilt making my cheeks blush. 'Sorry,' I mutter.

This time I close my eyes and firmly focus on my breathing instead of Sebastian's voice. One deep breath in, one deep breath out. Repeat. We do this for a minute before Sebastian seems happy that I'm sufficiently calmed.

'I want you to concentrate on your chest. There should be a warm, almost tingling spot inside of you. This is the source where you draw your talent from.'

I know exactly where he is talking about. Deep within my chest I can always feel warmth; a part of me that seems to hum and vibrate with energy. At the moment the orb of energy within me feels small, but as I focus down on the area it seems to grow, pulsing as it expands.

'Now focus on drawing the energy from that spot and spreading it through your body. Bring it to your hands and then imagine it seeping out of every pore on your fingertips.'

I allow the pulsing ball of power in my chest to continue growing and then urge it to disperse and flow through me. As it moves around my body it seems to pick up speed and suddenly feels like it is rushing towards my fingers like an unstoppable force, eager to escape.

In my head I imagine it bursting out of my hands in a huge inferno and engulfing Sebastian as he sits in front of me. I panic and tense my chest while closing my hands into tight fists. I desperately attempt to quell the powerful energy that pulses inside me and threatens to burst from my palms. But it's too late. Intense heat fills my hands and they burst open, sending two balls of fire flying up to the ceiling above. I look up and watch the flames crash against the stone roof, the flames licking outwards as they flatten before disappearing into thin air. All that remains are two scorched, black marks on the stone.

My eyes fall to Sebastian who watches me calmly. 'You panicked, didn't you,' he says. 'I saw you tense up and try and hold it in. You need to do the opposite. Just let your talent flow naturally—trust me, Elle.'

I frown and tilt my head back to look at the burn marks above us. Doing what Sebastian suggests goes against every ounce of reason inside of me. Allowing my talent to leave my body without restriction seems impossible and dangerous. Sebastian is right about one thing though. It did feel natural to have my talent flow through me, just like breathing. I just panic the moment it tries to leave my body. I need to trust him. I need to try this again. Plus, the church didn't come crashing down during my first attempt, so maybe I'm not as dangerous as I thought.

I lower my gaze to the candles in front of me and focus inwards on the talent I can feel humming inside. The ball of energy still pulses from my last attempt and it doesn't take much focus to get it moving through me once again. This time as my talent begins to hurtle towards my hands, I focus on staying calm. Instead of seizing up, I close my eyes and let out one long breath to relax. I open my hands to the sky and allow the energy to continue on its collision course to my fingertips.

When the intense heat returns to my hands I apprehensively open my eyes, expecting to see flames rocketing up into the air. But there are no balls of fire hurtling upwards. Instead, a calm sea of flames gently floats over my palms and between my fingers. The flames give off a soft golden light and the sight of the fire so steadily burning surprises me.

It takes me a moment to remember that I'm supposed to be lighting the candles. I reach my hands out over the candles lined up in front of me and face my hands down so the flames hover over the wicks. I slowly lower my hands closer and one by one the candles burst to life until they all burn brightly.

I pull my hands away and slowly clench them into fists, withdrawing the talent from my fingertips and urging it back into my chest. I smile when the last flame disappears from my hands.

'You did it,' Sebastian whispers quietly, the reflection of tiny flames dancing in his blue eyes as he stares in awe at the candles.

'I did it' I repeat, in just as much shock as he is. 'And the church still stands,' I add, feeling a wide smile touch my lips.

'The church still stands,' he agrees, looking back up at me before quickly dipping his head and blowing out the candles with one sweeping breath. 'Should we try again?'

I nod eagerly. We repeat the same process over and over. By the time we've finished practicing I'm actually getting good at it. I wish I could show Will how far I've come. He would have been so excited if he could see me using my talent with such control.

After a while, Sebastian stretches his arms up over his head and stifles a yawn. 'I think that's enough for one night. I don't want to exhaust you.'

I smile and nod, but I feel far from exhausted. I feel like I've barely even started to make a dent in the well of power that I can feel buzzing in my chest.

We stand and begin to make our way towards the front of the church. When I reach the door I stop and turn around, and Sebastian nearly runs into me. 'Whoa,' he says, as he steadies himself by holding onto my shoulders.

'I nearly forgot to say thank you.' I reach up on my tiptoes and gently kiss the corner of his mouth. He doesn't move; he doesn't so much as breathe. 'Thank you,' I whisper.

I take a step back, pushing against the door behind me. 'Same time tomorrow night?'

He nods, failing to find his voice for a few moments. 'Same time tomorrow night,' he agrees, his voice rough as he responds.

CHAPTER THIRTEEN

I open my eyes to find Kelsey shaking me. Her eyes are streaming with tears and her lower lip is trembling. 'What's wrong?' I ask, sitting up in bed, immediately alert.

'She's dead,' Kelsey says.

'Who?'

'Sleeping Beauty.'

My stomach drops and I feel my face drain of colour. 'Jane is dead?'

She nods her head.

I jump out of bed, throwing a jumper over my head. I take Kelsey by the hand and hurry into the carriage next to ours. April and Sebastian are both still sleeping, but April's eyes flicker open to the sound of the squeaking door hinges. 'Can you watch Kelsey?' I ask her.

She slowly sits up in bed, rubbing her eyes tiredly. 'What's wrong?'

'I have to go to the clinic. Can you watch her?'

April nods. She looks like she wants to ask me more, but I leave before she gets the chance. I don't know if what Kelsey has seen has happened, but if it's a premonition I need to warn Aiden as quickly as possible.

The clinic is oddly dark when I arrive. There's an uninviting chill to the air and I feel strangely repelled by the place that always feels so welcoming. Even in the middle of the night there are usually soft lights seeping out from Henry and Aiden's workroom. The place is immersed in shadows though, which almost seem to reach out and run their icy fingers along my spine.

My feet pad softly against the wooden floorboards, and I wrap my arms tightly across my chest as I walk down the corridor towards Jane's room. Each step I take becomes smaller and slower as I approach. I can almost feel death's presence in the air around me and I worry that Kelsey's warning has come too late.

The door to Jane's room is open and even before I look inside, I already sense what I'm going to find. The room is dark, like the rest of the clinic, and Aiden sits by Jane's bedside. His head is bowed down over her hand, which he holds so tightly to his chest.

'Aiden?' I ask, my voice soft and barely louder than a whisper.

He looks up at me. His eyes are filled with unshed tears and his lips are downturned in an agonising grimace. My heart grows cold and plummets down into the depths of my stomach. His one look tells me everything. She's gone.

Aiden turns back to Jane and a hand touches my shoulder. I tear my eyes away from Aiden and find Henry standing behind me. He nods his head away from Jane's room and I follow him from the door as he guides me further down the corridor to one of the larger rooms at the back of the building.

'She's gone,' I say.

'Yes.'

I nod, my own eyes becoming wet with tears. I had known it the minute I entered the building. I look back over my shoulder, towards Jane's room.

'Aiden...'

Henry shakes his head. 'He needs time alone right now. Time to grieve.'

I sigh sadly and look down into my hands.

'She'd been getting worse and worse for some time,' Henry adds.

I brush my palm against my cheek, rubbing a stray tear away, and look back up at Henry. 'Can I wait here for him?'

'Yes, that's fine,' Henry says, giving me a sad smile. He goes back down the corridor to his office while I make myself comfortable on one of the patient beds.

I never knew Jane, but I cared about her because Aiden did. I wanted her to recover because she had been in the hospital just like me. She'd been subjected to Joseph's horrible tests and now they have killed her. Her death is painful to process when we had held out so much hope that she would recover. She didn't deserve to die, and my heart is filled with sorrow that she is gone. Another innocent life that Joseph has taken from us.

The sun is just starting to rise when Aiden emerges. I jump off the bed and walk down the corridor towards him when I hear his footsteps leaving her room. His eyes are glazed over, and his face is so haggard it's almost grey in colour.

'I'm sorry about Jane.' I reach out and lightly touch his arm. He flinches away from me.

'Can I get you anything?' I ask.

He shakes his head and his gaze flits up and down the corridor as though he's searching it for something.

Henry emerges from his office at the sound of my voice. His eyes are sad as he takes in Aiden's dishevelled appearance. He approaches Aiden cautiously and puts an arm around his shoulders. Again, Aiden flinches away.

'Come on, let's get you to a bed,' he says, refusing to take no for an answer. He guides Aiden to another room and when he returns he's rubbing the ridge of his nose between his eyes, tiredly.

'You should go get some rest yourself Elle,' Henry says. 'There's not much you can do to help him right now.'

I nod and move to leave, but then pause. 'Is he going to be okay?'

Henry shakes his head. 'I don't know Elle. I really don't know.'

As I NEAR the entrance to the station, April comes striding out the front of it with Copper at her heels. I'm slowly coming to terms with Jane's death and anger is pulsing through my veins as I approach her. Joseph killed Will and now another person has died because of him. I thought I couldn't hate that man any more than I already did, but I was wrong.

'Is everything okay?' she asks.

I shake my head. 'Jane is dead.'

April's face pales and her eyes become large. 'How's Aiden?'

'Not good,' I whisper.

She reaches out and touches my arm. 'We have to go get Hunter this morning. You can stay and rest if you're not up to it.'

'No. I want to come. I need the distraction.'

April nods.

'Are we going for him now?' I ask.

'Yes, if you're happy to. Kels is already with Mia and we just have to wake Sebastian.'

I lift my eyes to sky. That should go down well. I glance down at the dog. 'I want you to stay with Kelsey while we're gone. Okay?'

The dog's eyes light with understanding and he quickly turns and begins trotting back down the stairs into the station.

April's eyes are wide. 'You really think he understood that?' she asks.

'I think so. He seems to understand quite a bit actually. The more time I spend with him, the more I start to think he'll just open his mouth and talk one day. He's very clever.'

We follow Copper down the stairs and into the station.

'It seems like he's more than just clever,' April says. 'Do you think he could be talented?'

'Talented? Do you think that's even possible?'

She shrugs. 'Who knows what is and isn't possible anymore.'

When we get to the carriage Sebastian is sleeping, as expected. April lightly knocks on the door and opens it slowly. 'Seb, you decent?' she asks, pushing the door wide.

He groans and sits up in his bed. He is completely shirtless—totally not decent. I try to avoid looking directly at him, but my eyes keep wandering back to his bare chest.

'What time is it?' he moans, glancing at his cuff. 'It's not even seven in the morning yet? You crazy April?' His eyes slide past hers to mine. 'And I definitely thought you had more sense than this Elle.' He looks at me in such a disapproving way that if I weren't so miserable I'd be tempted to laugh. He really does hate early mornings.

April ignores his complaints and throws a shirt at him from a pile on the floor. He catches it just before it hits his face. 'Put some clothes on before you give poor Elle a heart attack.'

My cheeks warm as he looks at me and grins, winking before he pulls his top over his head. 'Why such an early start?' he asks, his voice muffled by his top, which is over his face.

''M agrees that Hunter is telling the truth. He wants us to bring him in so they can talk. We're going to get him now,' she answers.

Sebastian grumbles, but throws his shirt on and follows us back through the train tunnel and up onto the street.

I'm silent as we walk. My chest feels heavy today and I can't stop thinking about how Aiden is doing. He loves Jane and has put so much into finding a way to fix her, I worry he won't recover easily from her death.

We arrive at the house Hunter has been staying in and April walks straight to the front door, knocking loudly against the wood. 'Hunter?' she calls out.

I close my eyes and extend my senses out, focusing on the sounds I can hear from within the house. Beyond the door there's the deep and constant sound of breathing, so my eyes flutter open and I tap April on the shoulder.

'He's in there, but I think he's asleep.'

April tries the door. She eases it open carefully and calls out to Hunter as she enters. He doesn't respond. We follow April into the foyer and Sebastian shines the light from his cuff around the front room, where we'd sat with Hunter yesterday.

'Where do you think he is?' Sebastian asks.

I close my eyes and focus in on the sound of Hunter's breathing. 'He's upstairs,' I respond.

'You're getting pretty good at that,' Sebastian says, making me swell with pride. Using my senses has always come more naturally than my other talents, and I've found I'm getting quicker at drawing on them over the past few weeks. Some days I'll be using my extended hearing or sight without even realising I'm doing it. I just hope I'll become this good with my other talents soon.

We move towards the staircase at the far end of the foyer. The polished wood has lost some of its shine with age, but it doesn't detract from how extravagant the staircase is. The wide steps and curling bannister elegantly sweep up to the floor above.

The sound of Hunter's breathing becomes louder with each step I take up the stairs and I follow the sound to a door on the first floor.

'I'll let you handle this one,' April says, turning to me.

'You want *me* to wake him up?' I ask. 'How is that fair.'

She shrugs. 'I've already had one foul-mouthed boy swearing at me for waking him this morning. I'm not quite ready for round two.'

'Fine,' I grumble, as I go to ease the door open. Hunter is already stirring, stretching his arms over his head as he slowly sits up. He's still wearing the same clothes he'd been in the night he escaped Headquarters and he looks weary.

'You guys really need to keep your thoughts a little quieter,' he says, yawning. 'I think I heard your *boyfriend's* thoughts from out on the street.'

'He's not...' I cross my arms over my chest, refusing to let Hunter get a rise out of me. 'Look, you need to get ready. We're bringing you back to our camp.'

Surprise flashes on Hunter's face. I guess he hadn't read *that* in our thoughts.

'We're bringing you back and, I swear Hunter, if you so much as think of screwing us over, I will never forgive you. I'm getting better at using my talents and if you think being frozen by me was bad that's nothing compared to what I will do to you if you betray us.'

He frowns in response. 'I don't want to hurt you Winters, or anyone else in The Movement. I just want to help take down my father.' His eyes are large and filled with sincerity, but I ignore him. He's fooled me with looks like that before.

'I'll see you downstairs.' I turn and walk back to the door. 'He's awake,' I tell April, moving past her to head back to the foyer. Sebastian follows me at a distance.

When I get downstairs I lean up against one of the walls in the foyer and stare at the chandelier that hangs overhead. It's haunting in the darkness; a thing of such beauty that's been abandoned and left to deteriorate with the rest of this part of the city.

Sebastian leans up against the wall beside me, watching me. 'Why do you let him upset you so much?' he asks.

I continue to stare at the chandelier as I respond. 'I thought he was my friend. I honestly thought he wanted to help me. Instead, all these bad things happened to me because of him. I know he says he was being controlled, but it doesn't change the fact that what happened to me was because of him.'

'Do you like him?' he asks.

'What?' My eyes dart to Sebastian's. There's pain behind his stare that I've never seen before.

'I heard you in there talking to him. You avoided saying I'm your boyfriend...'

My eyes soften as I look at him. How could he even think for a second I like Hunter? He's always flirted with me and once upon a time we were friends, but when I look at him my heart doesn't flutter the way it does when I'm with Sebastian. He doesn't believe in me the way Sebastian does and he doesn't bring out the best in me. I should tell him how I feel, but I know I can't. I won't.

I reach out and lightly touch his arm. 'I don't like Hunter that way,' I respond firmly.

He slowly allows a smile to crack at the corner of his mouth, and his eyes brighten at my words. Footsteps creak on the stairs and I drop my hand from Sebastian's arm but, before it gets too far away from him, Sebastian takes my hand in his and holds it tightly.

'You guys ready?' April asks, as she walks down the stairs with Hunter a step behind her.

'Yeah, we're ready,' Sebastian says in response.

Daylight is beginning to dawn as we step outside the house. There are dark clouds overhead and the wind has stirred since we were last out here. It blows at my hair, pulling the loose strands across my face.

The others look uncomfortable, pulling their jackets in close to their chests and covering their heads with their hoods. I don't share their discomfort though. The wind's keen whip lashes against my skin, but in no way does it chill me.

Sebastian wraps one arm around me, pulling me in close. 'Suddenly the ARC doesn't look quite so bad,' he says. I glance up at him to see him deep in thought. His eyes search the horizon as though seeking to see the ARC itself.

'Do you think we'll ever go back there?' I ask.

He sighs sadly and shakes his head. 'Even if we could, we wouldn't be welcome. They still don't know about the surface. How could we tell them where we've been when they can't come here themselves?' He looks like he's thought about this before, but he doesn't have all the information. If Aiden and Henry's cure works, then they would have that option. They would be able to return to the surface.

I want so badly to tell Sebastian what I know, but I keep my mouth closed and nod. I glance over at Hunter and April who walk side-by-side. She keeps flicking uneasy looks at him and I wonder how much she actually trusts him. She eyes him like he's about to unleash hell on us. I wish I could decide what to believe. Is he the damaged son of our ruthless leader or is he a spy sent to bring us down?

Hunter turns to look at me, seeking my eyes with his own. As he catches them, I see a question burning within them. In this moment I feel certain he's read my thoughts, as though they've been shouted across the distance between us.

I feel a light touch against my mind, like a soft feather that has briefly fluttered against it. *Do you really have so little trust in me?* Hunter's voice sounds in my head.

I break eye contact with him and look away. My action is answer enough. I trust him, but only to disappoint me, like he has so many times before.

CHAPTER FOURTEEN

When we reach the station, we find M waiting in the security office. He still appears to be recovering after his capture. His cheekbones jut harshly from his gaunt face and his clothes hang loose from his lean body. If anything, the tired bags under his eyes are more pronounced than when he first returned. His capture has clearly weakened him, but his stare is still discerning and intelligent.

'Hunter,' he says, eyeing his nephew as we enter.

'Michael,' Hunter responds, nodding his head. There's a stiff formality to the way they greet each other. I look between the two of them trying to see any sort of familial bond, but they approach each other like acquaintances rather than family.

M looks to April and his face softens slightly. 'Thank you for bringing him in. You can leave us.' His eyes wander to Sebastian's and then mine, dismissing us with one glance.

The three of us leave without saying a word. We walk down the corridor, but Sebastian pauses when we reach the door that leads from the staff only area.

'Can you hear what they're discussing?' he asks me, under his breath.

I raise one eyebrow at him. 'Maybe,' I wonder. I glance at April who has stopped just inside the doorway. Her eyes flick from Sebastian to me and I wait for her to sound her disapproval, but she stays silent. We all need to know what's being said. We're already suspicious enough of Hunter.

I close my eyes and proceed to extend my senses out towards the security office down the corridor. When I tune in to M and Hunter's voices it's like they're talking right next to me rather than through a door at the end of the hallway.

'I know all about the things Joseph did to you,' M says softly. 'No father should treat his son that way, and I know you want revenge, but that's not what The Movement is about.'

'Isn't it?' Hunter asks.

'You know I want to depose him, but we will do it smartly. I won't have innocent people killed.'

Hunter lets out a laugh of disbelief. 'He's willing to kill each and every member of your merry little gang to maintain control of this city. He's willing to put innocent children through endless experiments to gain power. The sooner you start fighting fire with fire, the sooner we can all be free of him.'

There's the sound of shuffling footsteps and a pause in conversation. 'Look, we have a plan and I want you to be a part of that, but only if you're willing to cooperate. I don't want you going off script because it's what you think is best.'

'I want to help...really I do,' Hunter sighs. 'I just want him gone. Do you know how many other people he made me torture? Elle wasn't the only one...'

Silence hangs tensely in the air and when Hunter begins to talk again, I draw my senses back to my body until all I can hear is Sebastian breathing. I don't want to keep listening in. It feels wrong to be eavesdropping on their conversation, when it's clearly so personal. I open my eyes and nod at Sebastian. 'I can hear them.'

He grins at me. 'Do you think we should listen in?' he asks.

I glance at the door at the end of the corridor that Hunter and M are behind. 'No, I don't think we should listen.' I've already heard enough.

He frowns and glances at April, as though asking for her support. 'I don't trust Hunter,' he says, keeping his voice low. 'I want to know what he has to say to M.'

'Well, you guys eavesdrop then,' I say to them both. 'I don't feel comfortable with it. I'd rather just ask Hunter to his face.'

'You really think he'll just tell you? I'd rather have a heads-up if he has something planned.'

I shake my head. 'He hasn't got anything planned.'

'You certain about that?' April asks softly.

My chest collapses as I heave out a long breath. 'No, I'm not certain. But we should probably give him the benefit of the doubt. Besides, don't you trust M?'

Sebastian's eyes soften at my words and the fight seems to rush out of him. April looks guilty. 'Yeah, you're right. We can trust M,' she says. 'If there's something we need to know about Hunter he'll tell us.'

I feel the tension in my back release as they both agree with me.

'There you are,' Mia exclaims, as we leave the corridor. She's walking past the turnstiles with Amber and Kelsey in hand, and Copper trailing behind. 'I'm helping out with breakfast and was hoping you guys would be back. The girls are full of mischief this morning and I can't keep an eye on the two of them at once.'

Sebastian's troubled eyes clear and he gives Mia a smile. 'We'll look after the girls,' he replies.

Mia's face lights up with relief. 'Thanks, I owe you one.' She gives us a little wave as she darts back down to the platform. We walk over to the two girls. Kelsey's eyes are bright and she proceeds to giggle as Copper gives her a massive slobbery lick across the face.

'Come on you,' I say, smiling as we move to follow Mia. Sebastian, April and Amber head down the steps to the platform first, but something in Kelsey's expression causes me to pause when I go to take her hand. Her lower lip is trembling and all traces of laughter have gone from her face.

'What's wrong?' I ask, crouching down beside her.

'I just miss him,' she says, causing my heart to flutter with a familiar pain. It's been weeks since Will left our life, but neither of us is over it. I'm not sure if I'll ever truly be able to move on.

I pull her into a hug. 'I miss him too,' I say.

'Do you believe in heaven?' she asks me, when I pull back.

I pause at her words. 'I—I'm not sure. Who told you about heaven?' I ask. It's been such a long time since I've heard that word uttered aloud. It's almost like a fairy tale adults tell children, though I've heard some people truly believe in it. I don't think it's true, but I hope it is, so I won't rule it out completely.

'Mia. She told me that's where Will is now. Is he with Sleeping Beauty?'

I give her a small nod, my words failing to find my lips.

'Can we go visit?'

My heart lurches in response. How am I supposed to answer her question? I'm not prepared for this. I slowly shake my head. 'No, we can't visit them. But we can think about Will and Jane and remember them every day. If they're still in our memories and in our hearts, they're never truly gone.'

She smiles sadly and nods. 'I think about Will all the time,' she says.

'Me too,' I reply.

Kelsey seems to brighten up as we head down to the platform. She climbs up onto Sebastian's lap. 'Can I open the can?' she asks, in her chirpy singsong voice.

Sebastian smiles and passes her the can. She purses her lips as she tries to go about opening it. I feel sad watching her and reflecting on our conversation. We've already lost too many people. I don't want to lose anyone else.

I hear footsteps on the stairs and I glance over my shoulder to look at who's walked onto the platform. Hunter stands there, appearing completely self-assured despite the glares people are shooting him. I turn my back on him and face Kelsey, decidedly ignoring him. He may have saved me at Headquarters the other night, but it hardly makes up for the other wrongs he's caused me.

I can feel him watching me, and the back of my neck tingles with his stare.

'You know what?' I say to Sebastian. 'I'm not really that hungry.'

I move to the edge of the platform, with Copper at my heels, and swing my way down onto the tracks. I don't look back. I don't want to see Hunter again and I can barely stand to be in the same space as him right now. Just being near him makes me angry and I can't afford to lose control. I head into the darkened tunnel and feel instant release once the platform is no longer in sight and I'm away from him.

'Winters, wait up,' Hunter says, coming after me.

I almost growl as I stop and turn to look at him. 'What?' I spit.

'I just thought you should know, M believes my story,' he says, seeming lost for words.

'Is that all it is? A *story*?'

Hunter crosses his arms over his chest. 'Look, I know you don't want to believe me, but it's the truth.'

'You once told me I could trust you, but everything that's ever come from your mouth has been a lie. Why should I believe you now?'

'Elle, I-'

'Look, you may have M convinced, but I don't trust you,' I say, cutting him off before he can feed me more lies. 'M may have agreed to let you stay, but I don't want anything to do with you. I've seen what you can do to people and I've been tormented by you before. If you're going to stay here, then make sure you stay out of my way.'

Hunter takes a step away from me, surprised by the vehemence with which I speak. I don't wait to see if he has another quick response for me, instead I stalk away from him down the tunnel.

I'm bristling as I walk along the train tracks and it takes everything in me to try and calm myself enough so I don't use my talents. I take a deep breath in and then out. I need to stay clear of Hunter. He brings out the worst in me and if he keeps trying to explain himself to me I'll probably end up losing control in a bad way.

I look back at the empty tunnel I've just walked down. Why did Hunter only break out of Headquarters now if he's been in control of himself since the day I froze him? Why is he so set on helping us?

Copper and I walk to the point where the train tunnel reaches the surface and daylight shines in through the entrance. I spot a solitary figure sitting by the entrance, looking out at the train tracks that move off into the light of day. As I get closer, I can see Lara's waist-long brown hair. She has her knees tucked up into her chest and she rests her chin on them as she peers up at the sky. She looks distant and thoughtful, and I hope I'm not interrupting her.

She's been so different since she was rescued from Headquarters —quieter and more withdrawn. I don't blame her for the way she's been, but I do miss my friend.

'Hey,' I say, sitting on the ground beside her.

She turns and gives me a small smile. 'Oh, hey Elle.' A frown creases her forehead as she looks at me. 'You're sad.'

I nod and try to resist the ache in my chest as I think of Jane. I'm not sure if Lara would have heard about her death yet, and I don't know how to tell her. It's difficult to control how I'm feeling though, so I know I need to let her know what's happened.

'Jane died,' I say, quietly.

She reaches out and rubs my arm, and I feel a wave of soothing warmth rush through me. 'Yeah, Dad told me,' she replies. 'Aiden must be really struggling.'

'I don't think he's doing well,' I agree. When I'd seen him this morning he'd looked like a part of his soul had been wrenched out of him. I hope he's able to make it out of this okay. I look past Lara to the world beyond the tunnel. The day is gloomy and there's a light mist rolling across the ground.

'There's something you should know...' I say, turning back to Lara and pushing away all thoughts of Jane.

She tilts her head and watches me closely. I can almost sense her talent reaching out to feel my emotions, to see if she can guess what I'm about to say. I shiver at the sensation. I've never felt it so keenly before.

'What is it?' she asks.

'Hunter escaped from Headquarters and he's here now,' I tell her. I go on to repeat his whole story to her. Lara stays silent the entire time, allowing me to finish in full.

'Do you believe he's telling the truth?' she asks.

'I'm not sure,' I reply, wishing I had a better answer. If I believed him I could try to move on, and if I was convinced he was lying I could hate him forever and be done with him. Sitting on the fence makes it so much harder.

'I never once sensed deceit in him,' she says, thoughtfully. 'Arrogance, yes, but never deceit. When I was in Headquarters he was the one to torture my mind, but the Hunter that came to see me was nothing like the one we went to school with. Even with an inhibitor band I could sense that.'

'So, you think we should believe him?' I ask.

She watches me closely, her eyes giving away nothing about the emotions I know must be rushing through her. 'I think we should give him a chance.'

As much as I hate to admit it, I agree. I do believe his story, but that doesn't make it any easier to trust him again, or be anywhere near him. I open my mouth to speak, but before I do she continues. 'That doesn't mean we shouldn't also stay wary of him. With a talent like his, who knows what web of lies he could be spinning.'

We both return to the platform together. When we arrive there are more people gathering there than usual. Lara asks a woman we pass what's happening and she tells us that M's called a meeting.

Lara goes in search of her parents, while I try to find a place to sit. Hunter is standing by the steps that lead to the surface, so I deliberately sit on the ground by the wall opposite—as far away from him as possible.

The platform is slowly filling with people, so I probably won't be able to see M very well from the spot I've chosen. As long as I'm away from Hunter though, I don't really mind.

Sebastian comes down the steps with Kelsey in hand and I see him searching the crowd for my face. His eyes almost immediately find mine and he makes his way over. He sits down beside me and Kelsey comes to my other side and curls up under my arm.

Hunter catches my eye and gives me a wink, making me groan out loud.

'What?' Sebastian asks.

I nod my head in Hunter's direction. 'I just didn't want to be near him,' I say, keeping my voice low.

Sebastian lightly places his hand on my knee and gives it a squeeze. I can feel he wants to comfort me; he just doesn't have the words. I place my hand over his and smile.

'Do you know what the meeting is about?' I ask.

'M hasn't said, but I'm guessing it has to do with Hunter being here. It's too much of a coincidence to be anything else.'

'Do you think he could have given him some new information?'

Sebastian considers my question. 'Maybe. Your guess is as good as mine.'

Kelsey tugs the sleeve of my jacket. 'Can we go to the park today?' she asks.

'Not today, you know it's too dangerous for us. Besides, it's freezing outside and we don't have any gloves for your hands. Your fingers will get cold.'

She gives me her largest pout, pleading. 'Sorry. We could play a board game though.'

Her eyes light up. 'Will you play too?' she asks Sebastian.

He smiles, but shakes his head. 'I'm on watch after the meeting, so I'm afraid I can't.'

'That's okay. You'll just have to play with me tomorrow,' she replies, causing him to laugh.

'She's a keen negotiator,' he says to me. 'We better watch out for that.'

I nod, smiling. 'I think she may already have you wrapped around her little finger. I wish I had that kind of influence over you.'

He wraps his arm around my shoulder and pulls me close, causing my heart to beat erratically. 'Don't be silly. I'd teleport to the stars and pick one out for you if you asked. She clearly learnt her persuasion skills somewhere.'

I smile into his chest before giving him a playful shove back. 'Teleporting to the stars? That's such a bad line.'

I shake my head as he laughs. He looks like he's about to respond but stops when M walks down onto the platform. Everyone falls quiet, with only a few whispers continuing on in the background as he moves to stand at the front.

April stands confidently next to him and I wonder if she knows what's going on. She certainly looks like she does. Behind her, Aiden and Henry walk into the room. It's strange to see them both out of the clinic, especially Aiden. His eyes are vacant and he appears completely detached, like he can't even see the crowd of people he stands before. There's only one thing that would have made him leave the clinic—the cure.

'Some information has come to light that cannot be ignored,' M begins. 'Aiden and Henry have been working hard on a cure that will stop the mutation that causes talents from developing. They have informed me that they have finally found that cure, but will need to start a series of human trials before it can be administered to those in the ARC.'

People mutter excitedly in response. This news is big. Everyone in the room knows that the cure could mean the chance to return our families and friends still living in the ARC to the surface. Most importantly though, they know it is the key to making Hope the place we all want it to be.

'I am proposing we send a team to the ARC to find several individuals who are willing to volunteer as test subjects for the cure,' he continues, raising his voice to be heard over the crowd.

'We have transport arranged to take a team this afternoon. This cure is our number one priority and we cannot wait to act on it. It is only once we make a cure available for citizens of the ARCs that we will be able to reunite broken families. We will finally have a platform from which we can truly oppose Joseph.'

With that, M turns and heads back up the stairs from the platform. There are mutters of agreement through the crowd as everyone digests what they've just heard.

'They've found a cure!' Sebastian says, excitedly from beside me. 'This is huge. I wonder who is being sent to the ARC.'

My heart starts racing wildly, and hope rushes through me at the thought of returning to the ARC. I've spent so long helping Aiden and Henry with the cure that it wouldn't feel right if I wasn't there to see this through to the end.

I see April making her way towards us through the crowd. 'Pretty big news, isn't it,' she says, when she reaches us. 'M wants to talk through the plans with the team,' she smiles at Sebastian, 'of which you're a member. You're going to the ARC, Seb.'

He grins. 'Really?'

She nods, smiling back at him.

'Who else is going?' I ask, nervously.

April's smile drops and her eyes don't meet mine as she turns to me. I already fear what she's going to say.

'Soren, Dalton, Luke, Aiden, Lara and Hunter are going,' she answers.

My heart sinks as I hear her words. I can't believe I won't get to be a part of this.

'I'm sorry Elle,' April says. 'M thinks it's too dangerous. You might lose control down there, or worse, you might be captured.'

'What about Lara?' I protest. 'Is she in the right shape to go after last time? How can you trust Hunter down there?'

146

'The team may need to use Lara and Hunter to convince the people of the ARC who they are. Soren, Dalton and Luke can fight if needed. Sebastian's talent can always comes in handy. Aiden needs to administer the cure. M has thought this through. He's made up his mind. I'm sorry. I know how much you want to go. I do too.'

'It's fine,' I reply, willing for my heart to feel okay about it. 'The most important thing is that the mission succeeds,' I add, not very convincingly.

'No, it's not,' Sebastian says. 'You of all people should be coming. April, we can talk to M.'

'Don't,' I reply. 'He won't listen. He's always thought I was a liability. A few words from you won't change that.'

He frowns, looking like he wants to argue back, but instead he turns to April. 'Which ARC do you think they'll send us to?' he asks.

'You'll find out in the meeting.'

'Could it be ours?'

She nods. 'It's the closest, so potentially.'

I try to be happy for Sebastian, and a part of me truly is. He might see his dad again. If I were going, I might have had the chance to be reunited with Quinn. But I guess that's not going to happen now.

April glances towards the staircase. 'You should go Seb...'

'I know,' he says. He watches me closely and I know he understands the pain that runs through me. His eyes plead with mine.

'Please, let me talk to M,' he says. 'I can tell him how you're improving with your talents.'

I shake my head. I may have looked in control in the church, but my talents certainly haven't responded well under pressure. M knows that, and Sebastian won't be able to sway him.

'I don't think there's anything you can say that will convince him. Just promise me you'll be careful,' I plead. 'And if by some stroke of luck you're sent to our ARC, give Quinn and your dad a hug for me.'

'I will.' He hesitates, like he doesn't want to leave me, so I give him a soft push towards the stairs.

'Go,' I insist.

He nods and begins walking in the direction of the stairs. When he gets there he pauses and looks back across the platform at me. His blue eyes are almost stormy grey in colour, and they swirl with determination. I try to give him a reassuring smile. His expression doesn't change though and, with a deep sigh, he turns and continues up the stairs.

'You're not going to the meeting?' I ask her.

'I am, I just need to go find Dalton. He was on lookout and missed the announcement,' she says.

'Why aren't you going to the ARC?' I ask.

'M told me I'm needed here,' she replies, sadly. Too sadly.

'You already know where they're going. It's our ARC, isn't it?' I guess.

Her eyes widen as I look at her, but she slowly nods.

'Sebastian is going home.'

CHAPTER FIFTEEN

I stay on the platform while M briefs the team upstairs on their mission to the ARC. The rest of the gathered crowd slowly disperses, but I can't bring myself to leave. I stare at the steps, trying to comprehend M's rejection of me. I feel empty inside and it hurts that he doesn't think I'm good enough. Especially when I was partly the reason that his rescue was successful. I've been growing more confident using my talents and I've spent all my spare time devoted to this cure.

Not only do I deserve to be on the team headed to the ARC, but also my knowledge of the cure and talents could actually be useful. M has underestimated me, and I want nothing more than to prove him wrong.

'Winters?' I hear Hunter's voice from behind me. I turn to see him approaching me slowly from the bottom of the stairs. He sounds as if he's terrified by the very mention of my name.

I try to ignore him, but the mere sound of his voice has me writhing inside. Unable to keep what I'm thinking silent, I look up at him. 'I thought I told you to leave me alone.'

'You did,' he replies simply.

'Then why are you here? Why have you even come to us at all?'

He blows out a slow, measured breath. 'Because I want to help Michael,' he replies. 'I want to make it up to you and Lara for the harm I caused you both. But, mostly, I want to take my father down and helping The Movement is the best way.'

I glare at him but struggle to find fault with his reasons, which only makes me hate him more.

He stands back and crosses his arms over his chest. 'I didn't come here to argue with you,' he says, before I can get another word out.

'No?'

'Look, Elle, I know you want to go on the mission to the ARC and I think you need to be there. I can help you.'

My gaze flicks up to meet his, weighing the truth I see in his eyes. 'And how will you do that?'

'I can get you on the team for the mission.'

'Sure you can,' I say, folding my arms over my chest and leaning back against the wall. There's no way in hell M would let that happen. He's made up his mind and I doubt he'll change it, even if Hunter is his nephew.

'I can,' he insists, his voice filled with certainty.

A kernel of hope begins to grow within me. 'How?'

'It wouldn't be easy, but I could manipulate all of the others on the team so they don't realise you're there.'

'So, you'd sneak me into the group?' I ask, the derision in my voice is completely gone and has been replaced by anticipation.

'Yes.'

'And you think that would work?'

He nods. 'Yes. We're getting ready to leave soon. We'll be heading to the edge of Hope where we'll meet our ride.'

'What do you need me to do?'

'Get a jacket with a big hood. It will make it easier to cover your identity. Then, I need you to wait in the station concourse so I can slip you into the group with ease.'

'Are you sure you can do it?' I ask.

'Just leave it to me,' he says. 'It will work.'

I take a deep breath in and then out, before nodding my head. 'Okay, I'll be there.' I turn from Hunter, my heart racing. I only have one shot at this and I hope I'm not wasting it by putting my trust in Hunter.

I WAIT in the station concourse for the others to arrive. They are all still in the security office and the longer I wait the more nervous I feel. I find myself pacing up and down, constantly glancing at the staff only door and jumping whenever I hear a sound. What if I can't get on the mission? What if Hunter doesn't help me?

I look over at the steps that lead down to the tunnels. Kelsey and Copper are with Mia now. I wish I could have warned Kels that I won't be coming back tonight, but I can't risk Mia finding out. Kels seemed aware that something was up when I said goodbye to her though. I wouldn't be surprised if she already had a feeling I was leaving.

She will be fine with Mia. I trust her completely with Kelsey who is as much a part of Mia's family these days as she is mine. Mia loves taking care of her, so I feel certain there will be no problem if I'm not back for a few days.

I hear the staff door opening, and I quickly move to stand behind one of the pillars in the hall. I keep out of sight as the group moves into the concourse, feeling uncertain how to proceed. Hunter hadn't given me any idea of what to expect or what I needed to do once they got up here.

'*Elle?*' Hunter's voice echoes in my mind.

I frown, not particularly liking his thoughts in my head.

'*You can come out here, no one will notice you,*' he continues.

I make certain my hood is low over my face before slipping into the group. I keep my back up against the wall and my eyes cast down on the floor. The people in the group are talking quietly amongst one another and haven't noticed my addition to the team.

My heart races as I focus my eyes on the ground. I keep waiting for someone to grab my arm and pull back my hood, exposing me. The talents on this team are formidable and I don't know how Hunter thinks he will manage to keep me hidden from them all the way to the ARC.

'*Has anyone noticed me yet?*' I direct my thoughts to Hunter, feeling a little silly and hoping he catches them.

I glance up to see him watching the group with analytical eyes. He looks away, considering them, and gives me a small shake of his head.

'*You're fine. For now, you're invisible to them.*'

I try to let his words sink in and relax me, but the tension in my shoulders refuses to budge.

The team assembled in the foyer hushes as April clears her throat. I draw further back against the wall, hoping she doesn't see me. Luckily she doesn't turn my way once. Although, it's probably more Hunter's doing than luck.

She moves to stand next to Dalton and Soren. 'I've just had word from our operative who's picking you up in the helicopter. He's scheduled to leave Hope for the ARC in two hours and can meet you by the edge of the city fifteen minutes after he sets off. He can't wait at the meeting point for long because they're expecting him at the ARC. If you're late, he won't wait. Good luck.'

Dalton nods seriously and then turns to the rest of us. 'You heard April,' he says, his deep voice booming loudly. 'Time to move.'

Everyone herds up the steps that lead to the surface. I catch sight of Aiden in the middle of the group. His eyes are red rimmed and his face is devoid of any emotion. I want to talk to him, to try and see how he's doing, but I can't expose myself.

I keep my head low as I walk past April towards the exit. Her eyes drift straight from the person in front of me to the person behind me and I smile. We're over the first hurdle.

Hunter and I stay at the back of the group as we follow the others onto the street. We're less noticeable here and so far it seems to be working. Not once has anyone glanced back at us.

Dalton and Soren are confident as they take the lead. The two of them look odd together, with Dalton so big and dark and Soren so small and pale, but whenever I've seen them working together they seem to make a great team. They walk quickly and with purpose, only pausing briefly when they reach an intersection.

The crumbled ruins of South Hope seem to stretch endlessly before us as we make a turn. I've become accustomed to the look of the area. Thick vines cover most of the buildings, and the uneven road is covered in deep, web-like fractures, which weeds and pools of water tend to gather in. Rusted cars dot the sides of the road, claimed by plants that wrap their way around the wheels and claw their grip around the bodies. The thick branches almost look as though they are about to rip the machines from the street and pull them down into the earth.

There are seven people in the team. Lara, Sebastian and Aiden stick close to Dalton and Soren, while Luke trails a little behind. I feel exposed walking beside Hunter, so worried that someone could turn around at any moment and ask what the hell I'm doing here. The more time that passes though, the less tense I feel.

I sneak glances at Hunter, trying to gauge if he's tiring from using his talent on the others, but so far he seems to be doing fine.

Dalton makes a sharp turn down one of the side streets and everyone follows without question. I get a bad, niggling feeling in my gut as we follow. I shoot a look at Hunter. Does he notice how the world seems suddenly quieter? Like the wind has stilled and even our soft steps have been muted.

'Elle, if anything goes wrong make sure you go back to the station. It's not worth you being caught again,' Hunter whispers to me, his words rushing out quickly.

'What do you mean if something goes wrong?'

Dalton raises his hand, causing the rest of us to stop. The quiet street has become unnervingly silent. I reach my senses out to see if I can hear anything, but there's not so much as a rustle from the breeze to be heard. Shivers run down my spine as I look around and I can almost feel eyes watching me.

I slowly raise my head to look at the rooftops of the buildings surrounding us, but a low hissing noise causes me to spin my head to look at the far end of the street.

'Get down!' I scream, throwing my body to the ground. The others follow suit and merely seconds later a huge funnel of crackling purple flames flows over our heads. Once it passes I look up to see a group of recruiters gathering in the street. There are only three of them, but I know what three well-trained recruiters can do.

'Recruiters!' Dalton hollers. 'Get out of here now!'

I jump up and turn, racing in the direction we've just come. My heart beats ferociously as I move, and I can clearly hear the slapping of feet as the rest of the team follow.

Hunter is running right beside me and coming up on my other side I can see Aiden. While Hunter looks calm and focused, there's true fear in Aiden's eyes.

A rumbling noise reaches my ears and the ground shudders beneath my feet. Small stones bounce as they roll across the uneven asphalt and the fractures in the ground groan as they stretch wider.

I hear a loud cracking noise echo down the street and I glance over my shoulder at the others who run behind us. The recruiter's aren't following and as I look at the street between us I can see why.

The ground just in front of the lead recruiter shudders before collapsing into the earth creating a huge hole. The abyss stretches from one side of the street to the other, the dark depths of it impossible to discern from here. The edge of the pit continues to tremor and slowly it begins to crumble. I watch in disbelief as the road between the recruiters and us starts collapsing into the darkness and disappearing from sight.

Slowly the imploding ground gains momentum, the gaping hole gathering speed as it chases us down the street. The fissuring earth pulls cars, fences, trees and lampposts into the void. Nothing is safe and it destroys everything in its path.

I turn and focus on where I'm going, running harder as I hear the quakes getting closer. I can feel my talent buzzing just beneath my skin, but as I race forward it fails to find an outlet and continues to build.

'Can you do something?' Hunter grunts between breaths.

'Like what?' I ask. About the only thing I'm good for under pressure is creating ice, and I don't think that will help.

'Anything!' he growls.

I glance over my shoulder again. Some of the others are falling behind and the large gaping hole in the street is getting closer. The cracking noise suddenly stops, as does the progress of the imploding earth. I naturally slow down to try and figure out why, and that's when I hear movement up ahead.

I turn to see five more recruiters standing there before us. With the hole behind us, it becomes clear we've been herded towards them.

I swallow tightly and when I look down at my hands, I can see sparks of electricity flying off of them as erratically as my heart beats in my chest. I take a small step closer to Hunter. These recruiters don't look like they have any intention of taking prisoners.

'The woman in the centre, with the red hair, she's the most talented. If we stop her, the others may just run. They're outnumbered, but they're not worried about it when they're with her.' Hunter speaks in my mind but I'm guessing he's also talking to the others in our team as they slowly seem to nod in response, their eyes zeroing in on the woman.

As talent continues to ripple wildly across my fingertips, I focus on the pulsing ball of energy I can feel deep in the centre of my chest, just like I did while practicing with Sebastian in the church. As I do it the sparks emanating from my hands begin to calm and I can almost feel the breeze brushing against my fingertips, whispering at me to pull it under my control.

As the wind begins to whip up into a frenzy around me, I instinctively gather it with my talent. Using the energy in my chest I draw in the coils of wind with my fingertips. The breeze twists and turns as it collects, whisking around my fingers and ricocheting between my raised hands. It feels like I've rolled a storm into an uncontainable ball in front of me, which pulses between my palms wildly as it fights to break free from my grasp. I don't know what I'm doing, or even if it will work, but I push the turbulent ball of air forward with all my strength, sending it hurtling towards the group of recruiters.

The woman in front dives out of the way, but the force of the wind hits one of the men, throwing him ten feet in the air and back into the street behind him. The rest of the group don't hesitate, charging towards us as one.

I try to gather the wind again, but it's slower this time, more sluggish to respond. Just as I bring it under my control once more, a ball of fire spins towards me and I throw myself out of its path. I can feel the heat as it passes by, so close to me it singes my jacket.

I glance up at the red-haired woman who has another fireball in hand. I need to find a way to stop her. As I watch the burning flames in her palm, the solution hits me. Fire needs air to burn and, for once, I seem to have control over the air around us.

I engage my talented senses with all my strength, going beyond my sight and hearing and the feeling in my fingertips until my whole body feels like it is reaching out to connect with the world around me. I can almost sense every molecule, every fibre of the air that fills the street. It's like the world around me is made up of tiny vibrations that bounce off my skin. The sensation is intense and overpowering all at once and my skin itches with the awareness, like the air itself is rubbing up against it.

I concentrate on the air particles that dance through and around the flames in the woman's hand and I urge them to disperse. I will them from the blaze, drawing them out and pulling them from the fire. Slowly her fireball gets smaller and smaller, until I've created a vacuum around the flames and suffocated it completely. I grin, when I see the confusion in the woman's eyes as Dalton approaches and backhands her, causing her to go flying across the street. She lands on her feet though and charges him, moving quickly as she launches herself towards him.

I try to focus on the air around her again, but I feel exhausted and my shoulders are slouching tiredly. The connection with the wind and air I felt is gone, and I'm swaying on my feet.

I watch in horror as the woman fights Dalton hand-to-hand. Every time she connects with his skin he yelps in pain as her burning hands scald him. Another recruiter descends on Dalton from behind, but is stopped in his tracks as Luke sends a fireball smashing into the ground at his feet. The explosion launches the man high into the air and knocks both Dalton and the redhead off their feet.

I hear a painful shout and look over to see a large man holding Aiden up against a wall by the cuff of his jacket. Before I can move to get to him though, Sebastian appears behind the recruiter with a broken slab of concrete and smashes it over his head.

The man barely flinches from the contact but drops Aiden, who crumples in a heap on the ground. The recruiter turns to face Sebastian, grabbing him with his powerful hands. Soren surges towards the man, but he's too slow, and the recruiter launches Sebastian up into the air like a rag doll, hurling him into the abyss behind us.

His body flies through the air almost as if it were in slow motion. My heart stills and my blood turns as cold as ice as I watch. I scream and race towards him, but he disappears from view, down into the chasm the recruiters have created.

'No!' I yell, falling to my knees, my heart wrenching inside. It can't be true. Please don't be true.

I feel the slightest shift in the air to my left and turn to see Sebastian appear just above me, his body hurtling through the air before he crashes into the ground.

I scramble to my feet and stumble over to him, completely oblivious to the fighting that goes on around us. He's not moving and his chest isn't rising and falling. Is he breathing?

I kneel down beside him, taking his hand in mine. 'Sebastian?' I say, but he doesn't respond. There's a whole lot of blood from a cut on his forehead, but I try to ignore that and lean my head down to hear if he's breathing.

My heart feels like it starts beating again when I hear his breath and he slowly opens his eyes, groaning aloud as he tries to move.

'Whoa, easy,' I say to him. 'Are you okay?'

He continues to ease himself up. 'Elle?' He looks dazed and his eyelids slowly blink open and closed as he struggles to remain conscious.

As I help him up, I feel the earth shudder beneath our feet. I look up to see the huge recruiter bounding towards us. I try to move, but Sebastian rests too heavily on my shoulders. The hulking recruiter bears down on us and I close my eyes, desperately willing us to teleport clear. I already know neither Sebastian nor I have the strength for it though.

A familiar coldness chills my skin and my stomach clenches as I feel myself teleporting. There's no surge of talent thrumming through my body though, and I can tell it's not me that's making it happen.

I open my eyes to find myself staring back at the spot where we had just stood, right by the edge of the vast abyss. The space is vacant now, and I watch on in horror as the recruiter, who had been charging towards us, wraps his arms around the thin air where we cowered half a breath ago. He loses his balance and stumbles forward, falling off the edge and plunging into the depths of the hole.

'Elle, are you okay?' a voice sounds in my ear. I jump with surprise and look to my right to find Ryan standing next to me. His hand grips onto my arm, and he slowly drops it from his grasp.

'Ryan? You...you saved us!' I exclaim. 'What are you doing here?'

'We should be asking you the same thing,' says another voice from behind me. I turn to see April has come to stand next to Sebastian.

'April?' I ask. 'I thought you were staying at the station.'

'No. We were following you guys to make sure you made it safely out of Hope,' she replies.

'But, how did you know—' A loud boom echoes behind me, and

the ground shudders beneath my feet. I glance over my shoulder to see a large plume of smoke wafting up from a burning car twenty feet from where we stand.

'I'll look after Seb; you two go help the others,' she shouts at Ryan and me.

Stunned, I instinctively follow her instructions and run towards the burning car. Lara is coughing as she makes her way through the haze towards us, supporting Aiden who staggers along next to her. I run over to help him, passing the red-haired recruiter who lies motionless on the ground.

'What happened?' I ask, as I sling Aiden's arm over my shoulder.

'The redhead threw a fireball that accidentally hit the car. There must have been petrol in the tank because it exploded. I think she got caught in the blast,' Lara replies, nodding at the woman's body lying stilly on the ground.

Dalton is on the ground near to her, slowly pushing himself to his feet. I can't see Luke, Soren or Hunter, but as the smoke begins to clear they appear in the distance, slowly walking back towards us.

Any recruiters that were left have run off, but that doesn't mean we're safe. They'll be back with others before we know it. We need to get out of here as quickly as possible.

The group looks a little battered as we gather together, but no one appears to be injured. Sebastian is slightly unsteady on his feet, but at least he's standing on his own. He steps towards me and drapes his arm around my shoulders. 'Fancy meeting you here,' he slurs, with a smile.

'Let's go,' Dalton bellows. 'More recruiters will be coming.'

'You're right,' adds April. 'Ryan and I will carry on to the helicopter with you in case there's another ambush.'

'What about *her*?' Luke says, spitting the word out as he glares at me. I can almost hear my heart pounding as Luke stares me down, with so much hatred clear in his eyes.

Dalton barely gives me a second look. 'We'll deal with her later. Let's move.'

CHAPTER SIXTEEN

A s we set off I let a deep breath out in relief. They haven't
sent me back and I still have a chance to get to the ARC. I
turn to check on Sebastian.

'Are you okay?' I ask him.

He nods. 'I'll be fine. I should have known you'd find a way to get
to the ARC with us. I had no idea you were here.'

I look over at Hunter who is just ahead with Aiden, the two of
them striding after Dalton. I still can't quite believe he was so willing
to help me when I've only been horrible to him.

I turn back to Sebastian. 'It's not just that I want to go, it's important that I'm there. I know M doesn't think I've got enough control to
be part of the team, but I honestly think I can help. This is our ARC
we're going to and if anyone can help us on a mission there, it's me. I
should be there and if M could only trust me, he'd see that.'

'I couldn't agree more,' Sebastian says, before he suddenly starts
to grin. 'And it looked like you had pretty good control over your
talents back there.'

He's right, I did, if only for a few moments. It felt different this
time. Usually when I'm under pressure my talents overwhelm me

and burst out without warning, or don't materialise at all. Today it felt like the energy inside me was ready and waiting to be called upon. Even now, as we run through the streets of Hope, I can feel my talent throbbing within me. It thuds in time with my heartbeat and flows through my body, just below the surface of my skin.

'April must be fuming,' says Sebastian, breaking into my thoughts.

'I don't want to think about that,' I say, groaning inside. I knew I'd be in trouble if I was discovered by the group, but now that April is here I'm certain she'll try and take me back with her to the station. April and Ryan are walking quickly ahead of us and they look to be deep in conversation.

'Come on Sebastian, we're falling behind.'

Dalton sets a fast pace and looks to be attempting to make up for the time we lost fighting the recruiters. I feel exhausted from using my talents before and it's difficult to keep up with the group, but I don't let out a word of complaint. I'm not the only one struggling. Both Sebastian and Aiden have been slower since the fight and I'm not sure they can maintain Dalton's fast pace for too much longer. As if reading my mind, Dalton slows to a halt as he turns into the shadows of a narrow back alley.

'We'll rest here for a few minutes,' he says. 'But we can't stop for long if we want to reach the edge of the city in time.'

I face Sebastian to see how he's feeling after his fall. The cut on his forehead looks bad, so I guide him over to Aiden who hangs back from the others with Hunter. There's still so much sadness in Aiden's eyes. I hate to ask anything of him but Sebastian's cut isn't good. His gaze warms a little when he sees me approach.

'Sebastian's got a bad cut to his face, do you think he needs stitches?' I ask.

Aiden takes a large gulp of water from his bottle before pouring some of the liquid onto Sebastian's forehead to clean out the wound. With the blood washed away, I can see the cut clearly slashes through his eyebrow.

'There's a lot of blood, but the wound isn't deep,' Aiden replies. 'Still, you might have a bit of a scar.' He pulls his backpack off and searches around in it for some antiseptic.

As I watch Aiden tend to Sebastian, April appears by my side. 'Do you want to explain what you're doing here,' she asks, glaring at me with her arms firmly folded across her chest.

'I'm sorry April, but I had to,' I protest. 'I need to go back to the ARC. I know I can be helpful.'

'He thinks so too,' she says, nodding at Ryan who stands talking to Hunter.

'What do you mean?'

'We both tried to convince M to let you go on the mission. When he refused, Ryan insisted that we follow the group to make sure they made it safely to the edge of Hope. It's like he knew you would be stupid enough to sneak onto the mission,' she says, rolling her eyes.

'So you're not sending me back?'

'I couldn't even if I wanted to, could I?' she says, with a smile.

Dalton's booming voice confirms it's time to move on, and we continue our push to the edge of the city. It doesn't take us long until we reach the marshland that marks the border.

We trek through the marsh, without slowing. There's no rusty fence and no airbase where we're headed, only an endless field of reeds softly blowing in the wind. I had expected to see the airstrip that our camp used to be situated by out here. I got so turned around in the South Hope ruins though, it's not exactly a surprise I'm disoriented.

The ground is sludgy beneath my feet and my shoes are quick to become coated in mud. 'Do you know how much further we're going?' I turn and ask Hunter, who trudges close behind me.

He looks up at Dalton, focusing on him for a moment, before settling his gaze back on me. 'Well, we're going to the edge of The Sphere,' he says, lowering his voice. 'So it could be a while yet.'

I look up at the sky to see if I can see the slight shimmer of The Sphere overhead. I've only caught sight of it a handful of times before, mostly when I was at our old camp. The sky overhead is covered with dark clouds though. There's no flicker of it visible today.

'We have to get as close as we can so that the helicopter isn't seen,' Hunter continues.

I know we are finally reaching the edge of the marsh when the ground becomes firmer beneath our feet. We no longer wade through mud and sludge, and instead we are able to walk with ease.

I almost stop in my tracks when I see the large helicopter looming up ahead. It is not the helicopter that surprises me though, rather the ice and snow I can see built up in the distance beyond. It's like a wall that extends along the horizon, as far as the eye can see. There's a slight shimmer to the air in front of the wall. It shoots up into the sky above between Hope and the impacted wastes beyond—The Sphere.

Looking at the phenomenon, I feel like we've been living in an inverted snow globe—us within the globe and the snow surrounding the outside, clinging to the mysterious transparent barrier that keeps the freezing wasteland at bay.

'It's not all like this,' Hunter says, coming to stand beside me.

I turn to him and raise one eyebrow, questioning his comment.

'The world outside Hope,' he explains. 'It's not all snow and ice. Some sections are worse than others, but it's almost like there are pockets that aren't affected as badly. It's been long enough now that the impact winter is losing its grip. Within our lifetime I reckon we'll see it recede almost completely.'

'You really think that?' I ask.

He nods. 'My father has a team of experts who analyse almost everything there is to know about the world we find ourselves in. They think it will happen.'

I close my eyes and try to imagine a world that isn't covered in heavy clouds and thick layers of ice. I think I would have struggled to really imagine it while still living in the ARC. But after living in Hope these last months, I know how amazing it would be.

The helicopter we approach is massive; much larger than the one I came to Hope in. As the door to the helicopter opens, an older man jumps out to greet us and I find a grin forming on my lips when I see him. It's Gord, the man who had brought me to Hope City in the first place. He'd been kind to me during our journey and I hadn't wanted to say goodbye when I'd arrived at the Reintegration Centre.

'Cutting it fine,' he says to Dalton, as we approach. 'I was about to leave without you.'

'Well, we made it,' Dalton says. 'And we need to leave right now.'

'I couldn't agree more,' Gord grins. His gaze moves past Dalton to the rest of us. 'Quite a bunch you have here for me. You said seven didn't you?'

'It's eight actually,' says April. 'Elle is joining you.'

'You're letting her come?' Luke asks, his anger making his words louder than I think he intended.

'Yes, she's going,' April responds. 'If you have a problem with it, you're welcome to come back with me and explain to M why you didn't want to go.'

That seems to shut Luke up and I struggle to hide a smile that sneaks onto my face. When he turns to me and sees me smiling, Luke's anger only seems to get worse. I quickly avert my eyes, not wanting to watch him seething at me.

Gord steps back and opens one of the doors, waving for us to get inside, and everyone begins to climb into the helicopter. Before I follow them I turn and walk towards Ryan who stands watching with April.

'How did you know I would be here?' I ask bluntly, not really expecting a straight answer. He looks to April before turning back to me, his brown eyes glowing under the dark clouds as they lock onto mine.

'You know you need to be there,' he says. 'And I knew you wouldn't let anything stop you from going back to the ARC. You're stronger than anyone understands Elle. You showed that today, and they'll need your help down there.'

For once I feel like he's making sense. A part of me has felt drawn to the ARC ever since I heard about the cure, and I'm grateful that Ryan understands.

'Thank you,' I say softly. 'For saving us back there.'

'I couldn't exactly let you and Sebastian get crushed by that recruiter could I,' he says, winking at me.

'You better get going, before I change my mind,' April says. I rush forward and smother her in a hug.

'I won't let you down.'

As I approach the helicopter, Gord gives me a smile and reaches out a hand to help me up into the back.

'Glad to see you again,' he says. 'I should have known you'd end up with this lot.'

I smile. 'How long have you been helping The Movement?'

'Too long kid,' he says. 'M got to me early. I didn't take much convincing when I heard what was happening to some of the kids I was transporting. I've been helping whenever I can.'

I feel excited and tense all at once as I take my seat next to Sebastian, pull the strap across my chest and buckle it in. A mixture of emotions war within me as I consider our return and as realisation dawns that I'm actually going back. So much rests on this mission and yet all I can think about is potentially seeing Quinn again.

Sebastian will be excited to have the chance to see his dad and I'm sure Aiden will want to see his grandfather. Who knows what will happen when we get down there though. Our mission is too important to risk failure by seeking them out.

I sneak a glance at Aiden, who sits on the other side of me. No emotions grace his features and he stares out the window, his thoughts a million miles from this helicopter.

When Gord straps himself in, I smile and grip the sides of my own seat tightly. I'd been so nervous about where I was going the last time I was in a helicopter, I can barely remember what it had been like. I actually feel excited this time.

As the helicopter lifts off the ground and takes off into the air, Aiden lets out a long breath.

'You okay?' I ask.

He nods, but he seems a little paler and there's a light sheen across his brow. 'I'm just not great with flying,' he responds.

'Really?' I tilt my head as I watch him, not quite able to understand. We've lived our whole lives underground and I can think of nothing better than being so high up in the air. I feel like I'm a bird when I'm up here. There's nothing to be nervous about.

'You know how you hate small spaces?' Sebastian murmurs to me.

I turn to him. 'Yeah...'

'Maybe that's what it's like for him.'

I feel a sudden wave of sympathy for Aiden. Hopefully the flight will be over quickly and he doesn't have to be scared for too long.

There's an immediate difference in the air around us when we pass through The Sphere between Hope and the outside world. It had just been starting to lightly drizzle in Hope but, out in the impact winter, snow falls heavily against the helicopter windows. The blizzard is so thick it's difficult to see anything at all.

The helicopter shakes as it is tossed back and forth between the clouds. The sensation causes my stomach to drop, and when I turn to look at Aiden his eyes are scrunched up tightly and he looks like he's about to pass out.

I reach out and take his hand in mine, clasping it tightly. He grips mine tightly in return. It's almost painful how firmly he grabs onto me, but I don't mind. I understand how much he's struggling with this.

I look around the helicopter and catch Lara's gaze. She is sitting against the wall directly opposite me and eyeing Aiden like he's the devil. His emotions must be affecting her pretty badly. He's not the only one freaking out as we are tossed around in the storm, but he's by far the worst.

'Can you do anything?' I mouth, nodding at Aiden.

Her eyes look to him and she slowly nods. Within moments, his grip on my hand loosens and he appears calmer, almost like he could drift off to sleep.

I smile at Lara. 'Thanks.'

She waves her hand like it was no problem and then slouches down in her seat, focusing intently on the ceiling.

The journey back to the ARC is longer and far rougher than I remember. Every time the helicopter jolts Aiden grips my hand tightly. Even with Lara's influence over his emotions, he's still struggling with the flight. I spend most of the trip silent as I reflect on how much has happened since I left the ARC and wondering whether things will have changed much there.

I've become a completely different person in the months since I left. Would Quinn even recognise me anymore? Will she be able to understand everything I've been through? To see past the monster they turned me into in that hospital?

As the clouds become even darker and night starts to surround us, we gradually begin to descend. Bright white light suddenly erupts around the helicopter, beaming up to us from the ground below as the roof to the ARC hangar recedes. It's almost blinding after being in the near dark of the snowstorm for hours.

I feel a thrill rush through me as the helicopter nears the entrance. My body hums with nervous tension and excitement. 'We're here,' my blood seems to sing. We're finally back where it all began. We've come home to the ARC.

CHAPTER SEVENTEEN

Dalton leaves the helicopter first, checking the coast is clear before waving us out into the hangar behind him. Memories flicker through my mind, consuming my thoughts, as I leave the helicopter and take a step down onto the hard concrete floor. This place had felt huge when I'd been here before. The corrugated iron roof had been so foreign and the chill in the air was so alien. It's just the same as it was when I left, but at the same time it feels completely different. I'd been blindly terrified at the time though, so it's not surprising really.

It's strange to recall my last moments here. The desperation I'd felt, the total uncertainty I had of what to expect next. I look around the space with fresh eyes. There are seven other helicopters of varying sizes in the space near us and the rest of the hangar is empty.

'That's strange,' Gord says, coming around the side of the helicopter and joining our group. 'There are more choppers here than usual and there's normally someone here to greet me.'

Dalton looks around the hangar and then shrugs. 'Maybe they got held up.'

'Maybe,' Gord replies, though he doesn't sound convinced.

Dalton moves to the centre of the group. 'Okay, you know the plan. When we get down into the ARC we're heading straight for the council chambers. There shouldn't be any problems, but if anything happens we'll meet back here.'

We all nod along with him and I feel tense as I look around the group. What if something bad does happen?

We follow Dalton across the hangar, towards the door that will lead us to the world below our feet. I should be excited, but instead I feel unease coursing through me. I glance back over my shoulder at Gord, who waits by the helicopter. Why hasn't someone come to meet him like they usually would? It's only a small thing but for some reason it has me on edge.

The sound of a door opening catches my attention, and I look back at the rest of our group to see I've fallen behind. The others are already moving past the door Dalton holds open and into the upper corridors of the ARC. I jog to catch up with them, and fall into place behind Lara as she steps through the doorway.

It's silent in the corridor and all I can hear are the sounds of breathing from our group. I try to see if I can hear anything further away, but am only met with more silence.

Dalton moves past us and walks over to a shelving unit just inside the doorway. It's filled with sets of the grey clothing I wore almost every day of my life in the ARC. Dalton grabs the clothes and passes them to the rest of us.

'Change,' he murmurs, his eyes darting warily down the long empty corridor before us.

These clothes had once felt so familiar to me, but now they feel like a distant memory. When I see Sebastian in his greys I am reminded of us growing up together and I smile. We used to get into so much trouble in the ARC and seeing us both in our greys makes me realise how much we've matured in the short time since we left.

Once everyone has changed we begin to move into the corridor. We are quick and silent as we move down one hallway after another, making our way to the lifts that will take us to the ARC. There are no officials in the upper ARC, but it's not surprising. The world up here is sectioned off from the rest of the ARC. There's no need for law enforcement when no one lives up here. Most of the ARC doesn't even know this area exists. Only those found tainted ever see it and then they're taken away, so it doesn't matter. No one has ever returned—until now.

Still, getting to the lifts seems too easy, and it makes me nervous when we reach them and we haven't seen a single person. I look around at the others, but no one else seems worried.

When the lift doors open and we step into the small space, my heart hammers as the reality of what we're doing hits me. We're finally returning to the ARC and I have no idea what will greet us when the lift descends and the doors open again.

We crowd into the lift and my stomach lurches when the doors slide closed and the lift begins to plummet at a rapid pace. I instinctively reach out and grab Sebastian's hand and he gives it a reassuring squeeze. His eyes are warm as he looks at me, telling me that everything will be okay.

The lift slows to a stop and when the doors slide open the blaring white florescent lights and white walls of a doctor's office greet us. Soren exits the lift first and as I step out after him he throws one hand against my chest to stop me. A man in an official's white uniform stands in the middle of the room. On seeing us his eyes widen and in the blink of an eye he disappears, reappearing next to us before throwing his fist at Soren's face.

Soren's eyes flare purple and he surges away from the punch, moving so quickly the man doesn't have a chance to react. Soren's body blurs as he darts to the man's side and places his hand against the side of his head. His hand glows a luminous blue and the man drops to the ground before any of us can react. Soren slouches slightly, resting his hand against the wall to support himself.

'What just happened?' I ask, my eyes darting from the man on the ground to Soren. 'I saw him teleport. What's someone talented doing down here?'

The rest of the group stand frozen still with identical looks of shock and worry on their faces, but Soren is straight into action. He begins to peel the man's uniform from his body.

'He must be a recruiter,' Dalton says, walking over to help Soren with the uniform. 'Something's not right.'

The others crowd into the room behind me and Soren changes into the official's uniform. Once he's dressed, he walks past the man lying still on the ground and over to the open doorway.

'Give me a minute,' he says, looking over his shoulder at us. 'I'll check there's no more officials nearby.' He then leaves the room, shutting the door behind him.

Sebastian glances at the man heaped on the ground before moving to the doorway to listen for any sign of Soren's progress. There's stiffness to Sebastian's shoulders and I can tell the talented official being in the ARC troubles him. I glance at the man, glad to see his chest clearly rising and falling. At least he isn't dead.

'Is he a recruiter?' I ask Hunter, as he comes to stand beside me. 'What do you think he's doing down here?'

'I didn't get a chance to read his mind,' he says, with a shrug. 'I sure hope there's not any more.'

If there's one though, it seems unlikely he will be the last we run into and, by the tension I can feel in the air, the rest of the group knows it too.

When Soren returns, he looks paler than when he left. His eyes are still flaming a brilliant colour of purple and, though no one says it aloud, he's clearly just used his talent again.

'There's no one out there,' he says. 'Sebastian, you know the ARC best; you should be up front to lead the way. I will bring up the rear.'

Sebastian nods, his eyes becoming focused as he moves to lead us from the room. The corridor is eerily quiet as we enter it. I feel nerves churning in my gut and I keep close to Sebastian who walks in front of me. We're such a big group and highly conspicuous if any official walks by.

It will be difficult to make it to the council chambers in the West

Wing undetected, but I feel certain we have enough talents to deal with any officials we come across—that's if they're not talented.

Sebastian moves with certainty as he leads us through the hospital corridors. He pauses by each corner, checking for signs of officials before waving us to follow him. We haven't seen a single nurse, doctor or patient yet. This place is usually a hive of activity, and the longer we go without seeing anyone the more nervous I feel.

We're almost to the front entrance of the hospital when I hear sounds of talking and movement up ahead. I grab Sebastian's arm and jerk him to a stop. He turns to me, a look of confusion furrowing his brow.

'What?' Sebastian mouths, as the rest of the group pauses behind us.

'There are people up ahead,' I whisper. My fingers tingle with talent as my heart begins to race. I take a deep breath in and blow it out to calm myself. The tingles dull a little, but I can still feel them humming in my fingertips. The thought makes me nervous, but I try to push it down. I will not lose control here. I refuse.

Hunter moves up beside Sebastian. 'Let me go first. I can manipulate their thoughts enough so they won't see us pass.'

He glances at Dalton who nods with approval, and allows Hunter to take the lead.

My heart beats so loudly I can hear it ringing in my ears and my fingers continue to prickle as we follow Hunter quietly. I try not to think about the talent that hums through my body. I can't waste energy now. I need to preserve my talent in case we get into real trouble, but it's difficult to convince my body I'm fine when I feel so wound up.

Hunter reaches the end of the corridor, which opens out onto the hospital foyer area, and pauses to look carefully around the corner. He holds up a hand, causing us to stop, before slowly turning to face us.

'*Is there another way out of here?*' his voice sounds in my mind.

Sebastian shakes his head and so do I. The entrance foyer of the hospital is, to my knowledge, the only way in and out of this place.

I cautiously approach Hunter and take a quick peek around the corner myself. Past the reception desk, there are two rows of people standing in their greys. They look like they must be teenagers and their faces are filled with fear. They all stare down at their feet, too scared to look up at the five officials who usher them into the hospital.

Hunter grabs my wrist, dragging my eyes from the group to look at him. *'Those people aren't officials. They're recruiters,'* he reveals.

My eyes widen and I glance back at the men in the crisp white suits. *'What are they doing with those kids?'* I think back at him, hoping he catches my thoughts. I can't stop looking at the grave faces of the teenagers assembled. One girl has tears in her eyes, while another boy is chewing nervously on his lower lip. Whatever's happening here isn't normal. At least, it wasn't when I used to live down here.

Hunter slowly shakes his head, frowning as he focuses in on one of the recruiters. *'They're taking them to a holding room in the hospital.'*

'What's happening?' Dalton whispers to Hunter, coming up behind us.

'Recruiters,' Hunter responds.

I pull back from the corner allowing Dalton to take my spot so he can get a look at the foyer. He assesses the room with one look before facing us again.

'We should find another route,' he says quietly.

'There isn't one,' Sebastian whispers back.

'Then we need to find a wall where I can make a window through to the rest of the ARC. This entrance is too dangerous. Something's clearly up and I don't want to expose our group until we know what it is.'

'I may have a way,' Aiden suggests softly.

We all turn to look at him and he lets out a slow breath.

'There's another way out of here,' he repeats, 'but I can guarantee no one is going to like it.'

'It doesn't matter; as long as it's not buzzing with recruiters,' Soren responds.

Aiden nods and turns, leading us away from the foyer. He pushes through a door at the end of the corridor, taking us deeper into the hospital. His steps are certain as he leads the way, and his face is calm as he checks for recruiters at each intersection.

I keep my senses extended as we walk, but the hallways are oddly quiet. There are no noises coming from patient rooms and the place feels like it's totally deserted.

'Through here,' Aiden says, pausing as he reaches a set of doors. He attempts to enter a pin into the keypad by the door, but it keeps flashing red.

Aiden turns to me. 'Any chance you can fry it?' he asks.

'I can try,' I say, giving him a hesitant look. Lara gently places her hand on my arm and her touch sends a flood of confidence flowing through me. I can almost feel the essence of her talent reaching every part of my body and instantly calming the nerves that restrict me. I smile at her gratefully and step towards the device.

My talent flows easily to my fingers as I place them over the pin pad and an electrical current erupts from my hand in a large white ball of light. As the sparks connect between my hand and the pin pad, I am thrown back from the door. I fly through the air behind me to land with a thud on my backside.

Ouch.

I groan and move to push myself up. I feel winded and my back feels tingly and slightly numb from the fall. Sparks of electricity still dance over my fingertips and move up my arms. I clench my teeth together as I try to calm myself enough to make them stop.

'Are you okay?' Sebastian asks, rushing to my side. He doesn't touch me, but crouches a safe distance away from the electricity still buzzing over me.

'Fine,' I say, a little breathless.

I look back up at the door to see the pin pad has been completely destroyed. I've reduced it to a melted, sparking clump of metal on the wall.

Aiden tries the doorhandle and the door pushes in. 'It worked,' he says, turning back to us. He steps through the doorway, holding the door open as we follow him in.

The room he's brought us to is dimly lit and much colder than the rest of the hospital. It's only when Aiden flicks on a light by the door that I can see where we are.

A collective gasp sounds through the group as my gaze settles on the rows of metal beds before us. The light dances along their flat, shiny surfaces, drawing in the eye to focus on what rests on each one. I don't want to believe what I'm seeing and I don't want to take another step into the room.

Aiden's brought us to the morgue and the place is filled with bodies.

CHAPTER EIGHTEEN

My eyes widen and I take a nervous step back. There are rows and rows of lifeless bodies before us. Some are covered in carelessly draped white sheets, while others lay there with their pale skin completely exposed. There's a pungent musty smell of blood in here and I cover my nose and try to breath through my mouth, but the sharp odour remains in my nostrils.

'Is this a joke?' Hunter asks.

'What are we doing here Aiden?' Lara says, taking a step closer to me.

Aiden doesn't respond though, his face has paled and his eyes are scanning across the dead bodies. There are no body bags and all the corpses in here are out on display. I try to avoid looking at them, but Aiden can't seem to tear his eyes away.

'What's wrong?' I ask him, taking a step forward and allowing the chill of the room to envelop me.

He slowly shakes his head. 'They shouldn't be out in the open like this. And there shouldn't be so many.'

'What do you think happened?' Sebastian asks.

Aiden slowly approaches the first body, pulling a chart out from a container at the end of the bed. He quickly reads through the notes, before moving onto the chart at the foot of the next bed and then the next.

He's almost at the end of the row when a chart drops from his hands and he staggers back against the wall.

'Aiden?' I call to him softly, but he doesn't respond. I walk over to him and pick the chart up off of the floor. Seeing the name at the top of it, I nearly drop the board myself. I look over at the body lying on the cold metal stretcher before us. It's Aiden's grandfather, Dr. Wilson.

'What happened?' I ask, my eyes skimming back to the chart.

'They tried to administer a trial cure on him.' Aiden's voice is deadened, completely flat of any emotion. 'They gave the other people in here the same thing. I don't understand why they would have gone ahead with something they weren't certain of. Unless...'

'Unless, what?' I whisper.

'Unless they were desperate.' He bows his head over, cupping his hands over his face.

I reach out to him, but his body stays frozen still as he stares at the body of his grandfather. My heart wrenches inside me as I watch him and I can't believe he's losing another person he loves so soon after Jane.

I look around at the other bodies and my mind whirs with questions. There are so many people here who needlessly died. Why would they be so desperate to test a cure they weren't certain of? Does it somehow tie in with the recruiters being here? Could the group of teenagers who had been waiting in the hospital foyer be about to face a similar fate? I don't know the answers to any of my questions, but an uneasy feeling in my gut tells me it's only a matter of time before I do.

'I'm so sorry Aiden,' I say, turning back to him. 'I wish there was something we could have done.'

He shakes his head. 'There is nothing we can do now for him, but we can help the others in the ARC. We need to find volunteers to trial the cure, *our cure*. The cure I have works and the sooner we trial it and succeed, the sooner this madness will stop.'

His gaze falls from his grandfather. 'He's gone,' he says. 'But, I can finish what he started.' His face hardens as he turns and walks back to the others. I slowly trail behind him, casting a glance back at his grandfather as I go.

The others in the group are huddled close, talking quietly with each other. Sebastian reaches out and pats Aiden's arm sympathetically as he approaches, and Lara comes up and gives him a hug.

When she lets go he coughs uncomfortably. 'We go this way,' he says, walking over and stopping in front of one of the walls. He presses his hand against one of the white panels and lifts back a large rectangular door. Behind the door is the metal rim of a deep and dark shaft.

'Aiden...' my voice quivers. 'Please tell me that's not what I think it is.'

He glances back and nods. 'Yes, this is how we dispose of the dead.'

'You're not serious...' Luke groans.

'Not going to happen,' Lara objects.

Aiden folds his arms over his chest. 'We don't have any other option. This is our only way out of here.'

I cringe, but take a step forward towards the shaft. Aiden needs us to be strong for him right now and this is clearly a last resort. 'I swear Aiden, if I land on a dead body I'm never getting over this...'

Then, before I have a chance to think twice about it, I climb into the shaft and push myself down the funnel.

I almost immediately regret the decision as I plummet quickly down the slide. The slope of the shaft is steep and I build momentum quickly. I squeeze my eyes tightly shut, but it doesn't stop them from watering. I try to remember to breathe as the air whips past my face.

As quickly as my plummet started, it stops and I roll out onto the hard concrete floor. I lurch to my feet and stumble away from the shaft's exit. The room I'm in is dim, but there are thankfully no bodies to be seen.

There are body bags piled up in the corner of the room and dark embers light a furnace against the far wall. The place is solemn and silent except for the subtle sound of crackling from the fire.

I hear a loud, 'umph,' as someone rolls out behind me.

'Can't believe you beat me to it, Winters,' Hunter says with a grin, as he stands up.

I roll my eyes at him and turn back to my inspection of the room. We must be on one of the lower levels of the ARC. I hope Aiden knows his way to the council chambers from here, because I've never been to this place before.

The others tumble out behind us, one by one. Soren is the last to come down, and he has a dark look to his eyes I hadn't noticed earlier.

'I assume you know the way to the council chambers from here,' Soren asks Aiden, his voice cutting through the silence like steel. He stands slowly, brushing his hands against his pants.

Aiden goes to respond, but Lara speaks before he has a chance. 'Are the council even in charge down here anymore?'

We all look at each other, but no one has the answer. With all the recruiters down here, and the hospital almost completely abandoned, it's clear that things aren't the way we left them.

Hunter shakes his head. 'I'm not sure, but we need to work out what the hell is going on down here.'

Soren shoots Hunter a dark look. 'You sure you don't already know? This has your *father* written all over it.'

Hunter throws his hands up in the air. 'Yeah, you're right. This probably is Joseph's doing, but that doesn't mean I know squat about it. I hate that man more than anyone and it's not like he pulls me aside to let me know his master plan.'

'What should we do?' Lara asks, turning to Dalton, who has been silent this whole time.

'We keep heading for the council chambers,' he says.

'Right, then let's keep moving,' Lara says, clapping her hands together and nodding her head at the door that leads from the room.

Hunter continues to scowl at Soren, but they both move silently over to the door.

'You do know how to get to the council chambers from here, don't you?' Lara asks Aiden, who gives her an affirmative nod.

'We need to go through the Atrium to the West Wing, which is where the chambers are located.'

I swallow tightly at his explanation. The Atrium is the mid-point of the ARC and the hub of all activity. I don't know how the hell he thinks we can get through there unscathed. If the Atrium is anything like the hospital there are bound to be recruiters or officials there, but it's the only way to get to the West Wing from here. The only positive I can think of is that it will be so busy in the Atrium, there's no way we will be noticed.

We follow Aiden down several hallways. They're darker than the usual bright, white corridors in the ARC, with pipes running along the ceiling and soft blue lighting filtering down the walls. Aiden leads us up one flight of steps and comes to a stop by the door at the top of them. He pauses with his hand reached out to the doorknob.

'We'll probably expect to see people beyond this door,' he says, in warning.

I brace myself as he pulls the door open, but the corridor beyond is empty. It's got the usual harsh lighting and sterile feel to it that I'm used to seeing in the ARC and I recognise the place instantly. It's the bottom floor of the ARC, and right near the Atrium. Aiden's right, people frequently use this corridor. We're going to have to be careful from here.

We slowly reassemble in our line as we follow Aiden through the doorway. My nerves are still on edge and I can feel them building the closer we get to the Atrium. All I can think is that we're going to be found at any moment.

When we reach the entrance to the Atrium, Sebastian moves to look around the corner of the opening. A moment later he stumbles back several feet, turning to us.

'That place is crawling with officials,' he hisses.

I cautiously approach the corner and peek around it to look at the Atrium myself. I quickly jerk my head back. He wasn't kidding. There has to be twenty officials out there and who knows how many of them are recruiters. The place is completely deserted of citizens though and nothing like the Atrium I expected to see. It was always heaving with people and buzzing with activity, but now the place is almost completely deserted.

'What do we do?' I ask the others.

'Our group is too big and there are too many of them for me to manipulate,' Hunter says, as he walks back from having a look himself. 'Especially if there are recruiters in there.'

Everyone falls silent and tension seems to hum through the group. I glance at Lara who shrugs at me. She's got no idea what to do and she's not the only one.

'We could fight them,' Luke suggests.

Sebastian raises one eyebrow at him. 'You really think that's a good idea?'

Luke's hands clench and unclench at his sides and I catch sight of a wisp of smoke dancing across his knuckles. He's been silent for a while now and he looks like he's itching for a fight. 'I'm sure we could take them.'

Lara shakes her head. 'One of us will get hurt if we fight them,' she says. 'We can't take them all.'

Luke glares at her. '*You* can't maybe.'

'Luke!' I hiss at him, causing him to turn his glare on me.

'Don't get me started on you, princess.'

'That's enough,' Dalton growls, catching Luke's eyes and signalling for him to back down. 'Is there another way around?' he asks, looking to Aiden.

Aiden shakes his head. 'We have to go through the Atrium.'

'Would it be better on another level?' I ask.

Hunter moves for the entrance again and sneaks a glance upwards. I can easily picture the glass walkways high above the Atrium floor. He comes back and shakes his head. 'They're just as bad. There are less recruiters, but the walkways are only narrow.'

Soren turns to Sebastian. 'Can you teleport to the wing?'

'Yes, with one other person,' Sebastian responds. 'But I don't think I could make the trip more than a few times and I'll be completely wiped if I need my talent again.'

Soren glances at Dalton, who gives him a small nod, before turning back to Sebastian. 'We'll have to risk it. I don't see any other way.' He readjusts the official's jacket he wears. 'Take Aiden first, then come back.'

Sebastian nods and reaches for Aiden. Once his hand is clasped firmly around Aiden's arm, the two of them disappear. Several moments later Sebastian reappears alone. His skin looks a little whiter than it was before, but he seems to be holding up okay. The furthest I can remember him teleporting was across the river from North Hope, and that didn't end well. The Atrium isn't quite as wide, but he can't be finding it easy.

Soren glances around our small circle. 'Lara, you next.'

Lara glances at me uneasily, but I give her an encouraging nod. I can tell she doesn't feel comfortable leaving me behind, but she needn't worry. I'll be in the West Wing soon.

Sebastian takes Lara and when he reappears again he is visibly struggling. He's sweating profusely and he looks shaky on his feet. He's going downhill quickly and I feel almost certain he won't make more than one final trip.

'Elle,' Soren says. 'You next.' I glance up at him, Dalton, Luke and Hunter.

'No, one of you should go next.'

Soren shakes his head. 'Sebastian won't make another trip, not unless we want him to collapse. Dalton and I will take Luke and Hunter through the Atrium. They're the strongest and will be able to defend themselves if needed. We will be fine.'

Feelings of guilt cause my stomach to curdle as I look at the four of them. I would be the strongest if I had better control of my talents.

'I could try to teleport myself,' I suggest.

Sebastian shakes his head. 'You've never tried something so far before on purpose, and now isn't the time to be taking that risk. Soren is in an official's uniform; it'll look like he's escorting them somewhere. Hunter should be able to use his talent to help. Right?' He glances at Hunter.

Hunter nods. 'There are a lot of minds out there to control, but I should be able to get them to lose interest in us. They hopefully won't question Soren since he's in uniform.'

I slowly nod and take a step towards Sebastian. I still feel uneasy about leaving the others here. What if something happens to them while they're trying to cross the Atrium?

Hunter reaches out and grabs my arm. 'Look, if anything happens to us in there, you guys run. Okay?'

I hesitate.

'*Okay?*' he repeats.

I give him a small nod, but I'm not certain that my heart agrees. I can't just abandon them if something goes wrong.

I step into Sebastian's arms. 'They'll be okay,' Sebastian says softly, as he takes hold of me. His grip is so gentle and he pulls me close, enveloping his arms around me. He rests his chin on my forehead and his proximity causes my stomach to flutter. He hadn't held any of the others this way and I smile as I close my eyes and place my head against his chest.

A rush of cold air flows over my skin, before disappearing just as quickly as it came. When I open my eyes I'm staring at Aiden and Lara.

Lara lifts an eyebrow at me and gives me a knowing smile. I take a step away from Sebastian's arms and immediately miss the feel of them around me. I glance back at him. His hands rest on his knees and there's a touch of blood at his nose, which makes me worry. He's overexerted himself. What if he needs his talent again later?

'You two need to get a room,' Lara mutters. I feel my cheeks grow warm with embarrassment and I struggle to meet anyone's eyes.

'Are you going back for the others?' Aiden asks.

Sebastian shakes his head. 'Soren is going to bring them over.'

I walk over to the West Wing entrance to the Atrium and look in. It's strange to see it so empty of people, with only the officials loitering in the large and open hall. Worry gathers in the pit of my stomach as I consider what has happened here. It can't be good.

The TV screens scattered on the walls that used to show the news are ominously quiet. Some of the TVs used to broadcast footage of the abandoned surface above the ARC, and even without those haunting images constantly flickering across their screens, the place seems truly lifeless.

I catch movement on the far side of the Atrium and watch as Soren emerges into the hall with Luke, Dalton and Hunter by his side.

'They're coming,' I whisper to the others. I turn back to watch them cross and I feel Sebastian come up behind me. His chest presses into my back as he lightly takes hold of my arms and peers over my head.

None of the officials have noticed the four of them yet, and they walk through the Atrium with such confidence, looking just like they're meant to be there. Watching them makes my skin crawl and my talent ripples across it. I can't stand to look, but I can't seem to take my eyes off of them either.

Time stretches as I watch them and an eternity seems to pass as they slowly make their way towards us. Most of the officials stand near the exits and the three of them look so exposed as they walk across the open expanse in the centre of the room.

Fear grips my insides as I stand and wait. Something could so easily go wrong for them. There are more officials in that room than I've ever seen in one place before, and if Hunter loses his concentration for even a second they could easily be caught.

Soren's confidence is effortless as he walks with Dalton, Luke and

Hunter in tow. With his head held high and his chest puffed out, he plays the part of an official well. Luke is scowling, but that's not anything unusual for him, and Dalton watches his surroundings warily. Hunter's eyes are locked on to the far wall. He walks without seeing, as his mind focuses fully on the men who surround them.

They are just past half way to the West Wing entrance, when an official steps out from the wall and moves towards them.

'Where are you going?' the man asks Soren.

Hunter's focus drops from the far wall to the man standing before them. His eyes become tense and I can see purple flaring in them as he attempts to manipulate the official.

Soren stands a little straighter. 'These three were in the hospital. I'm returning them to their quarters.' His voice is strong and filled with calm certainty. It's said so convincingly that I almost believe what he says, despite knowing it's not the truth.

Hunter takes a step backward. The movement is subtle, but I catch it all the same. There's a slight crease in his brow and the corner of his mouth is twitching. His gaze flickers past the official, in our direction.

'This man's a recruiter,' comes Hunter's voice in my head. 'Get out of here.'

The expression on my face drops and I take a rapid breath in as my body tenses.

'What is it Elle?' Sebastian whispers.

'He's a recruiter,' I reply, as the fear in my chest deepens. 'We can't leave them.'

'Elle...' Sebastian's voice holds a warning in it, but I'm not listening to him. We can't leave them with a recruiter. They'll end up being taken away, or worse, if he knows they are talented.

'Looks like you're heading to the West Wing,' the recruiter questions Soren. 'Their quarters aren't in the West Wing.'

Soren gives a short laugh and rubs his face. 'You're right. It's been a long shift. We were going to the East Wing.'

'You mean the North,' the recruiter responds, his voice filled with suspicion.

'Yeah, North, didn't I say that?' Soren responds.

The recruiter shakes his head. 'You should really get some sleep.'

'Tell me about it,' Soren says.

He moves to walk away, and I let out a short sign of relief, but then a group of adults dressed in their greys emerges from the North Wing. There's about twenty of them slowly moving in two rows, flanked by officials on either side. They look to be heading towards the hospital. Soren and the others halt as they look across the Atrium and see the group making their way across it.

'What are they doing with all those people?' I whisper to Sebastian, but he shakes his head, as confused as I am.

As I focus back on the group I see a man stumble out of line. An official leans over, grabbing him by the cuff of his grey top, and shoves him back towards the group.

'Back in line,' he growls at the man.

The man falters though and looks back at the official. 'Where are you taking us?'

'Do *not* ask questions!' the official replies. 'Get back in line!'

Another citizen in grey stops and turns to face the official. 'We just want to know what's going on,' he says.

The official's eyes darken and a smirk tugs at the corner of his lips. He holds out his hand and a coiling whip of sparking electricity unfurls from his palm, appearing out of thin air.

'What did I say about questions?' he yells, drawing the whip of hot, white, blinding energy back behind his head.

The men's eyes widen and they cower back from the official, pure terror lighting their faces.

The official begins to lower his arm, his whip lashing out in a glaring arc towards the men. But, just before it reaches them, a ball of bright purple fire rushes through the air towards the recruiter, completely engulfing him in flames. Luke stands there with his right arm outstretched, flames dancing from his fingertips, anger flaring in his eyes.

The room erupts in chaos as the group of citizens scream while the officials leave their posts and run towards our friends. Some officials stay still, shock evident on their faces, but most are straight into action. I move to run into the Atrium after them, but Sebastian pulls me back.

'What are you doing?' I shout at him, pushing against his hands.

'We can't go in there!'

'We can't leave them!' I yell back.

Aiden grabs hold of my other arm to help drag me back from the entrance, but he quickly jerks his hand away as though he's been shocked.

'Elle, you need to get control of yourself,' Sebastian says.

His arms are around my waist, trying to pull me away, but I shake my head and keep my eyes trained on the room before me. Luke is hurling balls of fire around him and Soren is a blur as he darts from one official to another. Dalton is using brute force on his opponents while Hunter stands completely still, his eyes flaring purple as he focuses in on any men who approach him.

An official tackles Luke to the ground and without a thought I grasp at the air around my fingers and hurl it at the man, throwing him off Luke's back. Luke quickly jumps to his feet and hurls another fireball from his fist.

Hunter looks in my direction. *'Elle, get out of here!'* I hear his voice speak in my mind before he turns back to focus on a man who has bolts of electricity dancing across his skin. It's another talented recruiter in an official's uniform. How many of them are there down here? Hunter and the others have no chance of escaping if the room is filled with recruiters. They need our help.

Sebastian won't let go of me and he keeps trying to drag me away to safety. Judging from the amount of recruiters in the Atrium though, nowhere in the ARC is safe anymore.

I glance back at Sebastian, looking him deep in the eyes. 'I know Hunter said to run, but they need our help in there.'

He looks intensely into my eyes and nods, slowly releasing his hands from my waist. I face the room and take a deep breath before blowing it out and launching into action.

'Stay here,' Sebastian shouts to Aiden, as he and Lara follow me in, hot at my heels.

The Atrium is chaos, with stray fireballs flying through the air and bolts of electricity dancing across the ground. Recruiters are using their talents recklessly as they battle to maintain control. Not all men dressed in official white are fighting though. Many of them stand still in shock, their mouths open and their eyes wide as they cower away from the fighting. Some have even joined the citizens in grey who are shrinking back against the wall by the North Wing entrance.

A fireball hurtles directly at my head and I dive forward. Lara and Sebastian throw themselves to the ground behind me, and I hear Lara gasp as she hits the floor. I glance over my shoulder. 'Are you okay?' I ask her.

She tries to get back to her feet but hisses in through her teeth again as she does so. 'It's my ankle.'

'Here,' Sebastian says, moving over to help her up. He slings her arm over his shoulder and wraps his arm around her waist to support her. He glances up at me. 'You keep going Elle. Help the others with the recruiters. We'll protect the citizens.'

I nod and push myself to my feet as the two of them vanish into thin air, reappearing in front of the people who cower over by the wall. Another stray fireball launches at me and I bolt forwards, continuing to run towards the battle.

I've almost reached Hunter when I begin to cough and I struggle to draw in a breath. I go to breathe in again, but no air enters my mouth. I drop to my knees, choking as I try to breathe, but no matter how hard I gasp, I'm suffocating. My eyes are wild as I look around the room for the culprit.

A recruiter in official white stands ten feet from here, his eyes narrowed in on me. The edges of my vision are blackening and my head feels dizzy, but I focus on the pulsing talent beneath my skin. I urge the energy down into my fingertips, creating a huge block of ice in my hand.

I can feel myself slowly fading but with one last push of energy I hurl the jagged block of ice at the man, propelling it across the room with a powerful thrust of wind. It rockets through the air, slamming against the recruiter's head. He sways on his feet and drops to the floor, unconscious.

As his body slaps against the ground, I gulp in a fresh breath of air. I look down at my shaking hands and brace myself as I gasp in and out. I slowly push myself to my feet again, feeling weak and light-headed.

There are only a few recruiters still fighting, and many men in white uniforms lie still on the ground.

My eyes land on Dalton's large figure as I survey the room. He's crumpled in a heap at one of the recruiter's feet. There's no rise and fall to his chest and there's blood, too much blood, pooling at his head.

Anger slowly builds in me, and I can feel my talent growing stronger as I glare at the man. It agitates within me, buzzing along my skin and rippling through my veins. Fire begins to envelop my fists and wind stirs around me, tugging at my hair. The man over Dalton looks up and gives me a sickening smile.

Hatred throbs through me as I stare him down and pain radiates from my chest. I hurl the fire burning around my fists towards him and the column of flames shoots out at him in a dizzying spiral. He reacts quickly and dives out of the way, but I lash out at him again with the torrents of air I can feel dancing at my fingertips. The gust of wind hits him directly in the chest and throws him up into the air. He slams against the far wall and slowly slides down it, sagging when he hits the ground.

My talents still rile out of control across my skin, but right now I don't care. There is electricity sparking along my arms and the air around me has become frosty cold, turning my breath into small puffs of steam.

I hear a shout behind me and I turn to see another recruiter bearing down on Lara with a whip of fire in her hands. I can still feel the air stirring at my fingertips, almost begging to be used. It whips up beneath my hand, gathering strength and speed as it spins into a swirling whirlwind. I release it from my grasp with one flick of my wrist, and it storms towards the woman and engulfs her. Her fiery whip is instantly extinguished as the raging wind spins her round and hurls her across the room. She lands hard against the solid floor, sliding before she comes to a stop.

The recruiters I've fought are littered around the room, unconscious or awkwardly stumbling to their feet. There are only a few others left fighting now, but as I turn on them they stop. Sparks crackle from my skin, engulfing me in searing light, and ice hisses around my feet, the ground stretching and cracking around me. I am a monster of pure, raw energy and they look at me with such panic in their eyes, I can almost feel their terror filled gazes rubbing against my skin.

'Let's get out of here!' one of them bellows to the others, causing the group to retreat backwards. The recruiters who are left standing stumble in their urgency, as they scramble to get back to the Hospital Wing as quickly as their legs will take them, while one or two others desperately stagger to their feet and follow suit.

Soren and Luke won't let them go that easily though, and the two of them launch after the men before any of us can stop them. They follow them from the Atrium and disappear into the corridors of the Hospital Wing.

The room falls silent and all eyes seem to turn on me as the sound of their slapping feet against the ground disappears into the distance. Sebastian comes towards me, while Lara staggers over to kneel by Dalton.

As I watching Lara rest her hand on Dalton's shoulder I can feel my anger rekindle. It's only when Sebastian gently touches my arm that I jerk back to my senses. My head clears of anger in a heartbeat and my talents fizz down to nothing.

'Are you okay?' he asks.

Several recruiters lie motionless amongst the debris littered across the floor. I'm not sure if all of them are dead or not. The ARC citizens are eyeing us with horror and the room has fallen so quiet that the terror in here is almost palpable. As I look around the damaged Atrium I feel far from okay.

Lara slowly stands and shakes her head as her eyes catch mine. Dalton is gone. I try to take a breath in, but my lungs feel shallow and I can't seem to get the air all the way into my chest. I swallow the lump sitting uncomfortably in my throat and push down my grief with it. I had known it the moment I saw him resting there, but it hadn't seemed real at the time. I clench my hands into fists, forcing myself to maintain control.

My gaze falls on Hunter who is bent over a barely conscious recruiter a few feet away. As if sensing my eyes on him, he straightens his back and faces me. He pushes up from the ground and takes cautious steps towards me.

'I read his mind,' he says, as he draws near. 'Those recruiters were rounding up people who aren't tainted for transport to Hope. My father wants more test subjects for his experiments. He must be getting desperate to find people who can adapt and absorb talents. People like you, Elle.'

'But, I'm the only one his experiments have worked on, right?'

'Yes,' he replies. 'Which means that most of the people he's taking from the ARC will die.'

CHAPTER NINETEEN

The ARC citizens and remaining officials are huddling together against the wall. They each give us the same look of panic that they gave the recruiters. There is fear in their eyes, but not surprise. I can't concentrate on them though, not after what Hunter's just told me.

I look away from him, unable to meet his eyes. I thought Joseph was only bringing people who were already tainted or talented up from the ARC. He couldn't care less if they live or die, as long as it gets him a step closer to his goals. Sebastian comes to stand in front of me and takes both of my arms in his grasp.

'We won't let them take anyone else,' he swears. I nod, but I can't stop thinking about the people we're too late for. The ones he's already taken to the surface for his experiments.

I'm distracted from my thoughts as I see a girl step from the group behind Sebastian. I recognise her immediately.

'Gemma?' I ask, pushing past Sebastian and taking several steps towards her. She shies back as though she's scared I might hurt her.

'Sebastian? Elle?' she responds, her eyes wide with fear. 'What's happened to you?'

I glance down at my hands. A minute ago I'd been commanding the very air around us, it's understandable that she's scared.

'You're just like *them*,' she says, quietly.

Sebastian approaches her, but she looks just as scared of him too.

'Gem there are a lot of things going on here, and we can explain, but you have to trust us,' he says. 'We have talents like the men you saw us fighting before, but we're here to help the people of the ARC. Those men pretending to be officials are here to take you in for experiments that could kill you. You can't trust them.'

She hesitates, her uncertain gaze flickering between Sebastian and me. She opens her mouth to respond, but a deafening boom echoes through the Atrium and the ground shudders beneath our feet, throwing us forward.

My forearms smack hard against the ground and a moment later Sebastian is covering my body with his. Screams of terror fill the air and the ground quivers and shakes beneath us. I hear a cracking, crumbling noise and the loud crashing of debris hitting the ground; then a shattering noise of glass splintering and smashing around us as it hits the Atrium floor. The room feels like it's collapsing and I keep my eyes clenched tightly shut until the rumbling quakes start to dissipate.

I slowly look up as Sebastian lifts his arms from over my head. Everyone in the Atrium is on the floor and some are slowly starting to stand. The room is darker than before and dust permeates the air. The ground near the Hospital Wing is covered in shards of glass from one of the walkways overhead that has collapsed.

'Are you okay?' Sebastian asks. I nod and scan him for any signs of injuries. Other than the dirt that covers his clothes and face, he seems to be fine.

'What the hell was that?' I ask, coughing to clear my throat.

He slowly points to the Hospital Wing and I turn to see thick dust pouring out of the completely black entrance way.

My face blanches. 'Soren and Luke are in there!' I shout. Sebas-

tian grabs my waist before I can even think of running to the wing to
see if they're okay.

'You can't go in there Elle. We don't know what's happened,'
he says,

'But, they might need our help!'

Hunter clambers to his feet and comes to stand at Sebastian's
side. 'He's right, Elle. We can't risk going in there. There might have
been a cave in. It could be unstable.'

'But, what if one of them is hurt?'

The sound of coughing reaches my ear from deep inside the
Hospital Wing, and I focus in on the entrance, willing for Luke and
Soren to emerge. We've already lost one member of our team—I can't
bear to see anyone else get hurt.

The sound of coughing comes again, closer this time, and then
two figures appear through the thick veil of dust that cloaks the
entrance. I can't make out their faces at first, but as the two men
stagger out into the Atrium I let out a cry of relief.

Luke and Soren are coughing violently, trying to clear the dust
from their throats, but then I notice their coughs aren't alone. A
moment later, the teens we'd seen in the hospital earlier appear in the
entrance, leaning on one another and rubbing dirt from their eyes as
they step into the Atrium.

The citizens in the Atrium rush over to assist the kids as they
stumble out of the Hospital Wing, and as the dust slowly starts to
settle I notice other inhabitants of the ARC cautiously approaching
the Atrium from the North and West Wings.

I can't wipe the beaming smile off my face as Luke and Soren
walk up to us.

'You're both okay!' I exclaim.

Luke frowns. 'Don't tell me you actually care what happens to
me,' he says, before giving me a small smile. 'Thanks though, for
helping me out back there,' he adds, nodding his head. I smile and
nod back. In that one moment, it's as though he's called a truce
with me.

'What happened in there?' Lara asks Soren, who is still coughing to clear his throat.

'The recruiters all retreated to the lift and took it up to the hangar. They set off some sort of explosion at the top so we couldn't come after them. The lift has been destroyed.' he says.

'What about Gord?' I ask. They'll be going right for him and without Gord there's no way for us to get back to Hope. That's if we can even get to the hangar now the elevator is gone.'

Without a word of response, Soren puts in a comm to Gord. It seems like an eternity before he finally answers.

'Gord, what's going on up there?' says Soren.

'I'm fine, thanks for asking,' Gord replies. 'I'm assuming you heard the explosion.'

'Yes. Is the helicopter okay? Did the recruiters see you?

'I managed to keep my head down and the helicopter is fine. They took off in a different one. We're still good to go whenever you find a way to get back up here!'

'We'll find a way. We still need to get our volunteers, but we'll let you know when we're ready for you.' Soren abruptly hangs up the call.

'You think those men are gone?' Gemma asks nervously, slowly approaching us.

'The recruiters?' I ask, getting a nod in response. 'They seem to be.'

'So, you'll be going too then?'

I shake my head. 'Not quite yet. We actually came to talk with the council about something.'

She purses her lips. 'There hasn't been much of a council these last few days, but you may want to talk to Rosa.'

I lift an eyebrow at her.

'Rosa was on the council,' Gemma explains. 'When your recruiters showed up and started taking so many people, everyone knew something was up, but the council did nothing to stop it. Rosa helped some of us hide and was planning to stand up against them. I guess you beat her to it.'

'Can you take us to her?' I ask, hopefully.

'Yes,' Gemma replies. I turn to look at the rest of the group who are all murmuring in agreement

'I'll catch up with you,' Soren says, causing us to fall silent. 'I need to make sure these people are okay and that there are no other recruiters who have been left behind.'

'Are you sure?' Sebastian asks.

Soren's eyes fall on Dalton's body on the ground. 'Yeah, I'm sure,' he says, roughly.

'I'll stay to help you.' Luke steps forward to stand next to Soren. 'I won't be much help with the others.'

Soren nods at him seriously, before glancing at the rest of us. 'Good luck,' he says.

Sebastian, Aiden, Lara, Hunter and I follow Gemma across the Atrium and over towards the East Wing. I'm surprised she's taking us there considering there are no residences in this area of the ARC. There's the plantation down here and other manufacturing zones, but nowhere I can imagine hiding.

There is only silence down the wide corridors of the East Wing, and it feels oddly empty in here. The orderly world I once knew is completely gone, and I worry if anyone will be willing to volunteer for the cure. I worry we won't be able to get out of here at all. Going back through the hospital to get to the hangar is definitely out of the question now.

Lara moves slowly, hobbling as she attempts to walk on her twisted ankle. Aiden puts her arm over his shoulder to help her, but even then our progress is still slow.

Gemma pauses when she reaches a door and looks over her shoulder at us before carefully easing it open. The corridor beyond the door is pitch black and silent. A layer of dust skims over the floor, with a few footsteps imprinted in the grime. She turns her cuff light on, beaming the light into the darkness.

'This way,' she says, walking through the doorway.

I step in after her, my skin crawling as I move into the darkness. It suddenly makes sense; she's brought us to the Old Wing. It was sectioned off years ago, after they closed the entrance to the ARC. It's the perfect place to hide as no one ever comes through here. I've only been in here once before, and I haven't been keen to return.

We follow her into the Old Wing, closing the door behind us. I've come a long way since I left the ARC, but being in such a small and dark space still makes me feel uncomfortable. We use our cuffs to light the way, but they do little to brighten the total darkness of the Old Wing.

'This is where you've been hiding?' Sebastian asks, moving to walk next to Gemma.

She nods. 'We've been here for a few days, but I was caught today when I went out looking for supplies. If you guys hadn't come along...'

I push down a shudder. Gemma could have become Joseph's next lab rat. I look over at Aiden and Lara who walk beside me. 'We have to stop him,' I say to them.

'And we will,' Aiden says. His voice is filled with more passion than I've heard from him in a while. 'With this cure he'll never be able to harm another person. Not in this way, at least.'

I nod but don't say another word to him. My mind is whirling with dark thoughts and spinning from the hatred I feel towards the one man who has caused us so much pain. I will stop him, no matter what it takes.

Gemma slows as we begin to hear the soft sound of voices nearby. She pauses by one of the doors that lead from the corridor. Her eyes dart in my direction before she focuses back on the door and turns the handle.

The dim room inside is cluttered with mattresses and people. It's lit by a couple of lamps and deep shadows line the walls. The voices inside stop as Gemma steps into the room, and the rest of our group follows her in.

There must be twenty faces staring back at us. Many are people I know, but there's only one face I'm desperate to see…

'Quinn…' I gasp.

I race forward, my feet flying beneath me, before Quinn has even had a chance to look up. Quinn's eyes brighten when she sees me and I throw myself into her arms. She hugs me back just as tightly and I try to stop tears from welling in my eyes, but they're nearly impossible to contain. She's here.

'Elle?' She chokes on the word. 'Elle!' Her body is shaking next to mine. 'I can't believe you're here,' she says, into my hair.

She pulls back to look at me, her eyes wet with tears. Her white blonde hair is pulled back in a tight ponytail and there are tired bags under her eyes. There is tension across her forehead that even her bright smile can't dismiss. She looks like she's been through so much since I left.

She lets out one of her easy laughs and shakes her head at me. 'This just doesn't feel real.'

I laugh with her. 'I can't believe I'm here either,' I say.

She studies me, searching my face for any clues as to what she's missed while we've been apart. So much has happened, but nothing has changed between us. It's clear she still worries for me like the little sister she's always treated me as.

'Your eyes…' she says, looking at them with uncertainty.

'Oh,' I rub at them tiredly. They must be flashing with purple. It's been happening more frequently since I took the inhibitor band off. 'They've started doing that sometimes. It's a side effect of leaving the ARC.'

She nods, but doesn't seem sure she likes the new development. She looks over my shoulder to the others standing behind me and grins when her eyes land on Sebastian. 'You've been looking after our girl?' she asks him.

'Trying to. She can be a bit of a handful sometimes.'

I scowl over my shoulder at him. He's grinning widely and shrugs his shoulders. 'What?' he asks innocently, laughter playing in his eyes. His face becomes more serious as he looks at Quinn. 'How's my dad?'

'He's ... he's okay. He's keeping watch at the moment, but he'll be back here soon,' Quinn responds. 'He'll be so happy to see you and Elle again.' She looks away and allows her gaze to travel over the others in our group. 'Who's the hunk?' she asks, eyeing Aiden.

I swiftly elbow her. 'Quinn, you remember Aiden. He's Dr. Wilson's grandson. And this is Lara and Hunter,' I say, introducing them.

Quinn grins, and then turns back to me. 'How the hell are you guys back here?' she asks. 'Why are you back?'

I glance at the others and Aiden steps forward. 'We have a cure for the tainted and we need volunteers to test it on.'

CHAPTER TWENTY

A woman steps over to stand beside Quinn. She's quite beautiful with vivid hazel eyes and touches of grey to her brown hair that only seem to accentuate her beauty. There is an undeniable strength to the woman's stance and confidence radiates from her expression.

'This is Rosa,' Quinn says, her tone filled with respect. I vaguely remember the woman's face from before I'd left the ARC.

'You are on the council,' Sebastian says.

'*Was* on the council,' she responds, without missing a beat. She turns and eyeballs Aiden. 'What exactly do you mean when you say you have a cure?'

He clears his throat and takes a step forward. 'The tainted have a specific mutation that has occurred within them, which enables them to return to the surface unharmed,' Aiden explains. 'Without this mutation, anyone brought to the surface will be overexposed to Lysartium, which makes them extremely unwell.'

Quinn shoots me a nervous glance when she hears this and I give her a small shake of my head. 'I'm fine,' I mouth, which makes her worried eyes calm a little.

Aiden continues. 'The cure we've created will stop the mutations from ever occurring. People will be able to come to the surface. They'll no longer need to live in the ARC.'

Rosa narrows her eyes. 'And you want to test it on people?'

Aiden nods. 'That's right.'

She pauses, her eyes clouding as she considers his words. 'The doctors here also thought they had the cure. They administered it to some of the patients in the hospital when the men came and started dragging people away. All of their test subjects were killed by it.'

Rosa must be talking about Aiden's grandfather and the others who were in the morgue. If the recruiters were taking normal people to the surface it certainly explains why they were desperate enough to administer a cure that may not have been ready.

'The cure I have works,' Aiden says, his eyes misting with tears. 'I have had access to the effects of surface exposure, and was able to use a combination of talents that stop mutations and adapt to the Lysartium. I would have no problem testing it on myself if I wasn't already tainted.'

Rosa looks uncertain, but Quinn's eyes are bright and a pit of worry enters my gut. I have a bad feeling Quinn intends to be one of the people who will volunteer.

'And there are no side effects?' Rosa asks.

'There shouldn't be.' Aiden hesitates before he continues. 'But, the tainted mutation has given rise to numerous gifts; we call them talents. If someone takes the cure they will never become talented. They will only ever be normal like you are now.'

Rosa glances at the rest of us before looking back at Aiden. 'Yes, we've seen these *gifts* over the last few days.'

Several people who have been listening in and are loitering nearby seem to recoil at her words. When the recruiters showed their talents for the first time it must have been so frightening for them.

Gemma steps forward. 'Elle and her friends used their gifts to fight the men who were taking people,' she says, coming to our defence. 'They fought them and they won. The gifted men have left the ARC.'

Gasps of shock echo through the group, and whispers rush through the crowd as the people in here eye us with awe.

A hint of respect enters Rosa's gaze. 'They're truly gone?' she asks, her voice edged with disbelief.

Gemma nods. 'And one of the groups they had taken was rescued from the hospital,' she adds.

Rosa turns to look at us. 'It seems I should be thanking you.'

Aiden inclines his head accepting her thanks.

'But,' she continues. 'After being subjected to those men and their gifts, I'm not so certain any of us will be rushing to volunteer to enter their world.'

'Not all talents are bad,' I say carefully. 'And talented or not, don't you want to see the sun again? To feel the wind against your face and the rain against your skin? The surface is beautiful and if this cure works everyone here can safety return to it.'

The room has gone totally silent, and every eye that is on me is filled with yearning and hope.

'Well, I'm convinced,' Quinn says, breaking the silence.

Rosa shoots her a look, her intense eyes admonishing Quinn for speaking out. When she faces us again she's regained her composure. 'I will call for the citizens to gather tonight in the Atrium and I'll tell them what you have told me. I will explain your request for volunteers and give people the choice to take part in your trial. How many people do you need?'

'As many as possible,' Aiden responds. He pauses and looks around the room, his brow furrowing. 'But, even just a few will be better than nothing.'

Rosa purses her lips as she considers his words. 'You will come with me and help explain the situation to the other ARC citizens,' she says, pointing at Aiden. 'But, I think it's best if the rest of you stay here and wait.'

I want to be a part of the discussion and open my mouth to

object, but Aiden cuts me off before I get a chance. 'Rosa's right, the four of you should stay here. You scared a few people by wielding your talents earlier. That might not help our cause.'

Rosa turns to Quinn. 'Why don't you take them next door so they can rest while we meet with the others.'

Quinn nods and leads us away. The room practically explodes with conversations the minute she shuts the door behind us. She takes us to another room down the corridor. It's smaller than the one we've just been in and there are a few mattresses scattered on the floor.

She places a lamp just inside the doorway, which gives us a small amount of light. Then lingers by the door as we all pile in. 'I want to stay, but I should go talk with the others. I can help convince them that this is the right thing to do.'

'You should go,' I agree with her.

She pauses by the door, ready to leave. 'Do you really have those gifts you were talking about?' she asks.

'Yeah,' I laugh softly, 'but I'm not very good at them.'

'Cool,' she says, with a grin. 'Okay, I'll catch you guys in the morning.'

As she leaves she shuts the door behind her and I let out a sad sigh. I miss her already and haven't spent nearly enough time with her.

'Do you think people will volunteer?' Lara asks.

Hunter shrugs and lowers himself to sit against the wall. 'We can only hope they will.'

She lowers herself to sit beside him. 'What will we do if no one agrees?'

'They'll agree,' he replies, sounding completely certain.

I don't have his confidence though. After seeing the way the recruiters treated the citizens down here, I won't be surprised if they are too scared to return to the surface. Not to mention that people have already died down here because they were given a cure that didn't work. It's going to take a lot to convince them that Aiden's cure can be trusted.

Lara falls asleep easily, and it takes a while longer for Hunter to start breathing deeply, but Sebastian and I struggle to keep our eyes shut. We both sit on one of the mattresses with our backs against the wall. The room is darkened, but not totally black. There's a soft glow from the small lamp by the door and I'm glad for it. I couldn't stand to be in the dark right now.

I hug my knees to my chest, resting my chin on them. I can't stop thinking about the possibility that there won't be any volunteers. That everything we've gone through down here will be for nothing. So many people have died because of Joseph and I want him gone more than ever.

'You okay?' Sebastian asks, keeping his voice low so he doesn't wake the other two.

'I'm okay. Just worrying,' I give him a small smile. 'Just for something different.'

I hear him shuffle closer so his shoulder bumps up against mine. 'This will work out, I'm certain of it.'

'I wish I had your confidence.'

'It will work out because it has to. You saw the way Quinn reacted when she heard. She'll be the first person in line to volunteer and there will be others who feel the same.'

'What if I don't want her to volunteer? Something could go wrong.'

Sebastian pauses, before reaching out and taking my hand in his. 'Or something could go right.'

I turn to look at him. His face is close to mine and his eyes hold such sincerity I can't help but want to believe him. As I look at him, I begin to feel nervous and I suddenly notice just how close he is. I can feel his breath against my face and his blue eyes become intense as he watches me. He glances down at my lips and I all but stop breathing. My worries seem to disappear and all I can think about is how close he is and how much I wish he would touch me.

As if hearing my thoughts, he slowly lowers his head forward and gives me a sweet, lingering kiss.

My lips tingle against his and my heart warms as I feel him lightly cup my face with his hand. When he pulls back to look at me his blue eyes seem to sparkle. They are brimming with the depths of his emotions and he pulls back slowly as though he's worried he's gone too far.

He lightly traces his thumb along the ridge of my hand and focuses down on our entwined fingers. When he looks up, he seems as nervous as I feel.

'Dad always used to tell us, that when you love someone, you tell them,' he says. 'You don't wait for the right moment, or hold back because you're scared. You say it aloud, because there are no guarantees of tomorrow. There is only ever today, and I don't want to imagine another tomorrow where you don't know how I truly feel.

'I know you told me that we couldn't be together for now, but I love you and I can't imagine my life without you in it.' His voice is husky and low, and my heart races in response to his words.

I had wanted distance while I tried to put back together the fragile pieces of myself, but now I realise more than ever that life is always fragile. In a moment everything can change and, for once, I want that change to be good.

For as long as I can remember, I've denied my feelings for him. I've brushed them aside or hidden them deep within myself, afraid of what it could mean to allow myself to care. Even now, my emotions feel so strong they threaten to burst from the very seams that hold me together.

I can't find the words to tell him how I feel, the depths of how much I care for him and how much I want to be his. So, instead of talking, instead of bumbling over words I can't get out, I lean forward and kiss him.

I kiss him softly at first, feeling the surging rush of warmth rise up inside. He seems surprised, but only momentarily. And then his arms come around me, pulling me towards him and I am lost in the swirling, dizzying, head-rushing perfection of his kiss.

I am slightly dazed when I pull myself away from him. I feel breathless and faint, but entirely wonderful all at once. His eyes are wide and heated as he takes me in, and a slow smile builds on his lips until he's completely beaming at me. He gathers me in his arms and I can't stop myself from smiling as I cuddle into them.

He kisses me on the forehead. 'I love you Elle Winters.'

My heart constricts at his words. 'I love you too, Sebastian Scott.'

A low growl escapes his lips and he pulls me in for another kiss. The surge of attraction I feel for him overwhelms me and for a moment I almost forget I'm back in the ARC. Almost.

His eyes are bright and filled with warmth as he pulls away from me, and the same large smile is still plastered across his face. I curl up next to him, resting my head on his shoulder. It feels so right to be with him this way and, resting in his arms, I finally feel like I am home.

'We should get some sleep,' he says, after we've been sitting there silently for several minutes.

I nod, stifling a yawn, and move to stretch out on the mattress we're on. He lies down beside me, and it's difficult to ignore the warmth I can feel radiating off of his body.

'Night Sebastian,' I say.

'Sweet dreams,' he responds.

I bury my face into the pillow, my eyes feeling suddenly heavy. I don't want to go to sleep, but I know how important tomorrow is. Everything could change tomorrow and I need to be ready for it.

CHAPTER TWENTY-ONE

When I wake in the morning I feel a twisted combination of elation and devastation for all the things that happened yesterday. How can such a short period of time have so many highs and so many lows?

I slowly push myself up. Sebastian is already sitting at the edge of the mattress, his eyes focused intently on the ceiling. The others are in similar states, their minds clearly deep in thought.

Lara clears her throat from the other side of the room. She's sitting against the wall with one of her legs out in front of her, propped up on a pillow. I can just make out a smile on her face in the dim light of the room. 'Sleep well?' she asks.

My cheeks warm in response and I'm glad it's too dark for her to see it. Unfortunately, she can probably still feel the emotions coursing through me. 'Yeah, you could say that.' I look at her leg. 'Is your ankle feeling any better?'

She chews on her lower lip, as if debating whether to tell me the truth. She sighs. 'If anything, it feels worse. At least Aiden thinks it's only sprained.'

'I'm sure it will be better in no time.' I give her a reassuring smile, before I glance at the door. 'No one's come yet?'

She shakes her head. 'No, it's still early though.'

Sound of movement down the hallway beyond the door reaches my ear and I wave for the others to be quiet. 'There are people coming.'

We all stand and move back from the door, drifting closer to each other as we wait to see who's coming. The door handle turns and a beam of light enters the room.

We all relax a little to see Rosa and Aiden standing there. Behind her walks Luke, Soren, Quinn and an older man. I hear Sebastian quickly gasp when he sees him.

'Dad?' he whispers. 'Dad!' He runs over to the man, shouldering past Quinn and Rosa, and grips him up in a hug.

I take a step closer. Sebastian's dad looks so different, I hadn't even known it was him. His hair has greyed and his face has so many lines on it that weren't there before. Adam Scott was like a father to me for a long time, but even I have trouble recognising him now.

Adam lets out a sob and collapses into Sebastian's arms. I can see them both clearly shaking from here and I wipe a tear from my eye as I watch their reunion. I move over to the two of them, keeping my distance, not wanting to interrupt, but as soon as Adam sees me he pulls me in to join their hug.

I struggle to keep my tears inside and I can hear Adam breaking down. He had thought we were gone forever, now he finally has us back.

When I step away from Adam and Sebastian I catch a glint of tears, unshed in Sebastian's eyes.

'They've told me what it's like up there. Is April okay?' Adam asks, as he pulls back from Sebastian.

'She's good.'

Adam grins. 'And Isabel?'

Sebastian's shoulders slouch and he slowly shakes his head.

'Mum died a few years ago,' he says softly. 'She was brought to the surface too soon.'

Adam slowly nods, the reality settling heavily on his shoulders. It was one thing to think that his wife might be dead, but another to know it was true. He'd spent years in the dark about her and it's painful to watch him accepting the truth.

Quinn rubs my arm and I turn to see Rosa watching us as she waits.

Hunter clears his throat. 'Were there any volunteers?' he asks.

She nods. 'Quinn and Adam have volunteered.'

My body stiffens as she says this and I slowly turn to Quinn. A part of me had already known she would volunteer, but I don't like hearing it confirmed. 'You don't have to do this,' I say, keeping my voice low.

She shakes her head and smiles. 'I know that, but I want to.'

'No others?' I ask Rosa, who shakes her head.

'People are scared of the talented and they are scared of leaving their home,' she says. 'After the recently failed attempt at a cure, they want assurances this cure will work before they take it. I have no doubt they will come around eventually, but it's going to take some time.'

Aiden sighs and rubs his face tiredly beside her. 'Two is better than none. We will make it work.'

Quinn turns to look at Aiden. 'What do you need me to do?' she asks, avoiding eye contact with me. She clearly saw the fear in my eyes; that I don't want her to take this risk and get hurt.

'I'll need to test you both to ensure you're not tainted already. If that comes back negative, I can administer the cure.'

'That's it?' Adam asks, taking a step closer.

I glance at Sebastian. He looks just as unhappy as I am about Adam and Quinn being the test subjects. We're hard pressed to argue with it though. Aiden has already told Rosa it's safe. How can we get her to convince others to take the cure if we don't believe it's safe enough to use on our own family?

'That's it,' Aiden confirms. 'Quinn, I'll take a blood sample from you first.' He walks to the corner of the room, pulls his backpack off his back and begins to remove the equipment he needs to administer the cure.

His motions become cautious as he removes a metal cold box from the pack. He places it on the ground next to him with such care that I know it must contain the vials of the cure inside.

When he's ready, he waves Quinn over and I glance at Sebastian to gauge his reaction. He's watching his father closely as though he's fearful of losing him again.

'Ah,' Quinn yelps, hissing in through her teeth as Aiden draws blood from her. He places the syringe carefully on the small metal tray he has on the ground beside him. He then looks up and waves Adam over for his turn. Adam moves slowly across the room and I worry about whether he is physically strong enough to do this. He's stoic though as his blood is taken, barely flinching as Aiden places the needle into his arm.

'The helicopter taking us back to Hope is in the hangar over the hospital. Do you know the place?' Soren asks Rosa.

She nods. 'Yes, all council members are aware of it.'

'Is there another way to get to it that doesn't use the lift in the hospital,' he asks. 'We need to find another route after the explosion yesterday.'

She seems uncertain. 'There isn't another way to get to the hangar, but there is another place I can take you to, where the helicopter could pick you up. Can you contact your pilot?'

'Yes, we should be able get hold of him,' Soren responds.

Rosa hesitates before continuing. 'It's dangerous though.'

Sebastian pulls his gaze from his father to look at her. 'We don't have much choice,' he says.

'I'll show you the way then,' she replies. Her voice is steady, but the uncertainty in her eyes makes me worried. Just how dangerous is her alternate route to the helicopter? I glance at Sebastian to see if he appears concerned, but his face still holds the same scowl he's had on it since he realised his father was here to volunteer.

'Done,' Aiden says. I look over to where he is checking the blood samples he's taken from Quinn and Adam under his microscope. He lifts his head away from the eyepiece, hesitating as he looks around the room at us. 'We have two viable candidates.'

My stomach lurches at Aiden's words. They're not tainted. I glance at Quinn who is grinning. How can she actually be pleased about this? The cure has never been tested on humans before. She could end up like Aiden's grandfather, or worse. I trust Aiden, but even he can't be certain it will work.

Aiden turns to the cold box and slowly opens it to withdraw two vials of the cure. It's clear in colour, though there's a slight purple shimmer to the viscous liquid. I swallow tightly at the sight of it—such a small vial, holding so much hope.

Reaching out, I touch Quinn's arm. 'You don't have to do this.' My eyes plead with her to reconsider. She must realise how risky this is.

She gently shakes her head. 'No. This is important and I want to help.'

'What if something goes wrong?'

'It won't,' she responds, sounding completely certain and almost a little too cheerful. She turns from me and crouches down beside Aiden, presenting her arm to him. 'I'm ready when you are.'

He nods seriously and begins to draw the cure into the syringe in his hand. I can barely bring myself to look, and I'm not the only one. Sebastian's skin has paled and I can tell he feels as worried as I do. There's nothing we can do to stop them though.

'They'll be okay,' Lara says, hobbling as she comes to stand beside me. 'I can tell how certain Aiden feels. He wouldn't do this to them if he didn't know it was going to work.'

She brushes her arm against mine and I can feel her trying to soothe me with her talent, but I pull my arm away. I don't want to be made to feel okay about this right now.

Aiden places the needle up against Quinn's arm and I look away. I can't watch him do it; not when I know this could end up hurting her. I grind my teeth together, hating every second of this and desperately hoping the cure will work.

I hear Aiden talking softly to Quinn after it's over and getting Adam ready for his turn. Sebastian watches them cautiously and scrunches up his face in a grimace when Adam has his injection.

'We should get moving,' Aiden says. He's already packing his tools away in his backpack when I look back.

I walk over to Quinn who is slowly standing. 'You feeling okay?'

'Completely fine,' she responds.

I frown, unable to tell if she's being honest with me or not. 'You'll let me know if you're not feeling great, right?'

'I swear, I'm fine!'

I still don't like it, but I give her a small nod. 'Do you need to get anything before we leave?'

'No. I grabbed a few things before we came here.'

I catch Adam's eye over her shoulder. 'Is there anything you need Adam?' I ask.

'No,' he responds, quietly. 'I have everything I need right here.' He gives Sebastian a quick glance before looking down at his feet. The reaction causes my heart to warm. Sebastian and Adam have always struggled to show their emotions to one another, but I'm hardly surprised to see how much Adam cares for his son.

'You guys all ready?' I ask the others, and grunts of agreement sound through the room.

Aiden's gaze moves to Rosa. 'Looks like we're ready for you—lead the way.'

Rosa strides over to the door and we follow her into the dark corridor. We don't move in the direction we'd taken to get here yesterday. Instead, she leads us deeper and deeper into the Old Wing.

There are no lights in the corridor and we have to use the lights from our cuffs to guide us as we follow Rosa. We're all quiet as we walk, as though we're scared of the sound of our own voices in the silent darkness.

I don't like leaving the ARC knowing that Joseph has been sending men here. I worry about what will happen if he sends more recruiters. The only way to stop that, and protect everyone down here, is by removing Joseph from power. And, if I have anything to do with it, I will personally be the one to stop him.

Rosa reaches what looks like a dead end in the corridor, before moving around debris that covers a narrow passage beyond. I know the passage is there before I even start to follow her. I've been here before.

'We're going to the entrance,' I whisper.

Sebastian glances at me. 'How do you know that?'

'I just do,' I reply softly, not wanting to go into how I explored the Old Wing in hopes of finding him after he was taken.

I chew nervously on my lip as I enter the narrow passage behind Sebastian. I've been so much better with small spaces, but it's a whole lot tighter and darker than I'm used to. I square my shoulders and push down the fear that once upon a time would have suffocated me. Sebastian reaches back behind him and grabs hold of my hand to give it a squeeze.

'You okay?' he asks.

'Yeah, I'll be fine,' I respond, my voice rough. I let go of his hand and give myself a moment before pressing on through the dark and narrow tunnel.

The passageway begins to widen and there's a soft light shinning into it in the distance. When we reach the end of the passage Sebastian stops ahead of me and there's a look of wonder on his face as he stares at the cavern beyond.

'Whoa!' Quinn's voice comes from behind me. She emerges from the passageway, supporting Lara as they walk out of the darkness. Even Luke and Hunter seem impressed as they appear behind the two girls.

The place is just as I remember it. Lamps light the massive, sprawling cavern we're in and we can easily see the large stalagmites and stalactites that grow from the ceiling and floor. On the far wall I can see the huge boulders of rock and debris that cover the opening that was once the entrance to the ARC. Whoa indeed.

There had been officials when I'd been here last, but they are nowhere to be seen today. I can only assume that they were pulled from their regular post here in the cavern when the recruiters arrived in the ARC.

Rosa leads us into the cavern and along a boardwalk that cuts between the huge rock formations that erupt from the ground around us. When she reaches the far end of the cavern she slows and approaches a door that's hidden away in a crevice in one of the walls.

She punches a code into the pin pad mounted to the wall and the door opens with a high-pitched 'beep.' Beyond the door is a small room with another identical door in the opposite wall. Heavy coats hang from one of the sidewalls, with a row of boots lined up below them. We all crowd into the room behind her and she nods at the coats.

'You'll all need to take one of these,' she says.

Aiden reaches out to take one, but pauses with his hand hovering just over the collar. 'Where exactly are we going?' he asks.

Rosa nods at the closed door. 'Beyond that door is the surface. You will be going to an airbase that lies just beyond the forest. It's the only place the helicopter will be able to land.'

'You can't be serious...' Quinn scoffs.

I push down a shudder myself. Surface temperatures are well below freezing over the ARC and the cold out there is lethal.

'Surely there's another way,' Hunter adds. Luke nods in agreement beside him.

Rosa folds her arms over her chest. 'I'm afraid there isn't. The trek to the base should take you about an hour. It's not far.'

'Yeah, it sounds like a really easy trek for us,' Quinn mutters, giving Lara an uneasy glance. 'Since when can anyone leave this way anyway? I thought the entrance was completely closed over after impact.'

'It was,' Rosa replies. 'They built these doors years later for easy access to the surface for experiments. Only, when people started getting sick from it we stopped venturing outside.' She begins to pull the jackets from the wall and passes them to each of us. 'This is as far as I come. Once outside you must follow the road that cuts through the forest. It will lead you to the base beyond.'

Aiden steps towards her and reaches out his hand to shake hers. 'Thank you for your help, Rosa. I expect we'll be back with a cure soon.'

Rosa grasps his hand tightly. 'I should be thanking all of you. I look forward to seeing you again. Hopefully, it will be under better circumstances next time.'

She moves past us and back towards the door we entered through. 'Good luck out there,' she says, before closing the door behind her. It clangs loudly as it shuts and I fight to push down another shudder.

Quinn smirks at me as she turns to face the door leading to the surface. 'I not only have to survive the cure, but now I'm expected to walk willingly into the apocalypse. It must be my lucky day.'

I shake my head at her and pull the coat on over my greys, before slipping on a pair of the large, heavy-duty boots. When I glance up I notice a hint of fear in Quinn's eyes and realise her words are just bravado. Looking to the others, I can see similar looks of apprehension on their faces.

Rosa had said the way would be dangerous, she hadn't told us it would be deadly.

CHAPTER TWENTY-TWO

'Hello?' Gord's voice comes in over Soren's CommuCuff. His words are cutting in and out and it's difficult to hear him clearly.

'Gord, it's Soren. Listen, we can't get back to the hangar and need you to meet us at the airbase beyond the forest. Do you know where it is?'

His question is met with a moment's silence before Gord's voice sounds again. 'What was that?'

'Can you meet us at the airbase beyond the forest?' Soren repeats.

'You want me to meet you at the airbase? How are you going to get there?'

'We're walking.'

'What? You're going to get yourselves killed!'

'Well, we don't have much choice. Can you do it? We should be there in an hour.'

'I'll be there,' Gord answers firmly. 'But I can't let the helicopter idle in the cold for long. Don't be late.'

'We won't be.' Soren lowers the cuff from his face and his eyes drop to Lara's ankle. 'Is your ankle going to be up to this?' he asks her. 'It's not too late if you want to stay here with Rosa.'

Lara shakes her head. 'I'll be fine. Promise.'

Soren turns to the rest of us. 'Okay, everyone else ready?'

'Yes,' most of us answer, sounding extremely uncertain.

'You're kidding me, right?' Quinn mutters, quietly.

It's clear that none of us are truly prepared to face the frozen world outside, but we haven't been left with much choice. We need to get back to Hope and this is the only way.

Soren pushes the door open and I brace myself, expecting to feel a rush of frigid air and flakes of snow to come billowing in through the door, but instead we are greeted with another tunnel. The way is wide and dark with a small rectangle of light shining in the far distance.

It's much colder than it was in the ARC, and I pull the hood of my jacket over my head in an attempt to keep my ears warm as I enter it. Small pockets of frost puff from my mouth as I breathe and my nose feels like it's become a frozen icicle clinging to my face.

There's a gradual incline to the tunnel and as we move closer to the entrance I can make out a large bank of snow mounded at the mouth of it. The world beyond is misted white with heavy banks of fog rolling through the air. The sight immediately makes me shudder. I can't believe we're expected to go out there.

'Rosa's crazy,' Quinn mutters beside me.

'Not crazy enough to come with us,' Hunter scoffs.

I brace myself as we reach the opening and prepare to leave the relative protection of the tunnel and step into the blizzard that rages outside. I slip and slide as I try to make my way over the icy mound by the entrance.

Hunter has taken the lead and Sebastian moves with ease ahead of me, despite the wind and snow battering at his jacket. Once he's past the snowdrift he waits with Hunter patiently for the rest of us to catch up. As I make my way out into the open I am almost knocked off my feet by the ferocious blizzard. Every step is a battle against the powerful, driving winds but I carefully drag myself over to where Hunter and Sebastian are waiting. The ground is solid and slippery beneath my feet, the wind having brushed away any fresh snow from the spot.

The forest quickly becomes dense with trees just past where the two boys stand and there's no clear space where a helicopter could land. The tree trunks are nothing like the trees of Hope. They are gnarled and crooked with branches that bend at unnatural angles and no leaves are anywhere to be seen. Blackened scars dot their trunks and thick icicles hang from their branches. They look like ancient chandeliers that have fallen from the sky and smashed into the frozen ground.

'Any sign of the road Rosa told us about?' Lara asks, stepping gingerly as she comes up beside me. Her face is pink from the cold and her lips are already turning a shade of blue. She's not the only one. Quinn, Luke and Adam appear to be just as cold as they clamber out of the tunnel. We've only been out here a few minutes. How can we expect to travel for an hour like this?

While I can feel the cold, it doesn't seem to bother me as much as I thought. I haven't noticed the cold for a while, but today is a true testament to how little my body reacts to it. As I think about it, realisation hits me. It must be part of the talents Joseph gave me. I shake my head unable to focus on my anger towards him right now. We need to get out of this blizzard and into the helicopter as fast as we can.

'It's over that way,' Aiden says, pointing off to the right. He has to raise his voice to be heard over the wind.

'You sure about that?' Quinn replies. 'I thought it was that way.' She points in the other direction. They scowl at one another as though readying themselves for a fight.

'Actually, you're both wrong, it's directly ahead.' Adam interrupts. 'The road has been buried in snow.' I look to where Adam is pointing. There seems to be a gap between the trees, but the ground below them is covered in a thick blanket of white snow. There's no sign of any asphalt but, after years of constant winter, it must be buried meters below the surface.

'Straight ahead it is,' I say, before Aiden or Quinn can object. I start off in the direction Adam had pointed. I trust his memory of arriving at the ARC more than I do Aiden or Quinn, who had only been kids at the time, and we can't stand here arguing all day.

The battering wind doesn't seem to lessen as we enter the trees. It's difficult to see more than fifty feet ahead, with the heavy snow falling in sheets onto the already thick blanket covering the surface. We are all silent as we try to conserve our energy.

Quinn has taken returning to the surface easily in her stride. She helps keep Lara steady as she walks through the snow and barely bats an eyelid at the world she's found herself in. Adam, however, doesn't appear quite so comfortable. His expression is dark and he keeps looking through the trees, almost as though he's watching for things that aren't there.

'Are you okay?' I ask him.

His eyes stare listlessly at the twisted branches of the trees that reach out to one another over our heads. 'It was so different before,' he says to me. 'These were once tall pine trees, covered in thick green needles, and there was a warm brown undergrowth below them.'

He seems to push down a shudder. 'Do you remember the day you came here?' he asks.

I shake my head. The haunted look in his eyes deepens as though the very ghosts that trouble him have materialised before his eyes.

'This road was littered with abandoned cars, buses and military vehicles. Where there were no cars, there were people. From one side of the road to the other, and as far as the eye could see, this road was covered in a sea of people. All of them were desperate and all of them were begging to be let inside.

'We were given less than a day's notice about the asteroid. People flocked to the asteroid refugee centres, and the wait to get in was terrifying. They only had so many spaces available for the general public. It wasn't nearly enough.'

He pauses, clearly still struggling with the horrible memories of that day, so long ago. I've never heard him talk about the days leading up to impact before. While I've learnt about it in school, I've never heard the story of that day told with such raw and vivid emotion. It's almost as though all the adults in the ARC signed a pact that they would never relive such a difficult time again. The whispers I always heard were just that—whispers. Small hints of the day everything went wrong.

'I can still hear the screams,' Aiden says, listening in. 'When they told the refugees there was no more room.'

A chill brought on by more than cold works its way down my spine.

Adam nods. 'We'd only just made it through the entrance by then. That was when we met you for the first time,' he says, smiling at me.

I'd heard the story of our meeting many times before. An official had found me walking alone through the crowd; my own family were nowhere to be seen. He'd brought me over to Adam's family and asked them to look after me. They had done that and more.

'What happened to the official who found me?' I ask.

'I never saw him again.' Adam shrugs. 'All I remember is the scar he had above his eye. I looked out for it every day down in the ARC, but never found him.'

'Do you think we're nearly there?' Lara asks. She's walking behind me and it's only when I turn that I notice how cold she looks. I can actually hear her teeth chattering from here.

Quinn rubs Lara's arm vigorously. 'We shouldn't be much longer,' she says. When she looks up at me though, her eyes betray the truth. We'd be lucky if we are halfway right now.

'We need to move faster,' Aiden says, and immediately strikes out in front to up the pace.

We all struggle to keep up with him. The snow is thicker on the road and with each step we take our boots sink into it, making it difficult to walk. Lara's pace continues to slow and I fall back to try and help her move faster.

Quinn and I each hold one arm to keep her steady as we walk.

'I'm just so cold,' Lara says, her chattering teeth now affecting her words. I can feel her body shaking under her jacket and her face has lost all of its colour as she struggles to walk.

'We just need to keep taking one step after another,' Quinn says, catching her as Lara's feet falter beneath her.

She looks past Lara to me, her eyes desperate. 'What can we do?' they ask me. I feel confused and worried. I have these talents within me, but I have no way to help her. No way to help her sprained ankle and no idea how I could even begin to make her warmer. I can create fire, sometimes, but setting her alight really won't help the situation. She needs to be off her ankle and on that chopper.

I grasp onto her sleeve tightly, desperately wishing I could help her. I long for her to feel warmer, to be able to move faster so we can get to the helicopter on time. If we keep going at this pace we'll never reach it within the hour Gord has given us.

She's slowing us down too much, but I would never dream of leaving her behind. There's no way Sebastian can teleport her; he has no idea where we are going. As the thoughts spin through my head, the familiar surge of my talent buzzing beneath my skin arises. The fear that usually comes with it is gone though. What could I possibly throw into this situation to make it any worse than it already is?

Lara stumbles again and Quinn and I both have to heave her up onto her feet. My talent is practically pulsating beneath my skin. I wish I could share the warmth that flows through me with her; that I could make her feel okay, despite the freezing cold blizzard we walk through.

My talent tingles along my skin and I feel a rush as it flows out of me in one massive outpouring. It's warm and electric as it runs through my fingers that latch onto Lara's arm.

I stagger forward, gripping Lara's arm tighter in an attempt to keep me upright. She steadies me as I right myself. I feel suddenly weak and exhausted.

'What did you just do?' Lara asks.

I shake my head, still clasping onto her arm. 'I-I don't know.'

She stands a little taller. 'I feel warmer, and my ankle isn't hurting anymore.'

I glance up at her. Even her lips have returned to their normal pink colour.

'What happened Elle?' asks Quinn, her eyes showing her concern.

'I don't know,' I gasp. I've never done anything like that before. Could I have somehow managed to share my warmth with her? 'It doesn't matter, as long as you're okay.'

She smiles. 'I feel much better. I can't believe it.'

She walks forward, no longer needing our help. I start to walk alongside her but slow as I feel a stabbing pain in my ankle. I try to keep moving but stumble in the snow and my left ankle caves inwards as I step on it. I clamp my teeth together, but can't keep the small cry of pain from hissing out of my lips as I fall to my knees.

I may have made Lara better, but in doing so I've somehow managed to acquire her injury myself.

Hearing my yelp, Lara and Quinn are at my side before I completely collapse onto the ground.

'What happened?' Quinn asks, holding me up. Her eyes are wide and full of fear. 'Did you hurt yourself?'

I nod, unable to come up with an adequate explanation. How do I explain to them that I've somehow obtained Lara's injury with my talent? I've never heard of a talent like that and they'll both probably think I'm mad. Looking up I see Sebastian making his way back towards us through the blizzard.

'I don't think I can keep up with everyone and we can't keep going this slowly,' I say to them. 'Gord won't be able to stick around for long and it's too important to get Adam and Quinn back to Hope.'

Quinn looks at me in horror. 'You're not thinking about...'

'What's going on?' Sebastian shouts over the snowstorm as he approaches. 'Are you alright, Elle?'

I swallow. 'I've hurt my ankle,' I reply, looking up at him as he comes to stand between Quinn and Lara. 'You guys have to go. I'll keep coming, but if I'm not at the helicopter in time, you need to leave without me.'

Before I can say another word Sebastian bends down and hoists me up into his arms.

'Sebastian!' I gasp. 'Put me down.'

'Stop trying to be the hero,' he says, winking at me through the storm. 'That's my job.'

CHAPTER TWENTY-THREE

I plead for Sebastian to let me try and walk, but he refuses. I can't believe he can carry me all the way to the base, but he seems intent on trying. I pray that we are getting close as the trees slowly begin to thin out and we reach a barren expanse of snow that extends beyond them. The snow that is falling is captured in torrents of wind that whisk across the plain. It's difficult to see too far, but all I can make out is an open wasteland. It's flat and bare with not so much as a tree or a building in sight.

The wind has picked up and it batters violently again our clothes. The freezing sting bites into the small areas of uncovered skin and the blizzard blinds us as we walk. We're too exposed out here and running out of time. We huddle close together, trying to gain some small protection.

'Where is he?' Sebastian yells, his words battling to be heard over the sound of the wind.

Soren looks confused as he scans the land before us. 'I don't know,' he yells back. 'I thought there'd be buildings or some sort of landing area, but there's nothing here.'

Adam points across the plain. 'It's all buried in snow.'

Sebastian lowers me from his arms, but continues to support my weight and hold me next to him. He checks the time on his cuff. 'We've taken too long. What if he's already been and gone?' Panic touches his tone, and my heart beats faster in response.

Will we be able to get back to the ARC without freezing to death if Gord has gone without us? My ankle throbs with pain and there's no way Sebastian could carry me the entire way back.

I search the skies, concentrating my talented senses on finding the helicopter. There's no sound in the sky though, only the whipping torrent of wind buffeting along the plain. The visibility is so bad that even my talented sight can't see more than one hundred metres away.

'We can't stay out here. We'll die,' Quinn shouts. She shoots a look at me and I can see how worried she is about my injury.

'We should give him more time,' Aiden shouts back. His eyes are hard and I can see he's not ready to give up.

'What if he's already gone?' Quinn responds.

Aiden turns to her. 'What if he hasn't been?'

A noise catches my ear and I glance up into the sky again, desperately hoping I'd heard what I think I did. The whipping noise of a propeller sounds again, clearer this time, and I grin. Gord is on his way.

'You stay if you want, but I refuse to freeze to death waiting for someone who isn't coming,' Quinn says.

'You can't leave' Aiden responds.

Quinn places her hands on her hips and gives him her most loathing stare through the snow. 'You're not in charge of me,' she spits.

'Actually, I am.'

'Stop!' I interrupt them. 'I can hear the helicopter.'

Everyone lifts their heads to scan the wild skies but there's nothing to see through the snow.

'It's right above us,' I shout. 'It's definitely getting closer.'

As I strain my neck to look up at the sky, I press my left foot down into the snow and let out a cry as pain shoots through my ankle. I tighten my grip around Sebastian and pray that I'm not hearing things. If my senses are deceiving me right now, we're all going to die.

'I can see the helicopter!' Lara exclaims. I look up into the sky to see the helicopter bursting through the blizzard and descending quickly. It's being battered about by the intense winds that whip across the plain, but it is definitely heading towards us. Relief rushes through me as I finally see it coming.

I'm amazed at Gord's skill as he lowers the helicopter. He makes it look easy as he lands on the snow in front of us. He eases the chopper onto the ground despite the winds that pound him, jerking the helicopter this way and that. The propellers create their own mini squall as he lands, with the snow on the ground gusting away from the helicopter.

I'm still limping, but Sebastian acts as a crutch, helping me over.

'Come on Elle, let's get you on the helicopter,' Sebastian says. He takes my elbow and helps guide me up the steps and inside.

'Are you alright?' Hunter asks, climbing in behind us.

'I'm fine,' I reply, beginning to feel like a bit of a talking parrot. I really wish people would stop asking me that.

His eyes watch me closely and I wonder if he's probing my thoughts for the truth behind my words. He merely gives me a nod though and makes his way to a seat near Luke.

I sit next to Sebastian and move nice and close to him, allowing his warmth to comfort me. He easily drapes his arm over my shoulders and I rest my head against his chest.

'Okay kids, it's time to go home,' Gord says, over his intercom.

I glance at Quinn and Adam who sit behind us and give them a reassuring smile. They both look so worried and overwhelmed by everything that has happened.

When I turn back, Sebastian is watching me closely. 'What happened to you back there on the road?' he asks, keeping his voice low.

'I don't know,' I respond, as I fearfully consider my new talent. 'And I don't think I want to know.'

He pulls me in close, resting his chin on my head, and I relish the comfort that being close to him brings. When I'm in his arms I can almost believe that everything will be all right.

Iт's dark when we arrive in Hope and we're all so exhausted that most of us would rather sleep in the helicopter than try to walk back through the South Hope ruins tonight. Everyone agrees that we need to get back to the station as soon as possible though. So, instead of resting, we all begin the walk home.

For the first part of the journey back I use Sebastian's arm to help steady me. It's especially difficult to stay upright while trekking through the muddy marshlands. He's already so tired, and I feel like I'm being a burden to him. He won't say a word of complaint though, no matter how often I tell him to let me walk by myself for a little while.

When we reach the first row of buildings that mark the start of South Hope, Hunter comes to walk beside us.

'Why don't you let me help Elle for a little bit?' Hunter offers.

'I don't need your help,' Sebastian responds, curtly.

'I can tell you're exhausted,' Hunter continues, as though he hasn't heard the tone in Sebastian's voice. 'Let me help.'

Sebastian stiffens under me.

'That would be great,' I say, before he can refuse again. 'Thanks, Hunter.'

Sebastian shoots me a worried look, but lowers his arm from around me. I already miss the feel of it against my back, but I'm glad I'm not continuing to burden him when he is so tired.

I hobble towards Hunter who takes Sebastian's position, placing his arm carefully around me. Sebastian's eyes darken as he watches us. 'I'm going to walk with Dad for a bit,' he says, rather stiffly. 'I'll be back before you know it.' His voice softens as he says this and he gives me one of his heartbreaking smiles. I give him a small nod, not trusting my voice to respond.

'He absolutely loathes me,' Hunter comments with a grin, as Sebastian walks ahead to his dad.

'I don't blame him,' I respond.

'Aw, don't pretend you don't like me Winters. I know deep down you do.'

'Maybe once I did, but not anymore.'

He shakes his head, his eyes filling with sadness. 'I wish you could forgive me.'

'Some things are unforgiveable.'

We fall silent as we continue to walk. The street we are on is almost pitch black and there's barely any moonlight to guide us in the dark. We can't use our cuffs to light the way for fear of being seen, so it's slow going as we try to navigate our way home.

I almost feel grateful for my talented sight. I'm able to make out bumps and uneven surfaces on the road with ease. I hear Lara and Quinn cursing a lot as they stumble along behind us.

'I never had a chance against him, did I?' Hunter says, suddenly, his eyes narrowed on Sebastian.

'A chance at what exactly?'

'You know what,' he says. He laughs under his breath. 'I've read your mind so many times, I feel I know it as well as my own. You've loved that guy since the moment I met you. And yet, a part of me always hoped you'd change your mind. That you'd stop feeling the way you do about him and finally see me in a similar way. People can be fickle like that, you know.'

I shake my head, feeling speechless and a little surprised by the turn in conversation.

'I'm glad you're with him though,' he continues.

'You're glad?' I repeat, confused. Wasn't he just saying he wished I would pick him?

He nods. 'He's good for you and you deserve someone who will make you happy, someone who will be there for you, who won't hurt you. I'm not that guy.'

I stop in my tracks and look at him. His blue eyes are sad, but so sincere. He truly believes he's the villain and I feel certain the way I've treated him these last few days hasn't helped. He had no control over what he did to Lara and me, and yet I've continued to blame him for it. I shouldn't blame him and in this moment, I realise that I don't. Not anymore.

I lift my hand up and push a loose strand of hair behind my ear as I consider him. He's handsome, there's no denying that, and a part of me does like him. But it's only as a friend. I don't feel the sparks between us that I feel with Sebastian and while his touch is comforting, it's the same kind of security I feel when I'm with Lara or with Quinn.

Hunter nods and I can tell he's reading my thoughts. *I'm sorry*, my mind whispers to his.

He gives me a sad smile. 'At least you forgive me.'

'Yeah, I do,' I agree.

We slowly continue to traipse down the road again, trailing after the others. I feel much better knowing I've forgiven Hunter, but a part of me stays unhappy. I don't want him to be alone, wishing for something to happen with me, when it clearly won't.

He chuckles out loud. 'Elle, I'm an eighteen-year-old guy. Don't feel too sorry for me just yet. There are plenty of other lovely ladies out there who I'm sure will be all too willing to console me.'

'You're impossible,' I groan.

'Impossibly awesome that is.'

I let out a laugh and a sense of rightness fills me. It feels good to have our old friendship back, even if it's not exactly what Hunter would have liked. I'm glad I haven't lost him.

I look ahead to the rest of our group and the smile on my face lowers as I consider them. There are so many people that I care about —too many people, and we're all in constant danger. Why do I feel like there's no way we'll all make it out of this alive?

CHAPTER TWENTY-FOUR

Copper barrels into me as we walk down the steps to the station. The concourse is dark with deep shadows crawling up the pillars and masking the empty ticketing booths. It's late and there's not a person to be seen, but I get the feeling Copper knew we were coming.

The dog's long tongue licks the side of my face in one big motion. He's so happy to see me again, but the excitement wanes once he knows that I'm okay. He walks off in a huff as if he wants to teach me a lesson for leaving him this way.

'You have a dog?' Quinn squeals, when she sees him. Her voice is loud and echoes in the deserted station.

Soren shoots her a dark glare and she scowls back at him in return. She leans in close to my ear. 'You have a dog?' she repeats, in an excited whisper.

'His name is Copper.'

She grins as she watches him and can barely contain her excitement as she walks over to the corner he's sitting in and pats him.

Aiden touches my elbow. 'Let me strap your ankle for you.' He leads me over to one of the metal bucket chairs near the staff entrance. I take a seat while he goes to the security office in search of a bandage.

My eyes are drooping as I wait, and I slouch further into the chair, struggling to keep myself upright. Aiden returns with a bandage in his hand, and proceeds to strap it around my ankle.

'I know we iced it on the helicopter, but I need you to do it again for fifteen minutes every two hours. Try not to walk on it too much and keep the ankle elevated,' he says, as he's finishing up.

I smile up at him. Seems like my talent to create ice will come in handy for once. 'Thanks Aiden.'

'It's my pleasure. Can you bring Quinn and Adam to the clinic in the morning? I need to monitor them,' he asks.

'Sure thing,' I say, stifling a yawn. Now that we're home, my exhaustion has hit me hard and I can barely keep my eyes open.

'Let's get you to bed,' Sebastian says, walking over as he sees me attempt to stand. He places his arm around my waist and helps me up. 'You look ready to collapse.'

'No kidding,' I respond. I want to stay awake to debrief M, but with the pain from my injury and my exhaustion I know I'll be of no help.

Sebastian helps me down to the tunnels and along the track to the carriage I sleep in. It's slow going, especially on the stairs, but my ankle does feel a lot better now it has been strapped.

As I reach for the carriage door handle I hear footsteps in the tunnel. I look over my shoulder and see April appearing out of the darkness, trailing along the side of the train towards us.

'You're back,' she says, relief evident in her eyes. She catches Sebastian up in a hug then proceeds to give me one. She's squeezes me tightly, and I can tell how relieved she's feeling.

'Not everyone's back,' Sebastian says. 'There were recruiters there. We fought them off and told the people in the ARC everything.' He pauses and glances at me before continuing. 'Dalton didn't make it though. They killed him.'

'He's dead?' April's eyes widen and she looks down at her feet for a moment. She roughly wipes her eyes, and when she looks up again her face has hardened. I can still see her eyes are glistening with tears though. 'We need to wake M up. He'll want to know.'

'Yes, we need to talk to him as soon as possible,' Sebastian agrees. His face lights up as he goes on. 'There's someone else here you'll want to see.'

She raises one eyebrow and I smile at her warmly. She's going to be so happy to see her dad again. I would love to see her face when they are reunited, but I really need to rest. I give Sebastian a nudge. 'I can find my bed from here. You should go with her.'

'You sure?'

'Of course I'm sure.' I stifle yet another yawn. 'I'll see you both in the morning.'

I stagger into the carriage, exhaustion making even the simplest task an effort. I close the door behind me and, fully dressed, I collapse down onto the bed. My head has barely hit the pillow when I fall asleep.

'Elle! Elle! Wake up!'

'What?' I groan, struggling to open my eyes. It feels like mere moments ago that I closed my eyes and went to sleep. My vision is hazy and it takes me a moment to recognise Quinn standing over me. A lamp lights her face, which is filled with such fear that I feel like I've been doused in a cold bucket of water.

'What's wrong?' I ask, sitting up.

'We have to leave.'

'What are you talking about?'

'Recruiters were spotted by a lookout, and the man in charge, M, thinks they tracked us back here.'

'And he wants us to leave now?'

She nods her head vigorously.

I slowly push myself to stand up. My leg is still shaky beneath me and pain shoots up through my calf whenever I lean on it too heavily.

Quinn reaches out and grasps my arm until I can steady myself by curling one hand around the back of a seat.

'There's a bag of my things in the corner,' I say, quickly and quietly.

She heads for the corner of the carriage and slings the bag over her back. 'Anything else?'

'I need to go get someone.'

'Who?'

'Kelsey. She'll be just a few carriages down with Mia.'

I open the door and find Sebastian reaching out to grasp the handle. Kelsey is already in his arms and rubbing her eyes tiredly.

'You're back,' she says, smiling.

I manage a grin for her. 'Of course I'm back. I missed you.'

'I missed you too,' she says.

'You ready?' Sebastian asks.

There's no worry in his stance, just sheer determination. I give him a nod and try to appear a little less concerned. 'Yeah, we're ready.'

We make our way along the train tracks to the platform where people are slowly gathering. Sebastian has his hands full with Kelsey, so Quinn helps me climb up off the tracks.

The people already waiting on the platform seem confused and lost. There's a tired tension to the air and, though everyone is exhausted, there is fear painted clearly across their faces. Sebastian winds his way through the crowd to one of the walls where his dad is already standing. Quinn and I follow him closely, and I try hard not to bump people as I stagger past.

'I can't believe we're being driven out again,' I say. As much as I dislike living underground, I hate the idea of picking up our lives to leave again.

'We shouldn't be,' Sebastian says, taking care to keep his voice low. 'We need to be facing Joseph, not running away from him.'

I nod with him, but don't feel as certain of his words as he does.

People will get hurt if we confront Joseph and I don't want to lose anyone else.

M walks down the steps to the platform and the people gathered fall silent. He falls into place next to April, who is standing several steps up so the crowd can clearly see them.

'What's going on M?' Thatch raises his voice to be heard over the soft chatter.

M clears his throat. 'Recruiters have been spotted nearby and our location has been compromised. I believe the group followed some of our members here. There are still a couple out there watching the station, but they have sent others back for reinforcements. We need to leave before they return with an army to take us down.'

The words are barely out of his mouth when whispers and mutters start shooting around the room. People are clearly scared, but aren't happy to be leaving again. I don't blame them.

'Surely there's another way,' Thatch says.

M hesitates before he continues. 'I'm afraid not. We can't risk a reoccurrence of what happened at the last camp.'

'This isn't right!' Luke says, his voice carrying from the back of the platform. 'We can't keep hiding.' For once I find myself agreeing with him. Are we really going to move every time Joseph's recruiters find us?

'It's time we did something about Joseph,' Sebastian adds, causing heads to turn and look at him as he stands beside me. There are mutters of agreement through the crowd. We've been hiding for long enough and everyone knows it.

M faces the rest of our group and lifts his hands up, calling for us to quieten down. 'The recruiters will attack us here with all their strength, and I will not have a repeat of what happened last time.'

'Then we set a trap,' I say, surprising myself for actually voicing my opinion aloud in front of all these people.

The room falls quiet and every head turns to look at me. My heart is racing quickly as I look out at all the faces watching me. 'If we know that

Joseph is sending an army of recruiters this way, we need to set a trap for them. While they are distracted here, we attack Headquarters. If we can keep the recruiters occupied here, it will be easier to get to Joseph.'

'She's right,' Hunter says. I catch sight of him across the room. His eyes are bright with defiance and there's a deadly look to them as he considers the plan. 'You know how desperately he wants to stop The Movement now, after everything that's happened. He will send every last recruiter he can spare if he thinks this could be his chance. Joseph has no talent. His power lies in the fear and brutality of his recruiters. Without them he has no way to control the people of Hope.'

'If we can take away his recruiters he would be powerless and we would have a real chance at finally stopping him,' I add. 'We just fought off recruiters in the ARC and won. They know we're no longer scared, that we won't sit by and watch them ruin the world we live in anymore. They are waiting outside for reinforcements because they know we won't go quietly this time.' I feel confidence building inside me and I know for sure that it is time to act.

'In the ARC we saw first hand the lengths Joseph is going to in order to advance his evil experiments and maintain his power. We have to stop him now, or it might be too late!'

A cheer of approval goes up through the room. Every voice is in agreement. Every person is keen to finally get the chance to fight for our future. The group turn to M to see how he responds. He appears thoughtful as he considers our words.

'We may never get another opportunity like this,' April says to him, keeping her voice low enough that only he can hear. 'We have to take it.'

He draws himself up tall. 'You are all right. It's time we finally dealt with Joseph. He is getting desperate and we will take advantage. The snake is finally exposing its body. Tonight we chop off its head.'

CHAPTER TWENTY-FIVE

M launches straight into action and doesn't waste a minute as he puts our plan into motion. Everything feels rushed, and I'm worried this is all happening too quickly, but we don't have the luxury of time right now. The recruiters could attack the station at any moment and, though M's plan sounds solid, there are so many things that could go wrong.

I approach the edge of the platform with Sebastian at my side. Kelsey is sleeping contently in his arms, and I chew on my lower lip as I watch her. I don't want to let her go, but I know she can't stay here when there's so much danger.

'It's okay Elle, we'll look after her,' Quinn says. She's already down on the tracks with Adam and the others who won't be staying to fight. Aiden is taking them to the next hideout, so they should be safe. Still, it's harder than I expected to say goodbye.

We climb down onto the tracks and Sebastian slowly passes Kelsey to Adam, carefully arranging the sleeping girl so she's comfortable in his arms.

Quinn watches them closely and then turns to me. 'I wish you would come with us Elle. I only just got you back.'

I give her a sad smile. I wish I could wait in safety for this to be over too, but that's not who I am anymore. The girl who would hide away in the shadows has been gone for a while now. I could never sit back and allow other people to fight my battles for me.

'It will be over before you know it.' I try to reassure her.

'Are you sure you won't come with us?' she asks.

I shake my head and pull her into a tight hug. 'I'll see you tomorrow.'

'Tomorrow,' she gives a short laugh. 'It feels like an eternity away. I'll miss you.'

'Me too.'

She pulls back from the hug and looks me in the eye. 'You'll be careful, right? I don't want to hear about some heroic stunt you've pulled. If things go wrong and there's the option between being the girl who stands and fights or the girl who runs. Be the girl who runs.'

'I've always been useless at running,' I say quietly. 'You be careful too. You and that cure are too important.'

'I'll promise to be safe if you do,' she says, giving me her best motherly look. 'I've told you once before and I'll tell you again, this isn't the end for us.'

'No, this isn't the end.'

I'm sad to see Quinn and Adam go, and it tugs at my heart to see Kelsey leaving too, but it's a weight off my mind to know they'll all be safe. Copper comes and nuzzles his head against my leg as the group starts to move into the darkness of the tunnel. It's a small comfort, but it does make me feel better.

I see Mia loitering by the tunnel entrance, watching the group go, and I walk over to her.

'You're not going with them?' I ask.

She shakes her head. 'I can be helpful here. I want this to be a better world for Amber, and I can't go and hide when I could be making a difference,' she replies. 'Aiden will look after her.'

I nod, knowing exactly how she feels. We both pause as we watch the last of the people leaving disappear into the darkness of the tunnel.

'We'll see them again,' I say.

'I hope so,' she replies, her eyes misting with tears.

I reach out and rub her arm. 'We will,' I repeat.

The two of us climb back onto the platform. With most of our group gone, it feels eerily quiet and uncomfortably empty here. People are even whispering as they discuss our plan for tonight. Everyone falls completely silent though, when M whistles for our attention.

'You all know the plan,' he says. 'Now, get to your posts.' His firm order shatters the silence and my heart begins to race. It's happening. We're finally doing something about Joseph, and I know deep inside that everything is going to change tonight.

'Are you ready Elle?' April says, as she rushes over to me. He eyes drop to look at my leg. 'How's your ankle feeling?'

'It'll be fine,' I say. It still hurts to walk on, but Aiden says it's just a light sprain. I've been much more mobile since it was strapped and, as long as I'm not trudging through mud or snow, I think I'll able to manage okay on my own.

She frowns, looking as though she doesn't believe me. 'If it's causing you trouble or too much pain...' she hesitates before she continues. 'If there's something I can do...'

'It will be fine,' I insist.

'Okay...' she says, sounding thoroughly unconvinced. 'Then we better get moving. You head down to the tunnel entrance and check the coast is clear. Any problems, let me know. Otherwise, Luke and I will meet you there soon.'

I nod and turn to make my way to the edge of the platform, but Hunter intercepts me before I can even take a step towards the train tracks.

'Winters,' he says, as he approaches. 'You're leaving without saying goodbye?

I roll my eyes at him. 'The team going to Headquarters is leaving via my exit, I'll see you guys in like five minutes.'

'Five minutes is too long to wait.' He smirks, but his eyes are troubled and I know it has everything to do with what will happen tonight. My heart lurches inside me as I consider how this is for him. Joseph is his father after all and I can't imagine this is easy for him.

'Are you sure you should be going to Headquarters?' I ask him, before lowering my voice. 'You know how this ends.'

'I know how this ends,' Hunter replies, his face a detached mask. I want to reassure him, but there's nothing I can say that will help. If things go the way we hope, this won't end well for Joseph.

I glance at the tunnel. 'I need to get to my post, but I'll see you soon.'

He nods, but doesn't reply. He still has the same haunted look on his face and I worry about how he's going to cope with tonight. Something tells me that sending him to Headquarters is a bad idea.

I leave Hunter and get down onto the tracks, with Copper right behind me. As I enter the tunnel, cold tingles creep up my spine and I try to keep myself calm. The darkness of the tunnel envelops me and seems to invade my senses. I struggle to contain the nerves I feel churning in my gut as I think about tonight.

Lara and Henry will already be waiting by the front entrance. Their group is essentially acting as bait tonight, luring the recruiters down into the station. Lara had seemed so certain that she could toy with their emotions, making the recruiters unnaturally confident enough to storm the station once they catch sight of her by the entrance. Not only will her group have to lure the recruiters in, they'll also have to escape through the manhole exit at the other end of the tunnel.

The timing tonight has to be perfect. Once all of the recruiters are down in the station, each of the three teams will cause their entrance to collapse, trapping them in the tunnels. If one entrance blows before the others, the recruiters will realise what's happening and escape.

My stomach sinks as I think through the plan, and what could potentially go wrong. Our chances of success aren't high, but it's better than doing nothing. We just need to buy M and his team going to Headquarters enough time to get to Joseph. Who knows; maybe we can actually pull this off.

Copper starts whining, pulling my attention away from my thoughts. We are passing by the carriages as we head towards the wide-open entrance of the tunnel.

'It's okay boy,' I say to him, softly running my hand through his coat. My words don't relax him though and his whines become more persistent, until he suddenly launches forward, running away from me down the tunnel.

'Copper!' I whisper hotly, chasing after him. He bounds along beside the train before moving past it towards the tunnel opening that lies beyond. I struggle to keep up with him and can't understand what's got him so spooked. Was M wrong about the recruiters? Have they come for us already?

Copper finally slows as he nears the entrance, stopping in front of a man who stands just inside the tunnel.

'Copper, get back here,' I hiss at him, narrowing my eyes as I take the man in.

The dog refuses to listen to me though, and he pants happily as the man leans over to pat him. I cautiously approach the two of them. The man's back is to me and in the darkness I can't make out his features. He could be anyone, but I can't believe he's a recruiter if Copper is so content with him.

I stop in my tracks as the man turns around.

'Ryan?' My brow furrows as I try to fathom his presence. 'What are you doing here?'

Why isn't he back on the platform with the others? Why is he lurking here in the dark?

He sighs. His face is in shadow, but I can still make out the wild-eyed bewilderment that's crossing his expression. He's usually so put together, but tonight he seems far from it.

'I'm trying to figure out if I should tell you the truth,' he says.

'What truth?' I respond, frowning as I take a step closer to him.

'This is when it all happens,' he continues, as if he hasn't heard my question. 'This is the moment I've been trying to avoid for years.'

'What are you talking about?' I feel completely lost and have no idea what he could possibly mean.

He groans and pushes a hand through his hair. The gesture seems so familiar, yet I can't fathom how. I can't remember a time I've seen him do that.

I dismiss the thought and stand tall, crossing my arms over my chest. 'What truth are you talking about?' I repeat.

He steps away from me and moves further into the shadow of the tunnel. 'Elle, this might come as a shock, but I'm not who I say I am.'

I let out a laugh. 'Not who you say you are? You've never told me a thing about yourself. One day you're an official, the next you're a lone rebel. You're a complete mystery to me, so you don't need to worry about wrecking any preconceived image I may have of who you are.'

'You really have no idea?'

I raise my hands up in confusion.

'I thought you might have guessed,' he says, more to himself than to me.

'So, what's the big secret?'

He hesitates, as though he knows the words he's about to speak will change everything. As though he's unsure he wants things to change.

'Elle, my first name isn't Ryan.' He pauses again, before sucking in a breath and continuing. 'My name is Sebastian Ryan Scott.'

CHAPTER TWENTY-SIX

I take a step away from him. My hands are shaking and my mind whirls with confusion. 'So, you have the same name as Sebastian. Plenty of people have the same name.'

He frowns. 'It's not just my name that's the same...'

'What are you getting at?' I take another step away. I can't even begin to comprehend what he's saying.

'I'm Sebastian. *Your* Sebastian.'

I shake my head. 'No. Sebastian is back inside on the platform, and I hate to break it to you, but you're much older than him.'

He takes a step towards me and slowly lifts one hand to my face, touching my skin so gently. I instinctively rest in to his hand, unable to help myself.

'I can't think of another way to prove this to you and we don't have time,' he says.

He takes a nervous breath and then leans in and lightly touches his lips to mine with a kiss. The kiss is chaste and sweet, but it makes my heart hammer and electrifies the blood pulsing through my veins. With one kiss he has me weak at the knees, in a way that only one other person makes me feel.

When he pulls back I frown. Yes, he brings out the same feelings in me as Sebastian, but that doesn't make believing him any easier.

'That doesn't prove anything,' I say, my voice gravelly.

He sighs and slowly raises his hands to his face. With careful movements, he begins to remove a pair of contact lenses from his eyes. As he pulls his hands away, his warm brown irises are gone and dazzling blue ones are revealed. They're the colour of a shimmering sapphire with a deep blue ring around them. They watch me intensely and are simmering with emotion, and there's no denying the connection I feel now that I look into his eyes—Sebastian's eyes.

Confusion colours my features. 'But, how?'

'I can teleport through time.'

I laugh out loud, the sound slightly crazed. 'Of course you can.'

'I'm serious Elle. I've spent years coming back, trying to change the future.'

I frown as I watch him. He seems so sincere about what he's saying. The more I look at him, the more I recognise Sebastian's features. He's the same height and while his hair is longer, it's exactly the same colour as Sebastian's. Ryan's skin is darker, but if what he says is true then he could have spent years on the surface. They have the same nose, the same mouth and the same eyes. There's stubble over Ryan's jaw and he's more filled out, but again that can be explained by time. Even the old scar through his eyebrow, is in the exact same place as the cut Sebastian received when recruiters attacked us the other day, though Sebastian's is still freshly visible on his forehead.

My eyes grow wide and I start visibly shaking. 'I need to sit down.'

Ryan steps over to me, but I shake my head and move to sit against the tunnel wall. 'This can't be happening.' It takes my mind a few minutes to try and work through all the times I've seen Ryan and to recall all of our past encounters and conversations.

I finally look up at him. 'Why come back?' He can't be here simply on a sightseeing tour of the past.

He slowly approaches me, taking cautious steps as though afraid I will scare and run off. He sits on the ground near me, far enough away that I'm not intimidated, but close enough to talk. 'Something happens tonight,' he says. 'Someone is hurt and you try to heal them with your talent, only you transfer their injury to yourself.'

'That's not too bad,' I say, softly. 'I can handle a little pain.'

His eyes are sad as he shakes his head. 'Their injury is lethal and it kills you Elle.'

My blood runs cold as I hear his words. 'I'm going to die?'

He nods. 'I thought if I could come back I could change that future, but nothing I do seems to work. I tried to stop you from coming to the surface. I tried to stop you from getting caught and taken to the hospital. I desperately tried to get you out of there before you ever acquired the talent in the first place. I even helped you get back to the ARC in the hopes that you might still be there when all this happened. But it seems that everything you do just leads to this outcome. Telling you the truth is my last resort.'

I pull my knees into my chest. I know I should be crying and afraid of the fate that lies before me, but I feel nothing but cold. I feel completely detached from my body—a body that won't see the sunrise again.

'Elle?' he whispers.

'I'm fine.' I shake my head. 'Why have you gone to so much trouble just for me?'

'I would have thought that was obvious,' he replies. He reaches out and takes my hand in his, squeezing it tightly. 'But, it's not the only reason. Because of your death Joseph escapes unscathed.' His eyes grow dark as he looks at me. 'I can't begin to tell you the future that unfolds because of this.'

'Bad, huh?'

He nods. 'Worse than you can imagine. He succeeds in creating the serum that can give a talent to anyone he wishes and the divides you see in Hope now only become greater. He enslaves whole masses of untalents to serve the talented, and the talented he creates become monsters. People aren't capable of handling such power without becoming unstable.'

'So, that's why you wanted me to stop acquiring talents?' I ask.

'No, I believe you're different, and so does Joseph,' he replies. 'Your ability to absorb talents is a part of who you are and acquiring talents is a natural progression. I was hoping if I stopped you from gaining more, then maybe you wouldn't obtain the talent to heal. Judging from your limp though, I was already too late.'

I glance down at my still swollen ankle and wonder how long I have had this talent for. Is it really as deadly as Ryan thinks? I look back up at him. 'So how do we change the future?'

'That's the thing; I haven't been able to. No matter what I change or what I do, events continue to eventuate just as they did before.'

'So, that's it, we're doomed?'

'No, I've been talking with April and we think that I've been going about things the wrong way. I can't change the future that is already written because I'm from it. If I'm right, I think that you will be able to change the timeline because you're in it.'

'You know you sound crazy right?'

'Yes, I realise it's hard to understand. But, we don't have any other choice. You have to make certain you don't heal anyone tonight and you don't end up anywhere near Joseph.'

I hesitate. 'Well, I'm not part of the team going to Headquarters tonight...'

He sighs and rubs his face tiredly. 'Just promise me you won't go and you won't heal anyone.'

I nod. 'I think I can do that.'

'No matter what, Elle.' His voice becomes stern.

'No matter what,' I agree. I shake my head, still feeling overwhelmed by everything he's told me. 'I think I'm going to need a therapist after all this is over.'

He smiles as I shake my head again. 'Wait, does Sebastian know the truth about you?' It's weird talking to Ryan about himself and it kind of hurts my mind to think about it.

'No, I can't imagine he'd take it too well.'

'Probably not.' I look past him to the train tracks that run outside and into the dark of night. Sebastian will flip if I tell him about Ryan. I'm not certain if I even want to. It's too weird.

'I should leave; April will be here in a moment,' he says. He goes to stand up, but I touch his hand to stop him.

'If tonight doesn't work out the way we hope, he knows I love him, right?'

He gives me a warm, but sad smile. 'Yeah. He knows,' he says before disappearing into the night air.

CHAPTER TWENTY-SEVEN

The sound of footsteps echoes from down the tunnel, and I jump and turn as a group emerges from the shadows. I had expected it to be April and Luke, but there are too many people coming this way.

As they near, I can make out M leading the group. Hunter, Thatch and Soren walk alongside him, and behind them are the rest of the members of The Movement who are readying themselves to attack Headquarters. I hope our plan to trap the recruiters works, because their numbers are not much more than ten and I'm not sure they are quite ready for what they are about to face.

M gives me a brief nod as he walks past, and Hunter throws me a wink. They follow the train tracks out into the moonlit night and once they are beyond the protection of the tunnel entrance M pauses to check the coast is clear.

Sebastian trails at the rear of the group and my heartbeat stutters as I see him. He looks calm and collected, and I feel a stabbing pain in my chest. If things go wrong tonight this will be the last time I see him.

He pauses when he reaches me at the tunnel entrance.

'You ready for tonight?' I ask.

His lips are firm and his eyes seem heavy as he nods. 'Yes, I'm ready. How are you feeling?'

'Fine,' I respond. My voice is small and I struggle to contain the information Ryan has just given me. I wouldn't even know where to begin to explain it to Sebastian, and I would hate for him to worry about me tonight. He needs to stay focused if he's heading into Head-quarters and I can't have him distracted by what my fate may hold.

He steps forward and pulls me into his arms to give me a hug. I rest my cheek against his chest and close my eyes as I breathe him in. I push down tears that attempt to well in my eyes. I feel so small in his arms, and also so alone in the knowledge I'm keeping from him. I don't want to lose him. I don't want him to lose me and I hate the idea that if I'm gone he will spend years trying to right that wrong.

I bury my face into his chest and for a moment I try to pretend that everything will be fine tonight, but it's useless. All I keep thinking is that this is the last hug I will ever get from him.

He slowly pulls back and cups my face in his hand. 'Hey, are you okay?' he asks, when he looks into my eyes.

I give him a series of small nods, not trusting my voice.

'We're both going to be fine,' he says. 'M's plan for tonight is brilliant and when the sun comes up in the morning everything will have changed for the better.'

I nod again, but struggle to continue looking into his deep blue eyes. Even though I haven't said a word, I feel like I'm lying to him. Everything is about to change, and if things go down the way they're destined to, it won't be for the better. I don't know how to part with him. I don't know how to watch him walk away knowing that this could be our last goodbye.

'I better go, or I'll get left behind,' he says sadly, without looking away from me for even a moment. He gives me one of his beautiful, heartbreaking smiles. 'I'll see you soon.' He leans forward and lightly kisses my forehead, before taking a step back and turning away.

With each step he takes away from me, I feel my heart going with him. I feel like he's taking a piece of me with him and it's killing me to watch him go. He has almost disappeared into the darkness with the others when I call out to him. 'Sebastian?'

He turns and I run to him. Ignoring the pain in my ankle I fly across the ground between us and throw myself into his arms. I kiss him passionately, desperately, like this one kiss is all the time I will get with him. An eternity that only lasts a breath.

When I pull back, he seems shocked. His eyes sparkle and there's a crooked smile tugging at his lips. 'We should go into battle more often,' he whispers.

I try to smile in response, but I can feel tears bubbling up inside of me again.

'Just look after yourself,' I respond, before my tears can really start to well. I turn from him and walk back to the tunnel. Once I'm out of sight, I crumble to the ground and hug my knees to my chest as I struggle to maintain my composure.

I'm not sure if it's moments or minutes before I can breathe again, but I slowly pull myself together and stand tall. Clearing my face of all emotion, I push down my feelings and ready myself for what's about to come.

When April and Luke appear, Mia is also with them and so is a girl named Ethel who has also agreed to help. Luke has a large back-pack slung over his shoulder, which Ethel keeps eyeing suspiciously. I scan the pack cautiously, knowing all too well that there are explosives tucked inside.

'So, what now?' I ask, as they approach.

Luke kneels down, pulling the pack from his back. 'We need to set the devices up and blow them once the recruiters are in the tunnels.'

'That easy, huh?' I ask.

'Hopefully,' he nods. 'Where did you find this stuff April?'

'We found them back at the airbase and have been saving them for a rainy day,' she responds.

'Was there enough for all three entrances?' I ask.

'Enough for Lara and Henry,' she answers. 'Mia and Ethel have their own way of closing the main entrance.'

Copper starts sniffing at Luke's backpack, so I quickly shoo him away. 'Is it okay that he's here?' I ask April.

She glances at the dog and shrugs. 'As long as he doesn't make any noise and give us away, I have no problem with it.' Her voice sounds tired, and something seems off. I want to ask her what's wrong, but Mia starts to talk.

'We better get in position as well,' Mia says, nodding at Ethel. 'You three be careful with those explosives. Look after yourselves.'

'You too,' I say. She steps forward and gives me a lingering hug. I don't want to say another goodbye, and I know she feels the same because without a word she and Ethel leave the tunnel. They move to the opposite side of the tracks from where Sebastian and M left, and scramble under the wire fence, quickly disappearing into the shadows of the bushes.

I turn back to April and Luke. April is quiet and still hasn't made eye contact with me since she arrived. She is focusing intently down on the backpack in front of Luke as he slowly pulls out one of the small black devices.

He hands it to April who proceeds to place it by the wall at the mouth of the entrance. Luke slowly lifts another device from the pack and carries it over to the large brick column in the middle of the entrance that supports the roof. The other side of tunnel opening has already partially caved in, so it hopefully won't take too much more to cover the entrance completely.

Once Luke has finished the three of us walk outside, sticking close to the bushes by the side of the track, and crouch down on the ground facing the tunnel. We're close enough that we have a good view of the entrance, but far enough back that we should be hidden by the shadows, and out of range of the blast.

'We'll stay here until we get the comm that the recruiters have entered the tunnels,' April says.

'How long will it be?' I ask.

April shrugs. 'It could be anytime from now. It depends how quickly the recruiters are able to assemble and make their way from Headquarters to here. Lara won't start luring them in until they're all here.'

'Does M really think Joseph will send all of his recruiters?' Luke asks.

April nods. 'Hunter and M believe he'll send a large number of them.'

'But what if he doesn't?'

'Then we will find another way to bring Joseph to his knees,' she replies softly.

Copper snuggles in close to me, resting his head on my lap. I'm grateful for his presence and it's comforting to run my fingers through his fur. Nothing I do can keep my mind off the events that are supposed to happen tonight though.

The others fall silent and I stare at the train tracks, the minutes passing like hours. No one speaks and the other two seem caught up in their own thoughts. I'm glad of the silence. I don't feel up to making small talk for the sake of it right now. I have too much on my mind.

The longer we wait, the tenser I feel. I'm not the only one. April looks troubled and it worries me. Something is clearly up and it feels like more than the usual concerns that she seems to shoulder.

'What's wrong?' I ask her.

'Nothing,' she responds, too quickly. 'I'm just thinking about what we have to do.'

I can't argue with her answer, but something about it doesn't ring true. 'You sure that's all?'

'Elle, we have to blow up the tunnel entrance tonight and trap recruiters inside. I think that's enough to worry about for now,' she retorts sharply.

I frown and drop the subject, falling silent again. I want to trust her, but I don't believe she's telling me everything. There's something she's holding back from me.

I'm distracted from my concerns when I catch sight of April's cuff glowing. All of our eyes fall on it and she slowly lifts her head. 'The recruiters are nearing the station.'

We all stand in one fluid motion and I glance between April and the tunnel.

'Do we blow it now?' I ask her.

She shakes her head. 'No. We wait until they're all in there or until we can see someone coming. We don't want them to realise what's happening and stop them from entering the station.'

I nod, my body tensing. The timing has to be perfect for this. If we blow it too soon the recruiters will hear and may escape out the main entrance before Mia can destroy it.

My heart is beating quickly in my chest, but I feel disconnected from the sensation as I am totally focused on using my talented hearing and sight. I can hear the gentle wheezes of April and Luke's breaths in and out, and the near soundless rustle of their clothes flapping in the light breeze. The rest of the area is quiet though.

Through the silence, I begin to hear something. It sounds like muffled voices and footsteps and gravel scuffing against the ground.

'They're in there,' I whisper to the others, my heart rising to beat in my throat.

'Can you tell how far off?' April asks.

I look at her. 'No, but they can't be far. Any news from the others?'

She glances down at her cuff, her eyes willing another comm to come through with an update. 'Nothing,' she says, flinging her wrist down with disgust.

The feet slapping against the ground draw closer. Men's voices shouting to one another become louder. I can hear their ragged breaths, their sniffs and pants as they run along the tracks. They have to be getting close now. I'm almost surprised we can't see them already.

'I don't think we can wait much longer,' I say to April.

'Just another minute,' she says.

Luke looks worried though and a flaming ball of fire erupts in each of his hands.

'Not yet,' April says, holding her arm out to stop him. 'Not until we see them.'

My heart thuds loudly and my skin buzzes with nerves as we wait. Each moment draws out and I forget to breathe as I focus fully on the tunnel entrance.

'I hope your aim is good,' I hear April whisper to Luke.

'It is,' he responds.

A man in recruiter black appears in the tunnel, making his way towards the entrance. His eyes fall on Luke's burning purple flames and he shouts over his shoulder to the recruiters coming behind him. A flash of light erupts from his hands, beaming in our direction and completely blinding us. The searing light gushes from the tunnel entrance, like a huge spotlight has been pointed in our direction.

'Now!' April shouts.

'I can't see where to throw!' Luke yells back.

Copper growls and launches forward, bounding towards the tunnel entrance at an unnaturally fast speed.

'Copper!' I yell, but he disappears from sight as he's enveloped in the white light, which pours from the tunnel. I can still hear him panting, his growls echoing off of the concrete walls.

'I'm just going to take a shot and hope for the best!' Luke shouts.

'You can't!' I yell back at him, grabbing his arm and yanking it down, paying no heed to the flames that hiss in his hands. 'Copper is in there.'

'He's just a dog, Elle,' Luke responds, yanking his arm from mine.

Copper's barks become louder and more aggressive and a moment later the blinding light disappears. It takes me a moment for my eyes to readjust, but when they do I immediately see a man on the floor with Copper on top of him. Behind them, other recruiters are racing towards the entrance, appearing like wraiths from the shadows.

Luke spares a glance at us. 'Get down,' he says, before turning back to the entrance.

'Copper!' I scream, wanting to run to him, but April wraps her arms around my waist and stops me from rushing forward. She drags me away from Luke, back along the train tracks and away from the tunnel entrance. Tears stream down my face and my stomach clenches tightly.

Luke's fireballs grow larger and he hurls them at the tiny black devices they've placed on the ground by the tunnel wall. Before I can gauge if his aim is true, a huge explosion erupts and I am thrown forward, landing hard on my forearms.

The noise of the explosion is so loud I feel like heaving and I throw my hands up over my ears in an attempt to quieten the din. Even after the initial roar, the sound still reverberates around me like an ongoing rumble I can't escape.

'Elle!' I hear April cry, her voice distant as though she's shouting at me from another room. There's a ringing echo in my ears and a wave of dizziness floods my consciousness.

Something grips my arm tightly and I look up to find April there, helping me to my feet. Her face is covered in dirt and bloody gashes run down her arms. 'Elle?' she yells again, though her voice is quiet and distorted to my ears.

She slowly helps me up and we support each other as we stand. I glance over my shoulder to see Luke staggering along just behind us. I can't see the tunnel beyond him, as the air in front of it is thick with fire and smoke.

My eyes search the wreckage for any sign of Copper, but there's only rubble and smoke to be seen.

'Did it work?' April asks, as we slowly stagger back to where Luke has retreated.

Luke looks over his shoulder at the entranceway. A gust of wind blows the smoke from the fire in the other direction and we can all clearly see the debris behind it. The entrance has been destroyed, and only broken slabs of concrete and bent poles of steel remain.

We all stare at it in shock. I know what we had planned, but never guessed the devastation those bombs would pack. My heart breaks as I look at it, knowing there's no way Copper could have survived.

But then I hear a soft whining noise, so quiet there's no way you could catch it without talented senses. I rush forward, pushing out of April's grasp, and run towards the fire that still blazes from the ruins.

I get to the edge of the wreckage, but endless piles of rubble lay before me. I wouldn't know where to begin to look for him. But his solitary whining sound comes again and my eyes zero in on a pile of rocks just beyond me.

I clamber over the broken concrete and exposed wiring to reach them. There's a large slab of concrete, too heavy to lift alone, but I hear Copper's painful whines again and I know he must be under it.

'Here.' I look up and find Luke beside me, crouching down to help lift the slab. Together we both grab the bottom edge and groan as we pull it up. I feel a brush of fur against my leg, and Copper crawls from beneath the concrete until he is free.

We drop the slab and I laugh, pulling the dog in for a hug and burying my face in his neck. His fur is covered in ash and dust, and he's stepping gingerly on a bloodied front paw, but miraculously he somehow seems to have survived.

'I think he must have been cocooned in there,' Luke says. 'I don't think the concrete fell on him at all.'

I look up at him, my eyes wet with tears. I don't know whether to hug Luke or punch him for setting the bomb off in the first place.

'I'm sorry, Elle,' he says, scratching the fur behind Copper's ear. 'I didn't want to hurt him, but we had to close the entrance. We didn't have a choice.'

I slowly nod with understanding. 'I think Copper knew how important that was too. Thank you for helping me get him free.'

'It still doesn't mean I like you,' he says, with a grin.

'Noted.' I grin back at him.

We are slowly making our way back towards April, when a loud explosion echoes through the night. The ground shudders and more dust and dirt seeps out through the cracks in the debris that blocks the tunnel entrance.

'That must be Lara and Henry closing off the other side of the tunnel,' April says calmly, as we reach her. Her head is bowed and her eyes are trained on her cuff. 'I haven't had confirmation from Mia that the front entrance is closed,' she says. 'Come on, we need to check it out.'

She takes off at a run, and we follow close behind her. I struggle to keep up on my sore ankle and Copper has fallen back completely, barely able to run at all. I duck under the wire fence by the tracks and push through the bushes to get to the road beyond.

The others are already halfway down the street when I get to it, and I try to push myself to keep up with them, but each step I take is harder and harder. And it's not just my ankle I'm struggling with. A part of me feels like I shouldn't be here, like I'm running in the wrong direction.

The others start to slow up ahead and when I catch up with them I gasp. Mia stands in the middle of the road before us, facing the front of the station, with her arms stretched out wide. I watch in shock as a huge black hole engulfs the ground beneath the station entrance. The walls of the building are crumbling inwards, falling and plummeting down into the deep abyss that waits below.

The hole is slowly expanding, crawling its way further out into the street. The buildings connected to the station begin to shudder violently and the asphalt beneath our feet quakes and rumbles. The hole grows bigger and wider, creeping its way towards Mia.

'Why won't she stop?' Ethel cries, from the other side of the street.

April doesn't hesitate as she launches herself towards Mia. Luke tries to grab her, but she's too quick for him. She easily avoids his grasp and races down the road to Mia and the black abyss beyond her.

'What's she doing?' I yell.

'Saving us all,' Luke responds.

When she reaches Mia, April grips tightly onto her arm and stares straight into her eyes. She completely ignores the bottomless darkness that inches towards them, and focuses her attention solely on Mia.

April's lips move quickly, her persuasive words rushing out as she attempts to control Mia. But it doesn't seem to be working and the black hole only continues to grow. The station entrance is completely gone, and the buildings surrounding it are beginning to crumple under the power of Mia's all consuming talent.

I shake my head. 'April's persuasion isn't working. Mia's too strong, and she's clearly lost control'

'Elle...' Luke warns, as I take a step forward.

I glance back at him. 'Mia needs to stop this herself.'

I race forward, ignoring the pain that shoots through my sore ankle, as I run towards the two girls and the gaping black mass that roils just beyond them. Wind rushes noisily past me, gathering speed as it whips and lashes its way towards the black hole. The violent gusts pull at my clothes and my hair, and I can almost feel the power of the dark black vortex tugging my body closer. This thing is going to devour us all if Mia doesn't stop it quickly.

April's eyes are set on Mia, while Mia's focus is fully on the hole before her. She doesn't blink as she stares at her creation and her eyes are glazed over in a hauntingly dark colour of purple. I approach Mia's other side and grab her hand in mine.

'Mia,' I shout, trying to be heard over the battering sound of the storm around us. 'You have to stop this.'

'I can't,' she moans, not breaking her gaze with the chaos in front of her, which is creeping closer to our feet.

'You can. I know you can.'

'It's too powerful,' she whimpers. 'I can't contain it.'

'Yes, you can,' I repeat. 'You created this and you can control it. It's part of you and there's no reason to be afraid of it. Imagine that

Amber is here. You wouldn't let your talents hurt her, just like you won't let it hurt the rest of us.'

She doesn't respond and the fear in her eyes only seems to become more pronounced. Her body is shaking and there's a touch of blood at her nose. She looks close to collapsing and it terrifies me to think of what will happen with the hole if she passes out.

'Listen, forget the size of it and just treat it like you would any other black hole you create. You are in total control of it. It doesn't exist without you.'

Mia frowns, but then slowly nods. Her eyes harden and she glares at the darkness in front of her. A minute passes and nothing has changed, but as I watch the churning shadowy hole I realise it's stopped expanding towards us.

'You're doing it Mia!' April exclaims, as the abyss ever so slowly begins to retract. At first it's a little, and then a little more. The wind that batters against me, tugging at my clothes and hair, dies down and the rumbling beneath our feet slowly softens.

Gradually the black hole shrinks back towards the station until it disappears completely. Already crippled from the carnage Mia's power has inflicted, the buildings either side of the entrance continue to quake and crack. Just as the hole blinks out of existence the buildings collapse down on top of it in a deafening boom. Nothing remains of the station entrance and only piles of broken brick and concrete lie where it once stood.

Mia sags to the ground, exhausted. Collapsing her head into her hands, she starts to cry. 'I lost control,' she sobs. 'It was too big and it got away from me.'

April kneels next to her and rubs her on her back. 'It's okay Mia, you did amazing.' Ethel and Luke cautiously approach us, looks of shock plastered across their faces.

'There's no way the recruiters are getting out of there,' Luke says.

'We saw them go in.' Ethel speaks quietly, her words almost tinged with guilt. 'M was right; Joseph must have sent nearly every recruiter he had. There were so many of them.'

I turn from them to look back at the remains of the station we once called home. After the two explosions and Mia's monstrous black hole, I wonder how many of the recruiters are actually alive down there. I shake the thought from my mind. They were coming here to destroy us. We had no choice.

I feel my attention drawn away from the station remains, and I look over in the direction of the bright lights of the inner city in the distance. The others will be at Headquarters by now and, even though I know I can't go there tonight, a part of me feels like I'm supposed to. It's like an itch that I can't scratch, a compulsion that is difficult to ignore, and standing here by the station ruins suddenly feels wrong.

'What are you looking at?' April asks, worry touching her voice, as she comes to stand next to me.

I shake my head, unable to look away from the city's glow. 'It's nothing. I just...I just feel like I need to be at Headquarters.' It's more than just a feeling. It's like an urge pulsing through my body to the beat of my heart.

'You can't go there, Elle.'

'But, I think I have to.'

She grabs my arm and pulls me to face her. 'You can't go!'

She had been her normal fiery self only minutes ago, but now her eyes are filled with fear and she looks truly shaken.

'Are you okay?' I ask.

She looks away from me, her eyes welling with tears. Fear licks its way up my spine as I watch her. April never cries. This is more than just recovering from the scare with Mia's black hole or aftershock from the explosion. Something is truly wrong and she's hiding it.

'April, tell me what is wrong.'

'I can't,' she says.

The bad feeling forming in the pit of my stomach gets worse.

'What do you mean you can't?'

She merely shakes her head again, tears beginning to rush down her cheeks.

'April!' I bark at her. 'Tell me.'

She stays silent, but then lets out a sob, her whole body shaking from the impact. 'It's Sebastian,' she says, so quietly I almost don't hear her.

I freeze, unable to move or even so much as breathe. 'What is?'

'I know Sebastian...Ryan...told you the truth...'

'Yes...'

Her eyes look up into mine again and the way she stares at me sends terror like an arrow straight through to my heart. 'Ryan told you not to go to Headquarters tonight because you save someone and it kills you...'

'Yes, I know. Someone is going to—'

My heart stops beating and the quiet world around us becomes completely soundless. I can't think. I can't so much as move as I try to comprehend what she's saying. There's only one person who could have her so upset. Only one person who I would risk everything to save.

'If I don't go tonight, Sebastian dies. Sebastian is the one I'm meant to save, isn't he?'

She nods. 'If you're not there, he's going to die.'

'But, if I do go, I'm the one who will die.'

'Yes.' Her eyes well up again and she buries her face in her hands. The strong girl who I've come to rely on has been stripped away and instead there remains a scared teenager who is unable to decide the impossible.

I slowly back away from her. My heart knowing exactly what I must do. My destiny is to sacrifice myself at Headquarters, transferring Sebastian's deadly injury to myself. But what if Sebastian is never hurt? I was told to avoid healing someone, but never warned to stop them from getting injured in the first place. I'm not afraid, not in the slightest. A cold calm settles over me and I know what I have to do.

'Where are you going?' April whispers, her fear turning to terror. 'You can't go there, Elle, you'll die!'

She launches herself forwards to stop me, but she won't be quick enough. I close my eyes and focus on the warm place in my chest where my talent seems to lie. I coax it out, feeling it fill every cell of my being. My body hums with it and feels alive with the bright and intense tingle it spreads through me.

It comes so naturally, so easily, now that my fear of it has been pushed aside. I almost want to laugh at the folly of how much I've struggled to maintain control over something that is as much a part of me as the blood running through my veins. I always fought against my talent, when what I needed to do was accept it and embrace it.

In my mind's eye I picture Sebastian. I imagine the way he smells, the sound of his voice, his smile, the way he brushes his hand through his hair. It is like there is an invisible thread that connects our two hearts and I can sense the distance between us. I know exactly where he is.

I open my eyes, my body brimming with energy. I only have a moment before it will burst from me, teleporting me away. April lunges at me, fear painted across her features as she realises she's too late.

'Goodbye April,' I whisper, disappearing in the blink of an eye.

CHAPTER TWENTY-EIGHT

The cold bite of air hits my skin in a rush. It crawls up my back and washes down my arms like I've been dowsed in ice-cold water. The discomfort only lasts a second though and when I open my eyes April and the ruined entrance to the station are gone.

I blink slowly as my eyes adjust to my new surrounds. A long corridor with high ceilings and plush, blood red carpet greets me. The lights overhead shine brightly, making me feel exposed. There is nothing warm or inviting about this place and I am overwhelmed by how repelled I feel by it.

Looking behind me, I stagger, catching my arm against the wall. There are several bodies lying at unnatural angles on the floor between the stairs at the end of the corridor and myself.

I swallow and drag a ragged breath in as I try to calm my wildly beating heart. The room smells of blood and death. I place my hand against the wall to steady myself as I try to stop myself from retching.

Coming here had seemed so simple, and I had been certain I was teleporting to Sebastian, but he's not here. Unless... I stumble over to the first body, bending down to look at the man's face, and then stagger over to the next. Feeling queasy, I look into several pairs of vacant eyes. Some I recognise from M's group who left the tunnel and the others are nameless recruiters. I only let out a breath when I can see that none of them are Sebastian. I haven't come too late.

A shout sounds out behind me and I turn to see two recruiters have stepped into the corridor. My body is trembling, but I bring my hands up in front of me in a show of defence. I'm not sure if I can fight two men at once, but there's nowhere to run and definitely nowhere to hide. My heart races as I take a step backwards, readying myself for attack.

The man out in front catches my eye and smiles at me darkly. 'Looks like we've got another visitor.' He raises one hand and his fingers begin to glow an inhumanly bright blue, as he pulls at the air around him in one sweeping movement. Crystals slowly appear in his hand, melding and meshing together as they grow. My eyes boggle as they form a long, jagged dagger of ice created from the very water vapours in the air.

'Now, sweetheart, you going to come quietly?' he asks, holding the dagger out before him.

Talent still buzzes along my skin, becoming more charged as I stare him down. 'Never.'

His dark smile becomes feral as he snarls. Raising the dagger, he hurls it at me, but my body reacts instinctively. Energy ripples along my skin and fire erupts from my hands creating a shield of flames in defence. It hovers in front of me, in a swirling spiral of protection, crackling happily as the flames melt the dagger into nothing. It by no means stops the man though, who growls and runs towards me.

I draw at the flames in the shield, which feel malleable to my touch, and coax them into a large violent ball, which I launch at the man as he races down the corridor at me.

He ducks out of the way of my fireball, slamming against the wall. Without missing a beat, he pushes off the wall and continues forward. His eyes grow steel cold and his grin becomes menacing as his legs pump hard beneath him. He looks like some kind of animal, his motions fluid and terrifying to watch, and I feel true fear as the man advances.

A trail of sharp icicles lies in his wake and slowly they rise up from the ground to hover in the air behind him. He stops suddenly and his body glows blue as he flings his arms towards me. The swarm of icy daggers behind him shoot forward, following the direction of his arms. They spark and glisten as they fly towards me, a beautiful deadly cloud of ice piercing through the air, with only one target—me.

I dive to the ground, landing hard against my already bloody arms. I scream out in pain and, looking down, I can see I was too slow and several of the small icy blades are already embedded in my arm.

Tears sting my eyes, but I push the pain aside. If I allow it to distract me for even a second, I'm dead. Talent surges around me, no longer contained to my skin. I can feel it vibrating in the air around me, enveloping me in a dome of sizzling power.

I rise to my knees and flashes of electricity ignite at my fingertips, crackling down my arms. They spark across my skin in a brilliant white shock of spitting and hissing anger. I throw my arm forward, yelling out as the terawatts of power surge towards the recruiter, leaving my skin and streaking across the distance between us.

He tries to dodge away, but the surge hits him square in the shoulder. He shudders violently and drops to the ground, convulsing as the current runs through him. His shaking slowly ebbs until he lies there completely still.

The man who had been standing behind him is gone, and I push myself to my feet. He must have gone for back up. I tremble as I look down at the man I've killed. His unblinking eyes stare at the ceiling. The feral look in his stare is now gone and his face has become blank of emotion.

I stagger back from the man, banging into the wall as I try to get away from him. I need to get out of here. I turn and begin to run down the hallway. I try to ignore the repulsion I can feel consuming me, but I am filled with self-loathing for the things I have done tonight. The worst part is that the night is hardly over.

I reach the staircase at the end of the hallway and proceed to run up the stairs. It's difficult to concentrate and I feel disorientated as I run. I don't know where I'm going and at the moment I don't really care. I just need to get away from that corridor so I can try to clear my thoughts.

I push through a doorway at the top of the staircase and freeze as it opens. Standing in front of me is M. Behind him are Soren, Sebastian, Hunter and Thatch. The five of them are approaching a large metal door that bars their way at the end of the hallway.

M turns at the sound of the door opening. 'What are *you* doing here?' he growls. His eyes are dark with anger and a thread of fear works its way into my belly.

'I came to help,' I say, my eyes darting to Sebastian, before flicking back to M.

'You abandoned your post. Get out of here!' M says, his words laced with authority.

'No,' I respond.

Thatch touches M's arm. 'We don't have time for this,' he says.

'She will ruin everything!' M roars. His eyes are wild and there is too much anger in his voice for this to simply be over my presence here. The only explanation is that Ryan or April told him the truth about tonight. M must know that if I'm here I will die and Joseph will get away.

I glance over my shoulder at the staircase I've just walked up, and then step into the corridor, allowing the door to swing shut behind me.

I turn back to M. 'I *know* what is supposed to happen tonight, but I think it can be changed,' I say, my words rushing out of me quickly in my desperation to convince him. '*Please*, let me try to change it, because I don't want either option to eventuate.'

My eyes naturally find Sebastian's as I say this. He appears confused, which means there is no way he can know the truth. Neither April nor Ryan told him of his fate tonight.

M's eyes are still dark with anger. 'You will doom us all.'

'Then send him away,' I respond, being careful not to look at Sebastian as I say this.

M shakes his head. 'No.'

'You would sacrifice him...' I pause as the sounds of footsteps reach my ears. 'There are people coming,' I say, glaring him down.

'In here,' Hunter says, pushing open one of the doors leading from the hallway. We all crowd into the room, leaving Hunter just inside the door to guard it.

The room we've entered is a bedroom. There's a window that takes up the greater part of the far wall. Through it, the lights of Hope City can be seen twinkling far below. It's dark in here, but not completely black. The outline of a large bed is evident in the dim light that seeps in through the window.

'Where are we?' I ask Sebastian.

'Joseph's private quarters.'

A cold shiver runs down my spine. 'But, I thought you were going to Headquarters.'

'We are in Headquarters,' he responds. 'This area is highly secured. That large metal door at the end of the corridor is the entrance to Joseph's safe room. It seems he decided to take extra precautions after what you did to his office.'

'How did you get this far?'

'Thatch helped us crack the security and Hunter manipulated some of the guards. But, we still had to fight our way through several recruiters.' Sebastian glances away from me and I know he's thinking back to the bodies I saw in the hallway when I arrived. He sighs and rubs his face tiredly. 'Elle, you shouldn't have come.'

'I told you before, I came to help.'

'M is right, it's too dangerous for you to be here.'

I take hold of his hand in mine. 'It will be fine.'

'Well, make sure you stay close. I won't have anything happen to you.'

I swallow tightly at his words, and push down the unease I feel growing in my stomach. I struggle to form a word of response. I can't make any promises to him. Not tonight.

'They've gone,' Hunter whispers. 'We can go now, but I don't know how we're going to get through the next set of doors. The security on them is insane.'

'Could I create a window through them?' I ask him.

Hunter hesitates. 'Maybe. These doors are incredibly thick though. There's a chance it won't work.'

'And I can't teleport past them,' Sebastian adds. 'I've never been here before, I wouldn't know where I was going.'

M turns to Thatch. 'Do you think you can you crack through the security on them?' he asks him.

'I can try,' Thatch replies, with uncertainty. 'It could take a while though if it's more complicated than the others.'

'We don't have much choice,' M says, before glancing at Hunter. 'Unless there's another way in?'

Hunter shakes his head. 'No. And this won't be the only door we have to pass. There are another two before we reach his office. Plus, there are cameras watching the door. Thatch won't have much time before we're noticed.'

'There may be something else we can try,' I say softly. 'Hunter, do you think he'll be watching the cameras closely?'

Hunter glances my way, surprise flickering in his eyes as they lock onto mine. 'Probably, it's the only eyes he has out here right now.'

I try to keep myself from smiling. We don't need to break through the door, because Joseph already knows we're here and he's going to let us in. I push my idea out to Hunter and watch his eyes, waiting to see a flicker of understanding in them. He blinks and his eyes focus on mine before he gives me a small nod.

'Okay, I need everyone to follow my instructions,' he says. 'Elle's got an idea, and I think it could work.'

We follow Hunter out into the hallway. The others form a line behind us while Hunter grips my arm tightly, tugging me along. As we approach the door, my heartbeat quickens and I try not to look at the camera perched above it. Hunter flings me forward when we reach the door and I fall down onto my knees, my hands smacking against the carpet.

'The rest of you need to fall to your knees.' Hunter's voice sounds in my head, as the others in our group collapse to their knees in unison behind me.

'It's been a while, Father,' Hunter drawls. 'But, I wanted to give you some time to cool down after our last little spat. I've been busy while I've been away. I brought you a gift.' He waves his hand at our group.

The door doesn't open and I begin to doubt my plan. Maybe Joseph doesn't want me that much after all.

'Give him a moment,' Hunter thinks to me.

'But it's hard to give it to you when you're hiding in your little panic room,' Hunter continues. 'I always knew you were a little intimidated by the talented, but I never realised you were scared. There's no need to hide, they are all completely under my control.'

Still, the door stays locked shut.

'I guess I'll have to keep these toys for myself,' Hunter says. 'It's been nice catching up.'

He leans over and yanks me to my feet, pulling me in close to him. He grasps my face roughly with one hand and smacks a cruel kiss against my lips. With his face away from the camera he gives me a wink. *'Sorry, just getting into character,'* his thoughts sound in my head.

'Now that I have you to myself, you and me are going to have some fun after this,' he continues. He tugs me in even closer and turns to the others. 'Everyone up,' he says to rest of the group. 'We're leaving.'

I hear the loud click of a bolt, and Hunter grins, but then covers the expression as he tugs me around to face the door, which slowly swings open. A long stretch of passageway greets us and I can see two similar doors, just like the one in front of us, opening ahead.

There is only one heavy metal door at the far end of the stretch that stays closed. *'Joseph's panic room is through that one.'*

I sneak a look at Sebastian and allow myself a moment to fear for him; just one moment to feel the terror that prizes at my heart and freezes me to the spot. I cannot imagine a world without him. I can't begin to imagine my life without him in it.

My destiny tonight is to save him, and I would give my life in a heartbeat to keep him in this world, but I know I cannot allow that to happen. Not when Joseph will doom us all if it does. If I allow him to die though, I know that I will die with him.

The cool calm that had settled on me earlier returns and I feel a complete detachment from my body as I look away from Sebastian and to the door at the end of the corridor. I cannot be emotional. I cannot allow the worries I feel tugging at my awareness to cloud my mind. I feel myself harden, as I push my fears into a small box in the corner of my mind. There is no need to fear, because tonight I will change our fate.

Our footsteps pad silently down the corridor towards the door. I push my senses out to it, listening for movement from the room beyond. I can hear the crinkle of paper, breathing and the soft sound of several voices inside. If Joseph is there, he is certainly not alone.

'There are others in there.' I push the thought out to Hunter. He looks back and gives me a small nod.

'I know. I can sense their minds. Joseph is there with three others,' he responds.

'Can we take them?'

He doesn't answer right away. *'We're going to have to,'* he eventually replies.

We approach the door, and my heart flutters with a mixture of dread and anticipation. The moment when everything changes has come. The moment we stop Joseph is finally here.

'Here we go,' Hunter whispers, as he reaches for the door handle.

I square my shoulders as I look at the door. This is the moment we've been waiting for. This is the moment when my destiny is decided.

CHAPTER TWENTY-NINE

Some moments in life move by in what feels like slow motion. The seconds take minutes to pass, and the hands on the clock seem to slow until you worry they've stopped all together. The moment the door opens on Joseph's safe room is nothing like that —nothing like that at all.

I only have a split second to take in my surroundings as Hunter pushes the door open. It's an office, almost identical to the one in which I froze Joseph all those weeks ago. Screens line the walls showing every inch of Headquarters and a large wooden desk dominates the centre of the room. Three recruiters stand around it and behind it stands Joseph.

Before I know it Hunter has burst forward into the room but he immediately crumples to the ground, grasping at his head in pain. M, Soren, Thatcher and Sebastian follow him in, but they too are down on the ground in crumpled heaps within moments.

The fear I had so easily pushed aside moments ago, surges back with a vengeance and it takes everything within me to take a step forward rather than one back.

Before I can make either move, pain erupts in my mind and a

squealing, high-pitched noise assaults my ears. I fall into the office and drop to my knees, clutching my head in pain. My thoughts become incoherent and screams of agony burst from my lips. I forget how to think, how to move, how to so much as breathe the torture is so bad.

One strong urge still pulses through me though, and I focus on it with all that I have. Vengeance. I can still feel the pain coursing through my body and mind, and I can barely form any thoughts, but the need within me to stop Joseph is strong. The more I focus on that, the stronger I feel and the more I seem to be able to push past the pain that runs through me and think clearly.

The others are on the floor beside me, clutching at their heads too. The three recruiters in the room surround us and I struggle to determine which one is targeting our minds. If we can take him down we'll have a chance. We have no hope of surviving while he holds us all within his painful grasp.

I attempt to push the pain from my mind. It seems easier to do now and I wonder if the man inflicting it upon us is struggling to hold all of us at once.

'Now, now, now, what have we here?' I hear Joseph say. I force myself to look up, despite the agony that pounds in my head. There's such amusement in his voice and in his eyes. It makes me hate him a little more—if that's possible.

'Did you really think I'd believe your little display out there *son?*' he taunts Hunter. 'I thought I taught you better than that.'

As he speaks, one of the recruiters who stands next to the desk steps forward, leaving just two men flanking Joseph. In his hands I can see the glinting black glass of several inhibitor bands. The recruiter bends down to where Hunter writhes in pain on the floor and locks one of them around his wrist.

'I do appreciate you bringing my favourite test subject back though,' Joseph continues. 'Especially after all the trouble she's caused me in the ARC.' He starts tutting and shaking his head, turning to look at me. I glance at the recruiter who has just placed an inhibitor band on Soren's wrist and is moving towards Thatch. Through the intense pain in my mind, I can still hear Joseph's taunts.

'You've been such a bad girl, Elle. I'm sure I can come up with an adequate punishment. And you, Michael, skipping out on your execution the way you did. I can guarantee you that won't happen a second time.'

His words feed the already burning inferno of hate I feel for him. My body pulses with anger, and my white, hot fury feels like molten liquid running through my veins.

'Now that I have you back where you belong Elle, it won't be long until I am able to create more like you. I will go through every single person down in the ARCs if I have to, in order to find more test subjects. Of course, I'll start with the ARC you so bravely liberated. It won't be too long before I can give myself those talents and nobody will be able to stop me.'

My talent is riling within my chest and I can feel it buzzing more powerfully with each word he says. The recruiter's control over my mind is weakening, but he still has me locked within his control. I need to get free of him now, before it's too late.

The man with the inhibitor bands begins to approaches me, and I look around to see that Sebastian and I are the only ones still free of one. If he puts a band on me, there'll be no escape for any of us.

'Take her back to the lab. Kill the others,' Joseph's order hits me like a bolt of lightning. I won't let things end this way.

I dip into my talent and force it to flow to every cell in my body. As it flows through me it propels the pain completely from my mind. My brain and my body flick into action, like my mind had been restricted by taut elastic bands, which have just snapped and pinged apart. One of the recruiters standing by Joseph staggers back a step, and a small smile tugs at the corner of my lips. He's our guy.

In one swift movement I launch to my feet. I pull at the air around me and force it in the direction of the recruiter who bears down on me, inhibitor band at the ready. He flies back against the wall, hitting it so hard one of the TV screens shatters and falls to the ground next to him.

Before anyone can react, I launch myself at the man who had controlled our minds. My talent rushes to the surface of my skin and sparks of electricity flare to life all over my body. I crash into the recruiter, driving him to the floor. The sparks totally envelop us, and I can feel him writhing in pain beneath me. It's over quickly and the life trickles from his eyes until he is still.

I roll off him and stagger to my feet, sparks still flying from my skin. I whip around and train my eyes on the last remaining recruiter. Out of nowhere, Sebastian appears behind him. He rips a lamp from Joseph's desk and brings it down hard on the recruiter's head. The man immediately slumps to the ground and lays completely still, his face buried in the carpet.

Joseph's eyes are wide and his lips are hard as he watches the tables so quickly turn on him. M and the others slowly stagger to their feet, finally free from the pain of the recruiter's mind control.

'If you come with us quietly, if you give up control, no one else has to get hurt,' he says to Joseph.

Joseph's lips pull up in a sneer. 'You truly think I will go quietly.'

'No,' M admits. 'But, we have your recruiters out of the picture. You are alone here. And you are not talented. You're not stupid Joe.'

The electric sparks singe to nothing on my skin, as I look back and forth between the two of them.

Joseph pulls a gun from the back of his pants and points it at M, the movement so fast I can barely track it, even with my enhanced sight. 'I may not be talented *yet*, but I'm not without power.'

I draw on the air around me and send a burst of wind in the direction of the gun. A loud bang sounds, just before the weapon spins out of Joseph's hand and flies across the room.

M screams out in pain, and I turn to see him clasping at his shoulder as he falls backward. Soren darts forward to try and catch him, but with his talent inhibited he moves too slowly and M hits the ground hard.

Joseph lets out a laugh as he launches himself over his desk and makes for the door. Hunter races to cut him off, a knife in hand and blind fury raging in his eyes. Hunter swings the knife at his father, but Joseph easily blocks his attack. He grips Hunter's arm and twists the knife from Hunter's grasp with his other hand.

Fire flickers at my fingertips, but the two of them are too close together for me to use my talent without hurting Hunter. I watch on helplessly as Joseph gains the upper hand. With the knife in one hand, Joseph throws his other fist at Hunter, hitting him square in the jaw and causing him to stagger back across the room. As he falls backwards, Hunter's head smashes against the bookcase behind him and his arms drop limply at his sides as he hits the floor.

Joseph bolts towards the door but I rush to block his path. The cold metal edge of his knife glints in the light as he advances and my heart beats wildly. I cannot let him escape.

The flames dancing from my fingertips grow into a swirling ball of fire in one of my hands. I can hear it crackling, the flames spitting and hissing as it thirsts to be launched at this man who has caused me such grief. I hold the burning sphere out like a threat in front of me.

'Stop,' I shout. 'It's over Joseph.'

He comes to a standstill before me. I could end this all in a moment with the power I hold in my palm, but I pause, looking around the room. M squirms on the floor, clutching his shoulder as Soren and Thatch attempt to help him up. The three recruiters lie motionless around the room. Too many people have died already, some of them at my hands. I just want this all to end, but now that Joseph stands before me, I can't bring myself to finish it with violence. I flick my gaze back to Joseph. I see no fear in his expression as he grins at me.

'I created you Elle,' he growls. 'And if I can't have you, no one will.'

He lunges at me, and thrusts the knife towards me. The action is so fast I don't have time to react. I feel a subtle movement of air, and a touch of coldness over my skin. Sebastian appears before me and I watch in horror as Joseph buries the knife into his abdomen.

My heart stills and the flames die in my hands. 'No,' I whisper. 'No!' I scream. Sebastian staggers sideways. His arm dropping to his side as his other hand moves to clutch at his wound. He stumbles against the wall, sliding down it until he hits the floor.

'No!' I scream again. The whole world around me seems to still and becomes oddly silent. Every cell in my body quivers within me, urging me to run towards him. In this moment, all I can see is Sebastian and already his eyes are barely staying open and his face has turned so white.

'Elle, Joseph is getting away!' I look up to find Ryan has appeared. He's standing in front of me, a pained look on his face, and he points at the doorway behind me. His body is flickering in and out of existence, solid one moment and gone the next, like a badly tuned television.

I look away from him, to Sebastian who lies motionless on the floor. I would give up anything and everything for him, and the urge to run to him pulses through me like a compulsion that's impossible to fight. But, something in Ryan's warning stops me and I am reminded of the promise I made him earlier. In this moment I know I can't follow my heart like I so desperately want to. Instead, I stop. With one foot barely off the ground, I pause and slowly turn to face Joseph.

The movement feels wrong, like I'm wading through water or my feet are stuck in thick mud. I ignore the sensation though, gritting my teeth as I force myself to go against everything in my being that tells me to run to Sebastian's side.

As my eyes lock onto Joseph running for the door, my anger builds within me like a violent storm of nature. I can feel it tearing through me, mixing with the raw energy that already flows in my veins. The feeling ripples down my arms and pulses through my hands. I can feel it seeping out of every pore in my body. The energy manifests as it gathers, surrounding me in a glowing orb filled with a deadly combination of electricity, ice, fire and wind.

The room begins to shake as wind whips at my hair and ice expands on the floor around my feet. The TV screens lining the walls spark and crack, and books fall from their shelves. I am the monster of my nightmares. The thing I always dreaded I would become. And, in this moment I relish in it. I hesitated before and it won't happen again.

I throw a gust of air at the door, slamming it shut, boxing Joseph in. He whirls around to face me and this time his expression is one of stunned fear as he watches my powers manifest around me. He staggers back against the door. 'You win,' he croaks. 'I give myself up.'

He puts his hands out before him in a gesture of surrender, but the monster in me only wants to see him suffer. The orb around me grows larger again as I smirk at him. He turned me into this monstrosity; it's only fair that I should finish him with the very powers he forced on me.

'Elle, you're not an executioner,' M says, choking through the pain of his injury. 'You don't want to do this.'

I let out a rough laugh. 'Yes, I think I do.'

'He's given up. We'll imprison him. It's the right thing to do.'

My eyes flicker to look at M. He's on his feet now and is slowly stepping dangerously close to me, while Soren and Thatch cower away against the wall. M's eyes are so sincere, and the anger within me falters for a moment. I turn back to Joseph and it reignites again. No, I feel certain I want this man to feel every ounce of pain I felt in the months he held me captive. I want to see him bleed for what he's done to Sebastian.

M takes a step closer. 'He's still breathing,' he says. 'Sebastian is still breathing.' The words are like cold water dousing me and my hands drop to my side, the energy that engulfed me suddenly disappearing into thin air.

'He is?' I turn to look at Sebastian. Ryan stands next to him, still flickering in and out of existence. I hesitate. Can I safely save him now? Joseph hasn't gotten away. He's trapped. Is that enough to change the future Ryan is from?

'I knew you didn't have it in you,' Joseph's taunting voice sounds again from behind me. 'I'm disappointed. I didn't realise I had created something so weak.'

As I turn back to face him, he lunges at me again with the knife. Before I can react I hear the distinctive bang of a gunshot behind me. The sound echoes through the room, which then falls silent. I can hardly breathe as I turn in the direction of the sound, for fear of what I will see.

Hunter stands by the bookshelf, his arm outstretched and his father's gun in his hand. There's a thud on the ground at my feet and I look down to see Joseph has collapsed, unmoving on the floor, blood already pooling around his body. I go cold as I stand there watching. Everyone in the room is silent, the magnitude of what Hunter has done settling uncomfortably upon us.

Joseph is dead.

M is the first one to find his voice. 'Elle, Sebastian is still alive,' he says softly. 'But, he's dying. He doesn't have much longer.'

Tears well in my eyes as I turn to look at Sebastian again. Saving him will kill me, but it's a price I'm happy to pay if I can just see his disarming smile one last time.

M grabs hold of my arm. 'If you do this, only one of you will live,' he says.

'This is the only way,' I say, dismissing his words and shaking his arm from mine as I rush for Sebastian. I only hope I have enough time to heal him. I stumble onto the floor in my haste to get to him, and pull his head onto my lap, tears falling freely from my eyes. My heart aches at the thought of being apart from him.

I place my hands on either side of his face and look at him. His eyes are shut, but I can see he's still breathing laboured breaths. I run a finger along his cheekbone. There's a slight sheen of sweat on his forehead and his skin is so pale.

'Please wake up,' I whisper, slowly urging the talent pulsing underneath my skin to flow through my fingers and into Sebastian. I close my eyes and concentrate on the wound in his abdomen, willing it to knit itself back together. I can sense the injury within him and the threads of energy from my talent slowly weave their way through him, healing him as they go.

I suck in an agonising breath as I feel an echoing pain in my own stomach. It's working. I try to ignore the growing sting, but it continues to get worse.

'Elle, if you keep going, you'll die,' someone says, but the voice is only a distant echo. All I can focus on is Sebastian. I haven't done enough to save him, and if I stop now he won't survive.

I scream out as a wave of pain stabs through me and I lose all sense of focus for a minute as I grip my side, which is in agonising pain. Waves of nausea roll through me, and it's a struggle to keep my eyes open. I refuse to let them droop though. I need to keep going if I can hope for Sebastian to live.

I look back to his face, and see his eyes slowly fluttering open. His bright blue eyes hold pain in them, but he smiles at me and it's the most beautiful thing in the world.

'Elle,' he whispers.

My name on his lips is all I needed to hear. The pain is rolling unbearably through me now and I know I haven't got long. I slowly lower my lips to kiss his. One last kiss. One last breath. One last moment that is over way too soon.

And then, I go happily into the darkness that awaits me.

CHAPTER THIRTY

Searing white light greets my blurry vision and I attempt to
blink it away. I feel drowsy, but warm and my senses feel
sluggish. 'Is this heaven?' I croak.

A head comes into view above me, and even though my sight is
still blurry Sebastian's face is unmistakable. He chuckles softly and I
smile. I'm definitely in heaven. I want to reach up and touch his
perfect features, but my hand feels too heavy to respond.

His hand brushes my face. 'How are you feeling?'

I sigh. 'Perfect.'

He laughs again, his voice low, before looking away. 'What drugs
did you give her?' he jokes.

Another head appears over me. It's Aiden. I frown. What's he
doing here?

'They should be wearing off,' Aiden says. He looks down at me.
'Elle, you're in the clinic, recovering. What's the last thing you
remember?'

The crease in my forehead deepens. 'I'm not dead?'

Aiden smiles at me indulgently. 'Not today.'

'But I thought...'

287

I feel Sebastian take hold of my hand and give it a squeeze. 'Hunter pulled you away from me before you could take on too much of my injury. Seriously Elle, you nearly killed yourself.'

The fog in my head lifts slightly and I look between the two men. 'So, I'm not dead and you're not dead,' I say, nodding at Sebastian.

'Maybe I did give her a little too much pain relief,' Aiden says.

I shoot him a scowl, feeling more awake by the second.

Sebastian ignores Aiden's comment and smiles at me. 'You absorbed enough of my injury to save me, but not enough to kill you. We were both in a pretty bad way, but our wounds weren't fatal thanks to you

I mull it over in my mind, trying to fit the pieces together. 'So we both have stab wounds,' I say, my mind slowly wrapping itself around the information.

Sebastian nods and pulls up his shirt to show a bandage around his torso. 'And matching battle scars.' He shoots me a mischievous grin. 'I'd been considering getting your name tattooed across my arm, but this is way cooler.' He winks at me.

I roll my eyes and fight the smile that pulls at my lips. A spike of fear suddenly tugs at me. 'The others—are they all okay?' I struggle to breathe as all the faces of my friends flicker through my mind. What will I do if something's happened to April? How will I cope if Kelsey didn't make it to safety? Hell, I even care if Luke made it out unscathed.

I try to push myself up in bed, but struggle to move my arms. Aiden and Sebastian jump forward to help.

'Yes, they're all fine,' Aiden says. 'I'm not sure Quinn will ever let you out of her sight again, but yes, they're okay.'

Aiden places a pillow behind me to prop me up, and then stands back to look at me. 'You've still got a lot of painkillers in your system. You're going to be a little slow for the next few days.'

'I can do slow. How long have I been asleep?'

'Two days,' Sebastian says. 'I only woke up this morning myself.'

I huff out a breath. I hate to think of how much I've missed while I've been sleeping. 'So much time,' I whisper to myself.

As if reading my mind, Sebastian continues to speak. 'We managed to take control of Headquarters the other night. Not many recruiters survived the cave-ins, or Mia's black hole. Those that were left have been imprisoned. M's been very busy. He's placed a council in charge until an election can be called, with members being chosen from each area of the community. The council has already removed the restrictions on the bridge to North Hope and they ordered the experiments in the hospital to stop. Teams are already working on taking down the wall between East and West Hope.'

'Really?' My eyes are bright with excitement but I find myself pushing down a surge of disappointment. I would have loved to see that happen.

'Really.'

We talk for a while longer, until Aiden insists I need more rest.

'I'll be back in the morning,' Sebastian says, as they both leave.

I smile up at him and nod, pushing down a yawn. For someone who's slept for two days I'm surprisingly tired.

Once he's gone, I shuffle down my bed to go to sleep, but when I close my eyes I feel a presence nearby.

I open my eyes to see Ryan by my bedside. His body isn't quite solid as he stands there. It's almost transparent, like how I'd imagine a ghost to appear or a faded projection of some kind.

'Ryan?' I push myself up in bed. 'What's wrong with you?' My voice is quiet and I know it's because I'm scared to know the truth.

'I think my problem is that I no longer exist,' he gives a sad laugh. 'Or that I won't very soon.' He sighs and looks thoughtful. 'When Joseph died, and you lived, the future I'm part of ceased to exist. Sebastian won't become the person that I am. His path will be different now.'

'So, you're dying?'

He shakes his head. 'I'm not sure what's happening to me. Can someone die if they never existed?'

I frown. 'Of course you exist.'

'Maybe. Maybe not.'

We both fall into a troubled silence. I struggle to come to terms with his fate. I don't understand anything of the physics of time travel, but surely there's another way?

'I don't want to lose you,' I say, my voice small.

He reaches out and softly touches my face. 'You won't ever lose me. Not really. Especially not now that we have matching battle scars to prove our love.' He rolls his eyes, making me laugh. 'Who knew I could be so smooth?'

I smile. 'I knew.' I look away from him, so he doesn't catch the tear that runs down my cheek.

'So, do you know what happens now?' I ask. I subtly wipe the tear away, before looking back to him. Ryan is nowhere to be seen though and the air where he stood is empty.

I want to call out his name, to see if he'll come back, but deep down I know that he has gone for good. I swallow and look down into my hands, tears now running freely down my cheeks. I shouldn't be sad. His disappearance is the final signal that our future has truly changed. I will miss him though.

Aiden enters the room and I glance up at him. I shake my head, trying to rattle my thoughts together. My mind is suddenly foggy and I feel like I've forgotten something.

I glance around the rest of the room, before turning back to Aiden. 'Was someone just here?' I ask him.

'Not that I saw,' he replies, before dimming the lights and leaving again.

I touch my cheeks that are wet with tears and frown. My sadness is a total mystery and I can't remember what could have caused it. I've probably had too many painkillers. Dismissing my tears, I pull my sheet in close to my chest and close my eyes.

There's a strange, empty feeling inside of me, almost like a small part of me is missing, but I have no idea what it could be. My thoughts drift away from the emptiness though as the minutes pass. And before not too long, I begin to forget I'd felt slightly hollow at all.

My heart warms and my being is filled with contentment as I focus on the people who I love. Their faces flit through my mind and I smile into my pillow because I know that I will see them when I wake in the morning.

I have no idea what will happen now. No idea what the future may bring, or what tomorrow holds. But, I know that for once it is going to be filled with happiness and laughter. Tomorrow isn't just the promise of a new day, but the start of a new life.

EPILOGUE

'There was a time when I was afraid of being tested.' I rub my arms as I stare at the bright white lights on the ceiling above me, and push down a shiver. The ARC is still the same sterile white place I grew up in, but the fears that once consumed me no longer seem to echo down its corridors. People now know the truth about what it means to be tainted. Instead of fear and mystery, the doctors in the Hospital Wing now offer freedom in the form of the cure and the people of the ARC are lining up to receive their injections.

'There was a time when you were afraid of your own shadow,' Sebastian retorts.

I reach down and pick up a pillow from my bed. 'Hey!' I exclaim, throwing it at his face. Sebastian ducks out of the way, but I call on my talent and make the pillow float up and hit him from behind. He laughs and rubs the back of his head. Reaching for me, he pulls me down onto his bed and on top of him. My hair falls on either side of his face and our noses nearly touch. 'What I meant to say, was that you are one extremely brave girl.'

'Exactly,' I say, grinning.

He brings one hand up to my face and pulls me in for a kiss. His lips are warm and my skin tingles with pleasure. I could lose myself forever in his kisses.

I pull back and look at him. 'You, Sebastian, are a bad influence...'

His eyes are bright and playful, and I get the feeling that being a bad influence is exactly what he wants.

'Elle, Copper won't play with me!' Kelsey calls out, from down the corridor.

I roll off Sebastian in one swift move. He gives me a conspiring grin, which I blatantly ignore as I look around for Kelsey and the dog. They appear in the doorway together, both with unique looks of frustration on their faces.

'Did you pull his tail again?' I ask.

'No,' she responds, looking down at her feet.

Copper's expression tells a different story.

Sebastian gives one of her pigtails a playful tug. 'You know he doesn't like that.'

She pouts and throws herself onto one of the beds in the small room the three of us have been sharing. Copper keeps his distance, sitting on the ground a little further away.

'Have you seen Hunter since we arrived here?' Sebastian asks.

I shake my head. 'Not really. I've seen him in the hospital a few times, but he's been keeping to himself since his dad died. It seems a change of scenery hasn't helped.'

'It's been months...'

'Yeah, but killing Joseph isn't something he'll easily forget.'

He scratches behind his neck. 'I suppose not.'

A knock sounds on the doorframe and I look up to find Aiden there, with Quinn beaming beside him in the open doorway.

'Are you two playing nice?' I ask Quinn, as they step into our room. I'm surprised I didn't hear them bickering out in the corridor as they approached. I've never seen two people who set each other off so easily.

Quinn shakes her head. 'I am, but Aiden's impossible.' Despite her words her smile is indulgent and I wonder at exactly what is going on between the two of them.

'We're not rostered to help administer the cure for another hour,' I say, glancing down at my cuff.

'Oh, I know,' Aiden replies. 'I have something I want to show you guys.'

I lift an eyebrow, questioningly. 'And that is…'

'A surprise.' He grins. He's clearly excited about something. I don't think I've ever seen him so happy. He waves for us to follow him, and keeps a hurried pace as he leads us through the long, sterile corridors of the ARC.

We've been here for just over a week, but that week has been draining. I've spent more time providing people with reassurance about life on the surface than giving any cure injections. The more I talk about life above ground, the more I can't wait to return to it. I hope it lives up to the beautiful picture I've painted for people.

As Aiden takes us through the hospital that's still under repair, and up the brand new lift that leads to the surface, I begin to have my suspicions about what the big surprise is. When he pushes open the door to the hangar though, I find myself unable to move.

Before us stands an endless crowd of people dressed in grey. A sea of ARC citizens slowly moves towards the helicopters on the far side of the hangar. Tears prick the corners of my eyes as I watch mothers and daughters, fathers and sons making their way towards their new future. Some have looks of trepidation etched onto their features, but mostly I can see expressions of hope and anticipation.

'We finally did it,' Aiden says to us. 'We just administered the last cure.'

I let out a laugh of happiness and tears spill down my face. Quinn grabs me up in a hug and then Aiden, Sebastian and Kelsey pile in. I can hear Copper barking happily in the background. Everyone is laughing and there's so much promise for the future in the air.

'*Do you guys have room for one more?*' I turn to the voice in my mind and find Hunter standing over by the doorway, with his hands shoved in his jean pockets.

'*Always*,' I respond, pulling myself from the group and walking over to him.

'Did you hear the news?'

He gives me a nod and a small smile. 'Yeah, it's pretty obvious.'

I glance over my shoulder at the masses of people gathered. 'True.' I pause before I continue. 'How are you?'

'I've been better, Winters,' he replies, his face dropping. 'I can't hate myself when I did the right thing. At least, that's what I keep telling myself.'

I know what he means. He killed his father and while he knows it was the right thing to do, it can't be easy to accept that.

'I'll be alright,' he continues. 'I have to be. I have a hot date with a talented fire starter lined up once I'm back in Hope.' He winks.

I laugh and bump his shoulder against mine, which makes him smile. His eyes turn serious again. 'I really will be alright.'

I wonder if Hunter's words were to convince me or to convince him, but inside I know he will be okay eventually.

We return to the rest of the group, who have been joined by April, Adam and Lara. The three of them are chatting animatedly and removing white lab coats. They must have been there when the last cure injection was administered. I can feel Lara's excitement tingling across my skin and I give her a warm smile.

'I think it's time to go,' April says, grinning as she looks across the crowd towards the helicopters.

'I think you might be right,' Aiden replies, with an even bigger smile plastered across his face.

We all slowly begin to make our way across the hangar towards the helicopters at the far side. Sebastian, Kelsey and I bring up the rear of the group. Kelsey is quite happy swinging between our hands as we walk and I think Copper is simply glad to have a reprieve from her ever-reaching grasp.

'So, what do you think will happen when we get back to Hope?' Sebastian asks. 'I know the election is in two weeks, but what do we do now?'

I pause. I've been asking myself this question for months now, but I'm yet to come up with the answer. What do we do when all is right with the world?

'We live happily ever after, of course,' Kelsey responds.

I laugh and give her hand a squeeze. 'Anything else while we're at it?'

'No, that's all,' she responds. She lets go of my hand and runs ahead to chase Copper.

'So, what do you think of the plan?' Sebastian asks, slinging his arm around my shoulders.

'I think it has potential.'

'Yeah, it sounds pretty good to me.' He pulls me close and kisses the top of my head. Kelsey squeals with delight as she catches Copper's tail. Sebastian smiles, dropping his arm from me, and jogs forward to catch up with her.

Watching them and the rest of my friends together makes my heart warm. It makes me believe that our future really will be a happy one.

I glance back at the door that leads down to the ARC one last time, knowing I will never see it again. The thought doesn't make me sad, but hopeful. It shows me how far we've come. How much I've grown since I first left this place. When I turn and face all the people that are gathered I know that everything we've been through has been worth it. That *this* is what it was all about.

'Come on, Elle,' Kelsey says, giggling as Sebastian picks her up and lifts her onto his shoulders. He holds out one hand to me and I know that whatever my future may bring, it will be our future, together.

As we walk to the helicopters waiting to take us home, surrounded by our friends, I can't help but feel that maybe we can't answer the question of what comes next. Maybe our destiny is yet to be written.

~

The End

~

ACKNOWLEDGMENTS

It is with mixed feelings that I write these acknowledgements. The ARC Series has been a three-year endeavour for me, and I still can't quite believe the journey has come to an end. I am sad to be saying goodbye to these characters, who I've spent so much time with these last few years, but I'm glad their stories finally have closure.

These books wouldn't have been the same without my amazing editor, Pete, who constantly drives me to be a better writer. His ability to pack more excitement into scenes has helped to develop this series into what it is today. He has worked tirelessly on the series, and I am so grateful for his input.

My family and friends have been my biggest cheerleaders and their support means everything to me. Thank you to Mum, Dad, Hen and Jen: your enthusiasm for my work gives me the courage to share it with the world. You guys are the most amazing people and I feel so blessed to have you in my life.

Finally, to everyone who has read and loved the ARC series: you have brought it to life, and I couldn't have done it without you. You guys are why I love to write and you make me excited to work every day. I look forward to hearing your reactions to how the series has ended.

The ARC Series may be over, but I have so many exciting new projects in the works and I hope you will enjoy them as well!

ALSO BY ALEXANDRA MOODY

The Liftsal Guardians Series

The Liftsal Guardians

The Brakys' Lair

The Oblivion Stone

The Rift War

The ARC series

Tainted

Talented

Fractured

Destined

ABOUT THE AUTHOR

ALEXANDRA MOODY is an Australian author. She studied Law and Commerce in her hometown, Adelaide, before going on to spend several years living abroad in Canada and the UK. She is a serious dog-lover, double-black-diamond snowboarder and has a love/hate relationship with the gym.

Never miss a release!
Sign up at: www.subscribepage.com/TheARCsubscribe

For more information:
www.alexandramoody.com
info@alexandramoody.com